Over the Fence

Holly Whitworth

This one is for those who dream of something more in their life. Don't ever stop looking for more. Go out and find it. Believe in yourself and your dreams, and never give up. Ever.

This is a work of fiction. Names, places, characters, places, events, and incidents are products of the authors imagination.

Text copyright © Holly Whitworth

Published by Holly Whitworth

Chapter One

Rell

I wipe the sweat dripping from my forehead with the back of my hand. I look to my left to see my friend Bree, wearing a purple sports bra with matching leggings, enjoying herself in the downward dog position. These hot yoga classes we have been taking together for the last couple of months are whipping us into shape and getting us out of bed in the morning. I look to my left to see a new girl joining us in the downward dog. I instantly get a whiff of a horrible smell.

Bree looks over at me. She must've got a whiff too. I clench my teeth and wrinkle up my nose, and Bree laughs.

"Ladies, quiet, please," The instructor yells out.

Bree rolls her eyes before nodding toward the lady next to me. I nod yes to her, and we both stand out of the downward dog position.

"Alright, ladies. Warrior pose, please."

I put one foot in front of me with the other behind me, squatting, and then spread out one arm in front of my face and the other behind me. The smell again appears, and this time it's much more potent. It's so bad that it makes me gag. What is it with some people in California not wanting to wear deodorant?

Bree makes a stink face while in her warrior pose. I hope this class ends soon because I can't take this horrible smell much longer. I may have to bring nose plugs next time. We seem to be getting into classes lately with at least one person who forgot to bathe.

"Okay. Great job. Let us end this class with the lotus pose. Meditate for a bit,"

Bree and I get down on our mats and meditate. It's my favorite pose because it is when I relax a little, even if I use this time to think about everything I have scheduled for today. I am finally relaxed and forget about the smell when I hear a squeaking sound. I open one eye and peek to the right. The new girl is waving her hand in front of her face, and I realize it is about to smell a lot worse here.

I raise my hand, "May I be excused, please?"

I stand and start picking up my mat before she even answers me. This class is over for me. Bree looks at me and then stands to do the same. We both hurried out of the room and started laughing when we got to the front entrance of the hot yoga studio.

"Rell, remind me never to sign up for that class again," Bree says, opening the door for the both of us.

I walk out the door first and am hit in the face by a breeze of fresh air.

"Ah, that is much better."

"Where are we off to now?"

I look around, thinking about our next stop before we walk home. The new girl didn't give me enough time to consider what today holds.

"Smoothies, and then showers?" I ask Bree.

We walk a few doors from the yoga studio to our favorite place to pick up smoothies. We both order the same thing we always get. I get a green smoothie that has spinach, banana, and mango. Bria gets a triple berry with a scoop of vanilla protein powder. After picking up our drinks at the pick-up window, we take off in the direction of home.

"Did you share that you were at the studio this morning?"

"Of course," I say. "Do you even work out if you didn't share it?"

Bree's not only my best friend and roommate, but she also doubles as my assistant. Most people call my job an "Influencer," but I call it a social media expert. I couldn't think of anyone better to be on this journey with me.

We turn the corner, and our cute little bungalow house comes into view. It's gray, with white trim and black shutters. It's small and charming. Perfect for Bree and me. We are almost to the front of the house when Bree turns around to start walking back.

"It looks like we are getting new neighbors."

I turn around to look at her. She's standing next to the enormous red SOLD sign out front of the house next door. The house has been on the market for a while now. We haven't seen a single person look at it.

"Hmm. I wonder who bought it." I say.

She returns to me, and we walk together to the front door.

"Hopefully, it's not a killer," Bree says.

I roll my eyes before laughing. Bree thinks anyone could be a murderer.

I stick the key into the lock and unlock the door. I open it to our cute cozy space. We have a white sectional with a vintage modern rug on the floor in the living room and a massive tv on the wall with a rattan sideboard underneath it. The house is older and updated in some areas. All the rooms are separate, and it is what I love about it.

I toss the keys down on the coffee table. Bree locks the front door behind her. We set our yoga mats by the front door, and then both fall onto the couch.

"Well, after showers, we can film the sponsored ad for that meal kit we got in yesterday. Then we have to test those cosmetics sent to us a week ago and send them our input. If we like it, they want to sponsor you too."

"That food kit was delicious," I say, trying to ignore everything she said.

Bree sits up on the couch and taps me with her foot. I lift my head from the cushion and look at her. "What?"

"Is that you that smells?" She looks disgusted.

I sit up, lifting my armpit to smell. "Ugh. It's me,"

Bree starts laughing, gets up from the couch, and takes off toward her bedroom.

I then head to my room to shower. I wash off the sweat and the stench from the new girl in our hot yoga class.

I throw on a robe out of the shower to get ready. Bree and I turned our extra room into our workroom. When I walk in there, I sit at the white vanity we have set up. There's a giant gold mirror set up against a wall behind me. We have clothes on gold clothing racks on both sides of the mirror, and on the other wall, we have glass shelves filled with products sent to us. A desk by the product shelves holds a computer we use to upload our content.

    Social media expert was never a job Bree and I intended to do. It just happened. Fresh out of college, we were flight attendants for the same airline. I started filming our travels and outfits in different cities, getting ready videos and makeup tutorials. People began to ask for more content which then led to more followers. We started getting things sent to us for free. It started taking up all our free time. That meant we needed to make a decision. So we quit the airline. Bree insisted I be the face of our account, and she just wanted to do all the behind-the-camera stuff. I don't blame her. Being the face of something we depend on to pay the bills is challenging.

    I pick up the makeup sent to us and start putting it on. I can tell already that I am going to like it. Plus, we need new sponsors. All the other influencers are picking up sponsors that are well above ours.

    "What do you think?" Bree asks, walking into the room.

    I tilt my head to the side, looking in the mirror. "Not bad," I shrug my shoulders.

    "Good. I'll email them today and let them know we are in."

    Bree heads to the desk and sits while I continue putting on makeup. I can tell she is turning on the computer from behind me. I pick up red lipstick and put it on my lips. I have never loved this color with my dark brown hair and light but fake-tanned skin, but it doesn't look too bad. I blot my lips on a tissue to wipe off any extra. I am looking at my full face of makeup in the mirror when Bree yells out, "Uh, Rell have you checked your messages today?"

    I look around for my phone, knowing it is on silent from yoga class.

    "No. Why?"

"Come look at this."

I get up from the vanity chair and walk to Bree at the computer. She has *The Gram* account open, and I see thousands of messages in our inboxes. She opens one, and it contains comments from a post from someone else. Words say I am uninteresting, claiming people are tired of watching the same thing from me every day, and the worst is that I am dull.

I gasp, "WHAT,"

"Looks like other influencers are talking smack about you. We have lost quite a few followers since yesterday," Bree chimes back.

I throw my hands to my chest, "Open the other messages."

Bree clicks on message after message of people saying the same thing and some encouragement to not listen to what others are saying. I have never once felt dull or uninteresting.

"What are we going to do?" I ask Bree.

"Ignore them," she points to the screen, "These words don't define who you are. You know that."

I know that, but I do not let things slide. These words will haunt me in my sleep. It will keep me awake at night, knowing people think these things about me, and I have no idea how to fix this situation. I walk back to the vanity and cross my arms as I sit. I look at myself in the mirror. You, Rell Campbell, are not dull. I try to tell myself. Am I?

I can feel Bree's eye on me while I look at myself. "Rell, stop,"

But I can't. I will figure out a way to let people know I am not dull.

I brush out my hair and then take the fancy blow-drying brush sent to us to try to dry my hair. I will fix this. I know I will because this job depends on me to be the one to come up with great content and engagement with our fans. People have loved us for too many years for this to be something to end us.

When I finish getting ready, we record the sponsored ad for the meal kit. Once Bree gets it uploaded to, *The Gram*, she meets me back on the porch. A couple of years back, we were sent a swinging daybed for the back porch, and it has become my favorite place to unwind when home. It's become peaceful outside since our noisy neighbors moved and put their house up for sale. They had three children constantly screaming and yelling while jumping in their small pool. The only time Bree and I would come outside was after dark, and we caught their parents' skinny dipping many times. While it was something we didn't want to see, it was hard not to, considering we had a great view of their backyard. A short wood fence only separates our houses, but since our back porch is high, we have no choice but to look over the fence.

Bree is lying opposite me on the daybed. We both have our legs down and our heads propped on pillows. "Bree, maybe we should give it up and go back to the airline," I say, setting my book beside me. We have been lying together for a while now, reading books.

"Rell, you can't let what they say get to you. Those people don't know the real you as I do. We make great money doing this, and all the free stuff we get is nice," she says as she continues to read.

I sit up and bring my knees to my chest. "It is, but I don't go out much unless a company pays for it. I feel like we always share the same things. All the other influencers my age are married, moms. They share kid content, and people love that. We share gym and smoothie content in our free time."

She says, "You don't want to be like everyone else. Let us continue doing the same thing we are doing now but maybe travel and go out more."

I lay back down on the daybed and opened my book back up. Bree is right. We didn't love working for the airline as much as we enjoyed doing this. It pays better, the gifts are lovely, and maybe I need to get out more.

Jansen

I put the last box in the back of the truck and pulled down the door. I turn around, taking one last look at my apartment building. I am ready to say goodbye to Kansas City, and hopefully, I will never return. This place holds memories that I will not miss. It will take me two days to get to the new home and adventure. I got a promotion at work, and when I learned it would require me to move eighteen hundred miles away, I was ready to go. I have spent the last six months waiting for this next step in life, and now the day is here.

I hop into the driver's seat of the truck. A bag full of beef jerky, sour gummi worms, and energy drinks is waiting for me in the passenger seat. The plan is to drive as far as possible, get a hotel room, and finish the drive the next day. Hopefully, I don't arrive at the new house around dark. I never looked at the new home in person and bought it based on the pictures. It is a little blue bungalow-style house with a small pool in the back. Since I know a thing or two about construction with work, I plan to fix anything myself.

The realtor on the phone said the house is in a neighborhood with older, retired folks. I look forward to living in a nice quiet area with no distractions. When I got this promotion, I knew I would need to work harder. I can explore the city when I get the time, and I look forward to it. I have never been to Cali before.

Chapter Two

Rell

It has been pouring rain most of the day, so Bree and I decided to skip yoga and content for the day. We are both bundled up with blankets on the couch, wearing sweats. We have been watching different types of movies all day, and I finally decided we should watch a scary movie. Bree hates horror movies, giving me all a reason to watch one. It is starting to get dark out, and the rain sounds like it is coming down harder. I decided to tone back the scary level for Bree by watching *Scream*. Older, but now they don't seem as frightening as they once were. I know it doesn't matter since scary scenes give her the creeps.

    We are to the part of the movie where Sydney's friends start dropping like flies. I decide it is an excellent time to use the bathroom and grab some more popcorn on my way back. I look over to Bree before getting up, and she is already holding the blanket in front of her face so she can hide it when bad parts happen. I smile, knowing she loves me enough to stick through this movie.

    I wash my hands before walking out of the bathroom. It is the perfect time for me to devise a plan to scare Bree. I should turn all the lights off and hide. I open the remote app on my phone to turn the tv off while I turn off the switch to the kitchen light. It's the only light in the house since it is just enough to see without any lights in the living room. I peek around the corner and see Bree with the blanket up to her face. She is looking at the tv like something frightening is fixing to happen. That's my cue.

    I flip the switch and the tv off simultaneously and then jump around the hall corner.

Screaming occurs before she yells out, "RELL."

I hold my hands over my mouth, dying laughing on the inside.

I can hear her footsteps and then a thump.

"OUCH," I hear footsteps again, "Rell, this isn't funny,"

Just before she flipped the switch, we both heard a loud crashing sound outside.

"What was that?" I say, coming around the corner.

Bree pushes me, "That isn't funny, Rell. What was that?"

"That wasn't me," I say, running over to the front window.

I open the blinds with my hand and see a huge moving truck outside. A man wearing a black hoodie is standing behind the moving truck assessing the damage he must have done by hitting his mailbox.

"Looks like our new neighbor is here,"

Bree runs up beside me and looks through the blinds herself.

"He looks like a killer to me,"

I look over at her, concerned. "Bree, it's pouring. The hoodie does not mean he is a killer. I wonder why he is here and in the rain so late in the day."

Bree shrugs her shoulders, "Maybe he didn't have a choice,"

"I bet Margret across the street is sitting on her front porch now, watching all this madness go down." I laugh.

Margret is a retired older lady who loves any action in the neighborhood. She will tell me about this tomorrow, I'm sure. She looks forward to talking gossip just as it happens.

I walk over to the coat closet and take out my raincoat. I start putting it on when Bree notices what I am doing.

"You can't go out there. You don't know that guy,"

"Well, he looks like he needs help. Just look out the window in case anything crazy happens. Call Margret if he captures me. She will love being able to tell everyone that story."

I turn around and open the front door. The rain is coming down hard outside. I walk down the steps to the sidewalk. He picks up the bricks surrounding his mailbox when I walk up behind him.

"Hey, need some help?" I ask him as I get slammed with rain.

He looks over his shoulder and stands when he sees me. He has to be at least six foot three and looks enormous compared to my five foot five body. I can't tell what he looks like because his hood is over his head, and it's pouring.

"I am fine. Thank you," Then he goes back to stacking the bricks.

I don't understand why this is an issue to him right now as he could be inside his lovely new house, but I guess this rain is holding him back from moving his things inside.

"We have a couch you can sleep on for the night. This rain will be gone by morning,"

He stands again and, after a few seconds, turns back to look at me. "You don't even know me, but thanks for the offer,"

I try to find his eyes to look into but fail in this ridiculous rain. He doesn't look like he could be a bad guy. "If you need a place to dry off, my roommate and I are nice, and we could fill you in on the neighborhood while we wait for the rain to go away," I say.

I know he has to be thinking of a nice warm cozy, dry place right now.

"Fine, but I won't stay long,"

I start walking to the house, and he follows me.

I whisper, "Margret is going to love this," as I walk through the door.

When we walk through the door, Bree is on the couch with the blanket back up to her face. I know she will be terrified that I just offered our place for the night to a killer. I slip out of my jacket and hang it on the hook behind the door. He takes off his hoodie and hangs it up next to my coat. We walk into the living room.

"Bree, this is...." I point my hands at him. Then I realized I had just let an insanely hot guy inside our house. He is shaped just right with black hair and dark eyes, straight from the GQ magazine.

Bree instantly loosens up and holds her hand out to shake his.

"I'm Jansen," he says, walking over to shake her hand.

"Nice to meet you, Jansen. I'm Bree, and this is Rell," she says, pointing to me.

He turns to me and then shakes my hand.

I point over to the couch, "Have a seat. Could I get you anything?"

He walks over to the couch and sits. "I'm good. Does it always rain this bad here? I wasn't expecting this when I drove into the city,"

"We have our worse rain during February into March. The rain should be mostly gone in a few days. Where did you drive in from?" Bree asks, obviously not scared of him anymore.

I take a seat on the sectional by Bree's feet.

"Kansas City. It's been two long days of driving."

The room gets silent and awkward for some reason. We don't want to ask him too many questions, but we both want to know more about Jansen, considering he is our new neighbor. Our new hot and sexy, mysterious neighbor.

"So, you two live here?" He asks, waving his hand between the two of us. "I am sorry, but when I bought the house, they told me mostly retired people live in this neighborhood,"

I finally look him in the eyes, and I can't help but smile. "Yes, sorry. We bought this house five years ago. And yes, everyone but us is retired. And well, now you."

I began to wonder why he asked such an odd question. Does it bother him having us next door?

"I'm sorry if that came out rude," he says.

"It's okay. I understand. You are new here." I sit back on the couch and take the remote from Bree. I turned the tv back on so we wouldn't be uncomfortable. I could continue watching *Scream* from where we left off. Maybe he will think we are strange. I hit play on the movie and then got up to grab the popcorn I was supposed to get earlier before this and all of us some boxed water.

When I get to the living room, he watches the movie, and Bree is back to being scared. I hand him the water, and he looks at it, confused.

"Sorry, but water is either boxed here in California or comes in glass bottles. I hope you said goodbye to the plastic bottles. You won't see them again."

He opens the water and takes a drink. "Scary movie?"

"I love scary movies," I look over at Bree. "Bree here is terrified by everyone and everything scary. She thinks anyone could be a murderer."

"And you went and let one in your house," He says.

Bree's eyes get so big that they will pop out of her socket. I laugh hard, "Bree, he is joking. So, Jansen, what brought you here to San Francisco, if you don't mind me asking?"

He finally relaxes on the couch and crosses his defined arms across his ample chest. His white shirt looks like it could rip right off of him. He seems like he visits the gym daily. If he were interested in hot yoga, the ladies would love him.

"Work. The company I work for is building some new condos here, and I am head of the construction project. I don't get my hands dirty, and I get to take care of the important things. What do you two do?"

I tap Bree on the leg to let me answer. We already have so many people around here that know us for what we do, but I would like someone for once to know us for just us. I can't tell him what we do yet.

I look over to Bree, "We work from home. nothing fancy," she nods. Then I look at him with a giant smile because I have at least told the half-truth.

He looks down at his phone in his lap. It must be going off silently. He looks up at me and then back to his phone.

"I have to get this. Give me one second," Jansen says, getting up and walking out the front door so he can talk while standing on the front porch.

Once she knows he is outside for good and talking on the phone, Bree says. "Oh, I like this guy."

"He seems nice and easy on the eyes too."

"Maybe we'll catch him skinny dipping in his pool out back," she laughs.

I peek through the blinds and notice it isn't raining anymore.

"He's probably leaving when he finishes his call."

I get up to walk into the kitchen. I want to look busy when Jansen steps back in. He doesn't need to think I was waiting for him to return. Bree has a boyfriend, so she isn't interested.

When I hear the front door open from the kitchen, I know it is him. I stand close to the doorway so I can listen to him.

"Thank you for letting me hang for a bit. I need to get going. Tell Rell thank you. I will be seeing you two around," then I hear Bree say, "No problem," before the front door shuts.

I walk back to the living room when I know he is gone. Bree is looking out the blinds, spying on him. I join her. We see him outside unloading some of the boxes from the back of his moving truck.

"Where did you take off to?"

I shrug, "I didn't want to look like I was waiting for him to return. I can't look interested." I pause to check him out through the window some more. "That doesn't mean I won't be on the back porch spying on him over the fence," I wink.

Bree laughs, shaking her head at me.

Today I have been trying to focus on changes Bree and I should make toward *The Gram* account content. It hasn't been easy when all I want to do is check on what is happening next door. I might have had one look, but I didn't see anything.

"Ready," Bree says, walking into the workroom.

I'm sitting at the vanity, putting the finishing touches on my hair. We received some new products in the mail to try. They sent an obscene amount to us, so we figured we could use some for a giveaway. We often get overloaded with products and gifts that we put together in cute gift baskets or bags to giveaway to followers who support us. It was a monthly thing for us at one time, but now we do it occasionally.

"Sure," I say, taking one last look in the mirror before getting up from the chair.

She lays out some products on the floor, and I find leftover overnight bags to put the products in as gifts.

"How excited are you about your date with Kent tonight?"

She has been seeing Kent for eight months now. He takes her out on some of the most romantic weekend dates. Since we don't share much content on weekends, I stay home most nights she is out. I usually read a book while episodes of One Tree Hill play for background noise, but tonight I'll take my book out back.

"He's cooking me dinner at his place tonight."

"Oh, cute and fancy."

Kent slid in our direct messages and asked about Bree. I know she prefers being behind the scenes. I always share fun moments so our followers can see a bit of our real life. We used to make dancing videos and post them on the account, but they were so much work, and we would never get anything else done. It just happened to be one of those videos that showed Kent a side to Bree most people have never seen. She was hesitant to talk to him at first, but I talked her into going out with him, and they had seen each other. She's happy, and it makes me happy.

We organize all the stuff, and then I place them in the bags.

"I got this. Go get ready," I tell Bree before she gets a chance to help.

She sits at the vanity, "What will you do while I am gone?"

"Read like I always do. Don't worry about me if you want to stay the night."

"Are you sure?" she asks, looking at me through the mirror.

"Yes, I will sleep in in the morning. I won't go to hot yoga without you."

I sit on the floor, watching Bree curl her short brown hair. She is the best at fixing hair. She should have gone to school to become a hairstylist. I always ask her for help when it should be the other way around. She is also the best at putting outfits together. She has a small frame, and everything fits her perfectly.

She finishes up, spraying it with some product before getting up. We always keep the newer clothes we buy on the gold rolling bars in the room. She walks over to one and scrolls through the clothes to find something to wear. It is then that the doorbell rings.

"I'll get it, and you finish up."

I walk down the hallway to the living room. When I unlock the front door and open it, there stands Kent. He flashes me a smile before walking in. "Hey, you can wait. She's finishing up,"

Kent is a big bearded guy with a sleeve of tattoos. He does Crossfit almost every night of the week and has a great job as a trainer there. He's much bigger than Bree, but they look so cute together.

I shut the door before walking back to the room to check on Bree, and Kent asks. "How's the new neighbor?"

I stop and turn to Kent, "Bree told you, didn't she?"

He smiles before taking a seat on the couch.

"Bree. Kent is here," I yell out instead of checking on her.

I don't want to talk about Jansen. I want them to get on their merry way so I can spy on him on the back porch.

Bree walks into the living room wearing a cute cream sweater that falls over one shoulder, paired with dark skinny jeans and high boots, which all look good with her curled short hair. I sometimes wonder why she isn't the face of our account.

She walks right up to Kent, and he kisses her before telling her she looks beautiful. They are indeed the most adorable couple. "You two get out of here. Have Fun, and I will see you tomorrow."

Kent takes her hand, and they walk out the door.

I grab my book off the coffee table and head to the back door. I look around when I open the door. Jansen isn't out there, but all his house lights are on. I still walk onto the porch and lay on the swinging daybed. It is getting close to dark, so I could get a little reading in before heading in for bed. These early morning yoga classes have me yawning throughout the day, and I desperately need extra sleep. I am still waiting for the best energy drink company to email us one day.

I read. Read some more. The words start blending. It's dark out now. Then I read some more. Then close the book. It's been at least two hours. I sit up on the daybed.

I was hoping to see a glimpse of him through a window, or maybe he would come outside, but I got nothing. There are still lights on at Jansen's house, but I'm getting too tired to wait outside. I head inside, changing into my pajamas before crawling into bed. Maybe tomorrow.

When I woke up the next day, I looked over at the bedside table to see that I didn't sleep like I wanted to. I'm not too fond of internal clocks. I walk into the kitchen and pull out the blender to make a smoothie. Bree usually comes home late in the afternoon when she stays at Kent's place. So, I will be looking for things to do alone today.

I go back into my room and grab my short black silk robe. I slip it on over my matching short sleep set and throw my hair into a nicer-looking messy bun. I blend my green smoothie, pouring it into a glass jar. I take a few sips before looking out the blinds in the living room. Margret looks to be on the sidewalk waiting for someone. I look over to Jansens to ensure he isn't outside before walking there.

I walk out the front door, looking like a mess. I slept in yesterday's makeup, and I know it is all over my face.

"Good Morning Margret. Are you waiting on someone this morning?" I yell out to her across the street.

She's standing on the sidewalk in her Moo-moo nightgown with her hands on her waist.

"Just waiting for Larry to finish mowing,"

I nod. Larry is her husband. He sleeps in on the weekends, and I don't hear a mower. I know Margret is outside, just waiting for some juicy gossip.

I turn around and walk back towards the house when Jansen runs by me, AirPods in his ears, wearing a zip-up jacket, joggers, and beanie. He stops his steps close to me and pulls his beanie off along with his jacket and shirt. All I can focus on is the sweat running down his chest and dripping off each abdominal muscle.

"Morning, Rell," he walks up to me and takes out his AirPods. I snap my head away from looking at his abs and walk right past him to head inside. I am so embarrassed.

He gently grabs my arm to stop me. "Woah, where are you going?"

I don't even turn around to look at him. "Uh, sorry. I. Uh forgot I had some eggs cooking. I was checking on Margret. Good day. I will see you around." Then I book it to the front door and close it quickly behind me.

"Ugh," I run over to the blinds. When I look out front, I see Margret's best friend Linda has joined her, and they have stopped Jansen so they can ask all sorts of questions. Great Margret saw this, and now she will give me a hard time.

Chapter Three

Jansen

I put my feet on my desk and kick back in my new rolling chair. My new office is what I pictured it to look like, fancy—walls of glass separate my office from everyone else. It has a modern black desk and a view of the city. I will finalize all the last details for the condos before they start construction. This new life here will be the greatest, at least I hope. It is already better than the cubicle I left in Kansas City, along with everything else I never want to think about again. So far, the only distraction is my neighbor wearing her silk robe right in front of my house. I would take it from the look on her face that I don't have to worry about that happening again.

I have a meeting with my boss here soon, and I haven't seen him since my last visit before I got this promotion. He isn't much older than me and is married to his wife, Laura. Last summer, when I was here, he and his wife took me out to dinner. He's the only person I know here, and I see more get-togethers with him in the future. I'm sure he will help tell me great things to do in the area. This job here could be long-term if this project works out as expected, and if it doesn't, then I will need to return to Kansas City. I don't want the option of going back. I want to stay here for as long as I can. I want to love this place.

My speakerphone beeps, "Jansen, can you come to my office, please,"

"Yes, sir. I will be right there."

It should be an easy meeting to talk about the upcoming job.

I walk down to his office, which is not far from mine. The only difference between his office and mine is that his office is larger. There are also blinds he can pull down for privacy.

I see him sitting behind his desk when I walk into his office. "Hello, Mr. Wilson,"

He points out his hand, "Take a seat, Mr. Davis."

I sit in one of the black leather chairs he has for guests.

"How are you liking the office?"

"I like it, thank you."

He crosses his arms and relaxes back in his chair. "And the move? Did everything go well, and you could get settled in your new house?"

I nodded and leaned forward in the chair, "Yes, sir. It went well, and I was able to get everything unpacked."

"How does your fiancé like the city? Have you been able to explore any?"

I pause for a moment. Unable to think about what I should say. When I last saw Jay Wilson, I had told him about my plans to propose to my then-girlfriend if I got the promotion. I wanted her to come to the city, but that was before everything. I don't want to tell him the story of what happened, and I don't want him to know I came here for a new life.

"Yes! She's excited about the city. We haven't gotten to see much yet," I lie.

"Ah, that is great to hear. The city is huge, so it will take time before you get to see the city." he rests his elbows on his desk, and suddenly I'm starting to get ridiculously nervous. I probably shouldn't have lied.

"I can't wait. I have a feeling I'm going to love it here."

"Yes, you will. I would love to have you and your fiancé over for dinner this Friday night. Would that work for the two of you?"

I want to smack myself right now for lying. There's no getting myself out of this now.

"Yes, we would love that."

"Great. I will have my assistant email you all the details later today. My wife will love meeting your fiancé. She loves making new friends here."

"Sounds good, thank you," I say, getting up from the chair.

He gives me a wave, and I leave his office.

I want to say every cuss word in the book, but I can't because that will only get me staring through all these glass walls. I also can't smack myself. Maybe I won't like these glass walls as much as I thought.

When back in my office, it takes me approximately 1.2 seconds before I start thinking about every damn excuse I can come up with that my "Fiance" can't be there. Maybe she went back to the city for her sick aunt? Or she came down with a cold? Oh, I know; tell him the freaking truth.

I turn and look out the window, "Sorry, Mr. Wilson. I lied. I don't have a fiancé because I caught her in bed with my best friend when I returned from my San Francisco trip."

See, that sounds ridiculous. I can't tell Jay Wilson anything. I will show up by myself and disappoint him and his wife. I already have the job, so it isn't like they will fire me over something stupid. Would they?

When I get home, I see the older lady across the street and her friend outside like they are waiting for something spectacular to happen. The other day, when I caught them out, they asked me what I thought of Rell, and I ignored them as if I didn't hear them. Then I went inside. When I came here, I said I didn't want any distractions, which still applies. If that means ignoring old ladies trying to set me up with my neighbor, then that's what I will do. The last thing on my mind is a woman, even one as pretty as Rell.

    I close my car door when I get out and give the old ladies a friendly little wave before heading inside. While unpacking what things I did bring, I made my house feel like a natural man cave. It was the first time in a while that I could do whatever I wanted to my place, so I did. I even hung a deer head on the wall above the mantel. Probably not something people do around here, but I don't plan on having guests here anyway. I want to get to know people here, but work will always come first, so I need to get these condos up and going first.

The pool in the backyard is heated, which is perfect during these cooler months, and after the day I had, I want to take a nice relaxing dip in it. It's what I need to help me come up with an idea to get out of dinner with my boss and his wife.

    After putting on my swimming trunks, I walk out back, throwing my towel on the ground. I take the little kid's approach when getting in. I jump in from the side of the pool, the water only coming to the middle of my chest. I return to the surface after jumping in and swim to the side. I cross my arms over the concrete and look into the back of my house. Out of the corner of my eye, I see two people kissing on the back of Rell's porch. Does Rell have a boyfriend? I can't help myself from looking over, and when I do, I see that it is just her roommate. *Brooke? Betsey?* Shit, I can't remember. I hear someone yell my name when I turn away from the poolside.

I turn back to see Rell's arms over the fence and looking at me. She must have been down in the yard while her friends are on the back porch. I swim over to the side to see what she wants.

"You called my name?" I ask her. She has her hair pulled up in a ponytail and isn't wearing makeup. She's wearing an oversized white sweatshirt.

"Just wanted to tell you, you did a great job putting your mailbox back together," she smiles at me, and now I want to talk to her more.

I put my arms over the poolside, closer to her, and rest them there. "Thanks."

"Isn't the water cold?" she asks me.

"The pool is heated," I keep it short.

She laughs, "Well, that explains all the late-night naked swimming from the last owners."

"You're kidding?"

She turns to her friend on the back porch, "Bree, the pool is heated. That explains why the last people were always out here skinny dipping,"

Bree, that's her name. Wait, she isn't kidding. I don't think. I'm swimming in disgusting water. *Gross.*

I jump out as fast as possible, grab my towel from the ground, and wrap it around my waist. When I look up, I see Rell, arms over the fence, watching me. It has been a while since I have had a woman look me over the way Rell does. This time, and the other morning, while wearing her black silk robe.

Then out of nowhere, an idea comes to mind, and Rell is the perfect person.

"Come with me," I walk up to her.

She put her hands up to her chest like she needed reassurance I was talking to her.

"Jump over the fence, and come with me." I nod at her.

"I can't jump over the fence," she says, not questioning why I want her to come with me.

"Fine," I reach over, putting my hands just around her ribcage, and then tell her to jump. She gives me the boost to pick her up over the short fence when she jumps.

She stops and looks over to her friends on the porch, "If I don't come home tonight. You know who captured and murdered me," she yells out, and I can't help but roll my eyes. I'm not going to do either of those things to her. I'm not doing anything to her at all.

She follows behind me when I open the back door. While I walk down to my bedroom, Rell stays in the kitchen.

"Give me a minute," I yell out to her.

"Okay," she answers.

"I need to ask you for a favor," I say as I look for sweatpants and a T-shirt to change into. I pull my gray joggers and a white shirt from a dresser drawer and take them into the bathroom with me.

She yells out so I can hear her, "What kind of favor?"

"A work favor," I yell out as I slide the shirt over my head before looking at myself in the mirror quickly and then walking down the hallway to meet her.

"I don't know anything about construction."

I laugh, "I guess you could say it's more of a personal favor."

Standing in front of her, I look into her eyes. She's so beautiful tonight without anything on her face, her hair in a ponytail, and comfy clothing.

"First things first, do you have a boyfriend?"

She laughs, "Definitely do *not*."

"Could you pretend to be my girlfriend this Friday night?"

She starts laughing hysterically. Which then makes me laugh. Then she gets serious with a slight smile when she finally contains herself. I can't help but think maybe she likes the question.

"Do I get to hear why you need this favor? I have a feeling this is a pretty great story."

I don't want to tell her everything yet. So I keep it simple.

"I might have lied to my boss today to impress him. He invited me to dinner and told me to bring my girlfriend. The thing is, I don't have one. It's just one night, but it might be more if his wife likes you. I don't know."

"Can I think about it?" she asks.

"Yes. Please don't wait too long to tell me your answer. If you tell me no, I may have to think of another idea."

"Like finding another girl to ask?" she asks, curious.

What is the correct answer to that question? I don't know. She seems to be the only woman I know here. I don't have time to find another woman to go with me, leading me not to go. I can't let my boss down now.

"No. I wouldn't go, and that isn't the option I want to do." I say, realizing I've never taken my eyes off her while talking.

She looks down, "Okay, I will tell you…" she puts her index finger up to her chin, "tomorrow. I will tell you my decision then."

She lifts her head, turning her eyes back to mine.

"Sounds great, thank you."

She starts to walk towards the back door and spins around.

"I don't want to jump over the fence. Can I use the front door?"

Pointing my hand toward the front door, I let her lead us. She starts walking that way, and when she enters the living room doorway, she lets out a scream and stops walking. I bump into the back of her, and she falls back into my arms. I let go of her quickly, and thankfully she stands. "What on God's green earth is that?" She points to the deer head hanging above the mantle.

"Rell, that's a deer...head."

"Well, freaking duh, Jansen, what's that thing doing on your wall? Here in Cali, we don't hang that crap on our walls. If you want any woman, that will need to come down, or they will leave immediately after walking in."

"Looks like it's staying, then," I say before opening the front door for her.

She smirks and then says, "See you around."

"Later."

I don't know why or when I decided it was a good idea to ask Rell to be my pretend girlfriend for this weekend, but I did it. Now I will wait for her answer. I hope she's leaning toward doing it for me. The only problem is I need her to be more than my girlfriend. If she decides to do this, then I will need to figure out how to pop the question. So much for no distractions. That didn't even last a week here.

Rell

Bree and Kent are making out on the couch when I slip in through the front door. Before I tell Bree all about Jansen's offer, I need Kent to leave. I clear my throat, and they both notice I walk back into the room.

"Well, looks like you made it out of there alive," Kent says.

"Yep, sure did," I stand there with my arms crossed, waiting. I don't want to be rude, but I need to talk to Bree like yesterday. She is going to flip.

"Let me guess. Do you need to talk to Bree? The model next door tried to get into your pants," Kent says, getting up from the couch.

I smack him on the arm, "Not funny, Kent."

He holds his hands up, "I got it, I got it. I'll go now."

"Thank you."

He kisses Bree and then leaves.

Bree sits back down on the couch, and I join her.

"So… spill. What happened?" Bree says.

"Well, nothing happened, but he asked me for a favor. It's something that you would never guess."

She throws her head back to look up at the ceiling. "He wants you to water his plants while he is working?"

"Not even close. Jansen wants me to pretend to be his girlfriend for dinner at his bosses on Friday night," I tell her, bringing my legs up to my chest on the couch.

Her face says it all. She's shocked. "What! Why?"

"Well, I didn't ask many questions, but I won't do it. I've known the guy for like four days. There's no way I'll pretend to be his girlfriend for one night."

"I feel like there's a good story behind this."

"Right, I think so too. I guess maybe one day he will tell me."

We both get quiet and think while chilling on the couch. The tv is on for noise, but neither of us is watching it.

"That's a bummer you don't want to do it because you could use this for great content for our *The Gram* page. You've never shared a boyfriend on there before, so that could make people more interested in you," Bree says casually.

Wait that isn't that bad of an idea. Bree isn't wrong that I have never shared a guy on our account. If he needs me, I could use him for a favor too. I may have to think about this myself.

"You think he would go for it?" I ask Bree.

"I mean, if he needs you, I'm sure he wouldn't mind helping you. He seems like a nice guy. When does he need an answer? That could give you time to think about it and put some rules in place?"

"Tomorrow. You think I should do it?"

Bree gets up from the couch to head to bed, "Definitely."

I never thought about this when he asked me, but since everyone seems to think I'm dull and uninteresting, maybe a boyfriend is just what I need on my page for more people to connect with me. I will need to set some rules and boundaries for both of us. I'm also not ready to let him in on what Bree and I do.

Chapter Four

Rell

I've thought long and hard about what I want to tell Jansen. I was up late last night thinking about how I want this to go if he agrees. I want to ensure it works for both of us and that no one gets hurt. I feel like there is more to his story on why he needs a pretend girlfriend, so I don't plan to tell him everything about *The Gram* account other than I need content.

Bree and I are hanging out in the workroom for the day, getting some work done.

"Nervous?" Bree asks, sitting at the vanity.

"Just a little," I say, organizing our product shelves.

Bree and I have been sharing sponsorship all day on the account, and we also gave away some bags full of goodies on our stories today. The direct messages about the comments made about me have faded away, and now we are back to getting happy and encouraging messages. Now that I have thought about it, I know once I share having a boyfriend, more people may be able to connect with me on that level. Most people who follow me are my age and married. I could turn this into sharing men's gifts and date night ideas. Things that I have never shared before.

"Welp, I'm finished. I am going to read on the back porch for a bit. If he comes by, just come get me out back."

"Sure thing,"

I walk into the living room and grab my book off the coffee table. Then I head to the back porch. I lay across the swinging daybed and rested my head on the pillows. I have been looking forward to this time all day. Between yoga, getting ready, and sharing content all day, I look forward to relaxing and having downtime. The sun has started setting, and it will be dark out soon.

I open my book, a romance novel, and start reading when I hear something. I sit on the swing and look over to Jansen's backyard when I see him making his way over to me. He must have jumped over the fence. He is wearing gray sweatpants, a black shirt, and tennis shoes. His black hair is a mess as if he has been asleep or stressed.

"Mind if I join you?"

I bring my legs to my chest and point my hand next to me. Jansen is walking up the stairs. "No. You can join me."

He sits, and I know exactly why he is here.

"You read?"

I look down at my book and then back to him. "Yes. When I get time, I'm almost always out here reading at the end of the day."

He runs his hand through his hair and looks at me. "Have you thought about what I asked you last night?"

"Before I say yes, I want to ask you something. Like a favor for a favor."

He looks at me, confused.

"I was wondering if I could document our outings as a couple. You said dinner and maybe more times that you would want me to be your pretend girlfriend. So, I was going to ask you if I could use you as my boyfriend for *The Gram* account,"

His face looks even more confused. "Tell me more."

"I get to share you as my boyfriend in exchange for being your girlfriend for your boss. I would also like to set rules for us, like only holding hands and putting your arm around me. There will be no kissing. We can take pictures together and share them on my account. I will be your girlfriend for your boss on Friday and more if you need me to. You get to say when I can't share you on my account anymore. I will share it as we break up. Also, we can exchange numbers, but we will only text each other with information about these dates, nothing else."

He nods as if maybe it doesn't sound like a bad idea. I know he needs me, so why would he say no?

"So basically, we would be in a relationship, but no kissing, touching, or feelings will be involved?" he asks

"Exactly."

"We would only see each other when these dates happen and only text about information for these dates—a relationship with no effort," he says, smiling.

"Uh, huh," I say, nodding.

"And you only need me for content on your account."

I continue nodding.

"I say that sounds great." He shrugs.

"So it is a deal then," I say.

He holds his hand out for me to shake, "Deal."

I put my hand in his, and we shake.

"Hand me your phone," I tell him.

He takes it out of his sweatpants pocket and hands it to me. I put my number into his contacts and gave it back to him.

"There, you have my number. It's under my name."

"You mean you didn't give yourself a special nickname," he laughs.

"No, you can do that yourself."

Opening his phone to ensure I had given him my number, he put his arm around me. "Let's take our first official photo."

I lean into Jansen's arm, and he takes a quick photo. Then I watch him set it as my contact picture.

"I'll send you that. You can use it as your first content photo," Jansen says, and it surprises me how quickly he's down for this crazy idea.

"Thanks," I say, pulling away from his hold.

He gets up to leave. "Thank you for doing this for me."

"Well, thank you too. I'll want to know in advance what I need to wear Friday for dinner, so don't wait until then to text me,"

"I won't," he starts walking down the stairs into the backyard. I watch him jump over the fence and step inside his house.

I pick up my book beside me, and my phone goes off. It is a message from Jansen containing the photo he took of us. I saved him on the phone as *J* and added the deer emoji. I don't plan on giving him a unique name on my phone. I also don't feel like messing with social media tonight, and I will share the picture when I think of a great caption. I may also have second thoughts about doing this. He agreed to the crazy idea too quickly.

Jansen

I don't get it, but I agreed to it. Why would someone as beautiful as Rell need a fake boyfriend? When she first mentioned a favor for a favor, I thought maybe she needed me for things around the house. I would have never expected her to want a fake boyfriend for social media. I don't know anyone around here, and I am sure she only has a small following, so I figured, why not. I need her to pretend, so why not let her show off the fake relationship?

It's now Thursday, and I haven't talked to Rell or seen her since we shook on the deal the other night. She set rules, and I will follow them, one being we only text about said dates. I don't need any distractions besides her showing up at my boss's house with me tomorrow night, so I don't mind all the rules she set for this. I want to control them by taking photos for her to post on social media. I need a little control over what she wants. I plan to send her a message tonight about what she must wear and all the details for tomorrow night. She said she didn't want to know last minute, so hopefully, tonight is okay.

I just finished walking to the new job site where the condos are going, and now I am back at the office. Since I was out all morning, I have plenty of work to finish here at the office, and there is a chance I could be here late. I don't mind considering it is so lonely when I get home at night. I need to start finding new things to do in this new city.

Before I head to my office to work, I stop by the breakroom for boxed water. When I walk into the breakroom, there are employees I have yet to meet, so I walk on by them since I don't have much time to waste and head straight to the fridge. I can meet everyone later.

I can feel everyone staring at me and whispering—two women at one table and three men at another. I ignore them and open the fridge. I can still feel everyone looking at me, so I look down at myself to ensure nothing is on me. I find nothing, not even a kick me sign on my back. I grab the water and shut the fridge. That is when one of the women starts checking me out.

"Excuse me, why is everyone whispering and staring at me?"

One of the men at the tables looks at his phone and then back to me.

"How did you score Rell Campbell?"

Confused, it takes me a minute to process what he is saying. Campbell? Shit. She was my fake girlfriend, and I didn't even know her last name. And how does everyone know who she is?

"Uh, lucky, I guess," I say, unsure what else to say.

I jet out of the breakroom so fast and down to my office. I shut the door to my office behind me like it matters, considering the room is freaking glass walls. I have to look up Rell on *The Gram*. I take a seat at my desk and open my computer. I haven't been on my account in months, so it takes me a minute to sign in. When I finally get the stupid password right, I type *Rell Campbell* in the search bar. She's the first account to show up, and when I click on her name to my surprise, I see she has one point five million followers. One point five freaking million followers?

I run my hand through my hair. What did I get myself into, and why does someone with that many followers need me? She looks to be making it just fine without me, so why me? I clicked on the photo I had taken of us and saw the caption "Soft Launch." Nice, Rell, charming. We are slowly introducing ourselves to millions of followers.

Crossing my arms and leaning back in my chair, I pull my phone out of my pocket to text Rell. I am so annoyed, as this is something she could've mentioned. I thumb over her name and know she won't respond to my text because it has nothing to do with tomorrow night, and she will know I know her secret. I can't get upset with her because that means she won't go tomorrow night. The deal would be gone.

I want to text her, but something is stopping me. She withheld this from me, but then again, I have my secrets I am holding back from her. We both seem to have something we could use against one another. I put my phone back in my pocket, ignoring this issue. I go back to Rell's page. She told me she worked from home, and now it makes sense. Looking through the thousands of posts by Rell and some with Bree, I see they mostly share clothes, products, and other things influencers share. I find an occasional dancing video, but I never see a photo or video of Rell and a guy. The only guy on her page is me, and while I want to feel special, I know this is just a deal between us.

After tomorrow night, I should reconsider this whole thing. If Jay and his wife don't mention wanting to get together again, I think I should end this. I came here for work, and that is all. I don't want to worry about anything, I left that life in Kansas City, and the last thing I want is a relationship with someone, even if it is fake. Everyone in the office thinks I am dating someone out of my league.

It's late when I get home from work. I need sleep for tomorrow also so I can get Rell out of my mind. It took me longer to finish working because I thought about why Rell needed me most of the time. You would think even though she was on my mind, I would remember to text her, but I didn't. I walk to the back door and peek out. I see her reading on the swing on her back porch. I pull my phone out to text her.

Me- Dinner is at seven. Be ready by six. Dress casual.

I look to see if she will respond to my text, but she doesn't move and continues reading. It is not that big of a deal for her to answer right now, but I feel like going over there. I know I shouldn't because I will bring up all the information I learned about her today. I continue spying on her for another minute before closing the door. Now is not the time. She will see my text eventually.

I walk down the hallway to my bathroom and turn on the water for a quick shower. This has been a day. After slipping out of my clothes, I get into the shower. I wash and still can't get Rell off my mind. This is precisely why this whole thing needs to end after tomorrow night. I can't do this for many reasons.

When I'm done, I get into bed and check my phone on the nightstand before falling asleep. There is one message from her.

Rell- Thanks.

For some reason, I was hoping for more of a response from her.

Chapter Five

Rell

Casual, dress casual, I think to myself while trying to find an outfit. Hundreds of options are in front of me, but I can't figure out what I want to wear. I want to look nice for his boss and wife. For Jansen, I would wear sweats to look less impressive. I am scrolling through the clothes hung on the workroom clothing racks. I should at least wear something newer and stylish. I pull out an oversized cream sweater cardigan, lace black silk tank, and leather leggings. Bree has worn this together, but I haven't. I want to be comfy because I know there's a chance tonight will be uncomfortable.

    I put on the outfit and look at myself in the mirror. My long hair is in curls from fixing it earlier. I slide on some leather slides and then look in the mirror again at my finished look. I look over at the time and see that Jansen should be here in a few minutes. We've hardly spoken this week, and I know that won't be good, considering we should know more about each other tonight. Knowing this could turn into a disaster, I'll try to keep positive thoughts.

    The doorbell rings, and I let Bree get it. Jansen can wait for me to finish getting ready. I sit at the vanity, and I hear Bree answer the door from the living room. I touch up my makeup and then spray some perfume on me. *Well, here goes nothing.*

    When I enter the living room, Jansen stands by the front door, leaning against the wall on his phone. Bree must have gone into her room.

"I'm ready," I say, getting Jansen's attention. He doesn't just look - he stares me up and down. Which then makes me second-guess my outfit choice. I should have gone with sweats.

"Let's go," he says in a grumpy voice. I grab my bag from the coffee table and yell "Bye," to Bree before we walk out the front door.

Jansen doesn't say a word and walks in front of me, which I find rude. We get to his truck in his driveway, and he gets in before me. When I finally get in, he seems annoyed, so I stay quiet. I pull out my phone for entertainment. I am still getting sweet messages from followers who are so excited for me to be in a relationship finally. Oh, if they only knew what a messed up relationship this is. I look over to Jansen, who seems focused on backing out and driving. I continue to look down at my phone so the silence is not awkward. I could feel Jansen's eyes, so I put my phone away in my bag and looked out the window.

"Don't you think we should ask each other simple questions about ourselves? Just in case they ask us questions." I say, breaking the silence.

He is straight-faced, looking forward, "We can make stuff up. I don't think they'll see us together again after tonight,"

"You're so cranky."

He opens the glove compartment by my legs and pulls out a box. He tosses the box on my lap. "Put that on," he says to me.

I pick up the box and open it. It's a diamond ring. "No way, I am not wearing that. What do you think you are doing?"

"I forgot to tell you that we are supposed to be engaged. Before you tell me *No*, I want you to know that I know all about your one point five million followers on The Gram."

Crap. Jansen looked at *The Gram*. I probably should've told him about my followers when we made the deal.

"Fine." I retort because I know what he's doing. He's holding my not-so-little secret against me so that I will wear the ring. I want this night over with already.

I take the ring out of the box, sliding it on my finger before throwing the ring box back into the glove compartment. I will give him some credit for the ring. It's a lovely oval solitaire, but I am sure it was for someone else.

"So, why don't you tell me what you are doing? With that many followers, you don't need me. I need to know why you made this deal with me?"

I ignore his question and look out the window while he continues driving. He didn't want us to get to know each other and threw a ring in my face. I don't feel like telling him anything.

He is getting angry. I can tell, waiting for me to answer him, but I don't care. He is cranky, and I already have to deal with that, even if I tell him.

He stops the truck on the side of the road in front of an enormous house. He turns the car off before turning his body in my direction."Tell me. I want to know."

"Ugh, I'm only telling you this, so you'll leave me alone, but surprisingly I lost a lot of followers last week because people were calling me boring and dreary. I depend on this as a job to pay my and Bree's bills. For people to say those things about me hurt. When you asked me to be your fake girl…" I held up my hand with the ring on it, "fiancé, I figured you could help me out a little too with better content. So people my age would connect with me better. So, there, does that answer the question for you?"

He holds his hands up, "Thank you, that answers the question."

Jansen then opens his door to get out. I guess this is the place we were supposed to go. I just thought he maybe pulled the car over to get me to talk. I get out before he even gets to put on a show for his boss by opening my door. He has been rude all night, and this is only the beginning.

Once out of the car, I situate my outfit before we walk together to the front door. When we get to their door, I cross my arms while we wait. I don't care what I said. I won't hold hands or let Jansen wrap his arm around me. I *will* pretend to be the best fiancé he has ever had, though.

When the front door opens, we are greeted by a dark-haired man who looks the same age as Jansen. Behind him is the sweetest looking blonde-haired shorter woman who looks to be my age. Great, someone who I can connect with for the night. I was expecting them to be an older couple.

"Why hello there," the man says.

I uncross my arms. "Hi."

"Jay, this is my fiancé, Rell." Jansen says, putting his hand on my lower back.

"Rell…" Jay's wife said, making me and Jansen pause and look at each other. Does she know me?

"Yes," I say while clenching my teeth.

"What a beautiful name," she holds out her hand. "I'm Laura."

I sign with relief and shake her hand, "Well, thank you. It's nice to meet you,"

That could've been bad if she knew who I was. If Laura's a follower, she would never believe Jansen and I were a real couple, knowing I don't post him besides the photo from the other night.

"Come in," Laura says, and when they turn around, I swat Jansen's hand away from me, which then gives me an angry look from him. Something I will have to get used to tonight.

I walk closely behind Laura as she walks us through their home. It is gorgeous, all white inside with lots of charm. Close to the Marina and a view of the Golden Gate bridge just out back. It is dreamy and has to be worth millions of dollars.

"Wow, this place is incredible."

"Thank you, Rell."

We continue walking around while they show us everything. I choose to stay closer to Laura instead of Jansen. She leads me out onto their rooftop deck, where you get the best bay view. When I turned around, I noticed the men didn't follow us and must've taken off to a guy's room.

We stop at the railing and look out. "So, how long have you and Jansen been together?"

My first lie of the night was, "Two years."

"That's about how long Jay and I were together before we married. When is the wedding?"

My second lie is, "It's next summer. Since we had just moved, we would need time to adjust to the new city before planning a wedding."

I don't know how many more lies I can tell. I need to find Jansen so he can answer some of these questions. It was his idea not to talk about this stuff beforehand.

And what do you know, the men are walking out on the rooftop deck to join us. Jansen walks over to me, placing his hand on my back again while I look out at the bay. I decided to be friendly and let him touch me there even though it wasn't in the rules. We're looking out together while Jay and Laura are talking. I decided to whisper my lies in Jansens ear. "Together for two years and marrying next summer," I want him to know so we don't mess this up.

He then whispers back in my ear, "I told him we were getting married in the fall,"

I look him in the eyes, and he looks down. "See, I told you we should have talked about this," I whisper again.

"Are you two ready for dinner?" Laura asks.

We both turn to her and say "Yes," in unison.

While we walk down the stairs and into the dining room, Jansen keeps his hand on me in some way: my arm or my back. He has been sweet since we arrived for someone so rude and cranky before getting here. He helps guide me to our seats at the table and even pulls out my chair. I know it is all for the show we are putting on tonight.

Once we are all seated, Laura asks, "So, Rell, what is it that you do?"

"I'm a clothing stylist," not much of a lie but not the whole truth. Jansen looks over at me, impressed by my answer. It was one thing I thought about before coming here. I knew I wanted to tell them it was a job I did.

"We should go shopping together sometime," Laura says.

At this moment, I know I shouldn't say yes because I know Jansen doesn't think we should see them again after tonight, but I can't help myself.

"Yes, we should."

Then, I feel a hand squeezing my thigh, and instead of being mad about it, I kindly smile. I'm officially Jansen's worst nightmare. No one said the guy's needed to go on the shopping trip with us. I know I would like Laura outside of this little dinner.

Our dinner was served to us by some wait staff, and that's when Laura mentioned they had a chef cook dinner for us tonight. I feel so fancy and far-fetched. My only fancy dinner is the one Bree and I have to cook from our meal kit delivery. Before those dinners, it was disgusting airline food. Jansen must work for a great company if his boss has a chef preparing food for a pretend-engaged couple.

We all begin to eat, and Jay and Jansen talk about work. I take this time to enjoy the food and not let out any more lies. It's also lovely to hear Jansen talk about how invested he is in the project he is starting at work and how much this job means to him.

"When are the condos going up?" Jay asks.

"Soon. I've already got all the supplies set to be delivered. The crew should be starting in no time, and I'm more than ready to get started on it all." Jansen says before taking another bite.

"Well, I'm excited to see your work. I heard a lot of positive feedback from everyone at the Kansas City office," Jay says, smiling.

"Thank you," Jansens answers him with a slight smile.

I haven't seen this side of Jansen in the week that I've known him. Now I know how important this dinner was for him, and I should probably take the rest of the night seriously.

I finish my plate and set it to the side. Jansen is still eating since he has done more talking than eating. Laura is just a supportive wife and listens to Jay while discussing work. I find this the perfect time to show some affection to Jansen. I place my hand on his thigh since I can't take his hand while he is eating. He smiles at me and then puts his hand over mine under the table. It's just enough movement and a sweet moment for Laura and Jay to think that whatever is between us is genuine. While his hand is on mine under the table, he brushes his thumb over my knuckles, taking me by surprise. I can't help but smile while he continues to talk to Jay while finishing his dinner. It is almost too much playing around for me.

"So, Laura, is there anything else you want to show me around the house?"

"Oh yes, there is." She gets up from the table, "Follow me."

Before getting up from the table, Jansen squeezed my hand like he wasn't ready for me to leave the table, but I got up anyway to follow Laura.

I follow behind Laura, and she takes me into a double-door room. When she opens the doors, we walk into her office. There's a substantial white desk in the middle of the room, a glass chandelier hanging above it, with built-in bookshelves behind it. Every shelf had an expensive purse box and books labeled Chanel and Tom Ford. She has clothes hanging on a clothing rack to the side with a vast gold-framed mirror. This office is a fantasy. It's what I would want our workroom to look like if we made more money. I want to say many things about this room, but I must keep my thoughts to myself. I can't let her in on who I am.

"It's amazing, isn't it?" she says, walking in behind me.

"Yes," I walk over to look at the clothes hanging up. They are all expensive clothing brands. I need to take back that I would go shopping. There is no way I could afford any of this.

"This is where I like to hang out all day while Jay works."

"I can see why. It's a woman's dream office."

I can hear the men walking down the hallway. When they reach the office door, Jansen's eyes get big when he sees the space. He thinks I told her what I really do.

"It's getting late. Are you ready to go?" He says to me.

"Yes, we should probably get going. Thank you for dinner and for showing us your amazing house.' I walk over to Jansen, and he takes my hand when I stand beside him.

"We are so happy to have the two of you over. We will have to do this again sometime. And shopping. We could have a girl's day." Laura says to me while taking Jay's hand.

"Yes," I say as we walk to the front door.

Jay opens the door for us, and we say our goodbyes before walking out. I keep my hand in Jansen's until we get into the truck. I get in before he does and feel my body relax once I know we are finally done pretending for the night. Jansen gets in, and I can tell he feels the same. We both stay quiet for a second, just sitting there.

"I didn't tell her if you think I did," I tell Jansen.

"I know you didn't, but that office was…." He starts the truck and looks out for any traffic before getting on the road.

"A dream. I know."

I feel mentally exhausted from lying most of the night, so I stay mostly quiet the rest of the way home. It must be the same feeling for Jansen because he hasn't said a single word either. Once he pulls into his driveway, I jump out once he turns the truck off. I walk around his car's back, hoping Margret isn't watching tonight across the street.

"Hey, thanks again." Jansens yells out to me.

I stop before crossing the fence to my house, "No problem, see you around."

I fish my keys out of my purse and realize I still have the ring on. "Shoot."

While slipping the ring off my finger, I walk back to Jansen's house and find him standing by the fence, watching me as if he was making sure I got in okay. I hold the ring up to show him I forgot it and then hand it to him. "Sorry, I forgot I still had this on,"

"Keep it. You may need it again," Jansen says with a sexy smile.

I look at the ring, then hand it to him again. "Nah, I think tonight was enough. Thank you."

He takes the ring from my hand and slides it into his pocket. "Do you want a photo for content? The night isn't over yet."

I smile at him, thoughtful of him to ask, but I think I am good. "It's okay. Goodnight, Jansen." I say to him before walking up the stairs to my house.

The worst part about tonight wasn't that Jansen and I had a bad start to this disastrous date. It was the fact that there could maybe be something there between the two of us. Something that I'm ready to feel again. It all felt like more real feelings and less of our deal when it came to pretending throughout the night. It was almost as if something changed inside of Jansen once he discovered why I needed him. The agreement between us seems like a bad idea, and now I'm reconsidering it.

Chapter Six

Jansen

One week. That is how long it has been since dinner with my boss. It's also the last time I have seen Rell. I found myself taking late-night swims, hoping she would be outside reading, but she never was. I went on some morning runs, hoping I would bump into her when I got home, and she was never out there. I don't understand why I want to see her, but I do. That night at dinner started rough for us, but once it was time for us to be an engaged couple, I had this deep feeling I didn't want it to end.

As I sit in my office before I leave for the day, I decide I should check Rell's *The Gram* account to see at least what she has been up to this week. I feel like the only way I can get her off my mind is to see at least what she's doing. When I sign in and find her account, I notice the photo of us is missing from her page, and she has no new post for the week. Why would she take the picture down? I never told her I had a problem with it, and where had she been? Last Friday night was not a good start, but I thought it ended well for both of us. It seems strange that her job is her account, and she hasn't been on there once this week.

I sign out of my account before closing my laptop for the day. Wishing I could contact Rell if I needed to text her, but I'm not allowed to use her number for anything but if required for our agreement. But what if I needed her for something that had to do with our deal?

Before leaving, I stop by Jay's office to tell him bye before the weekend.

"See you later, have a good weekend," I tell him, standing in his doorway.

I haven't seen him much this week between being in and out of the office building, but he mentioned that Laura wanted Rell's number one day.

"Thank you," he says before lifting his head from his computer and seeing me standing there; he says, "Hey, I was just about to come down to your office to see if you were still here. Laura wanted to know if Rell would want to go shopping this weekend."

"She is out of town," I say because that's where I think she is, "But I will give her Laura's number if you'd like. They can get together when she gets back in."

"That would be great," he says, writing her number down on a post-it note before getting up from his desk to bring it to me. "Give this to Rell. Laura liked her. She is just the type of friend she needs,"

"Same for Rell. This will be great for her." I hold up the post-it note. "Well, thank you. She'll be in touch. Have a good one."

It looks like I got exactly what I needed to message Rell.

Once I leave the building and get into my truck, I waste no time pulling my phone out to text Rell. I could easily message her Laura's number but let's be honest, that's not what I want to do. Seeing her in person feels like the right thing to do.

Me- Sorry to bother you. Laura wanted me to give you her number. I have it on paper to bring to you later if you want me to.

I put my phone back into my pocket before leaving the parking lot to head home. It's the middle of the day, and there's still plenty of time to see Rell.

It takes hours before I hear a response from Rell. It is now dark out, and I've already had dinner. There still hasn't been a sign of anyone being at her house, so I'm surprised when she responds that she's on the back porch. Before walking out the back door, I grab the note containing Laura's number. It's why I wanted to see her, or at least that's what I'm telling myself.

When I walk out the back door, I look over to see Rell on the swing lying down with a blanket and book. She is wearing her go-to sweatshirt and ponytail. I jump over the fence, and she looks up when she hears me. She sets her book down before saying, "Hey."

"Hey," I say, walking up the stairs and then taking a seat on the swing by her feet.

I hold the post-it note with two fingers, and she kindly takes it from me before sliding it into her book. "Thanks,"

We both sit quietly for a few seconds. All these questions were running through my head to ask her, but I knew it wasn't a good idea to ask any of them. I will let her be the one to tell me anything she wants.

"So, anything interesting happened in the neighborhood this week while I was away?" she says, breaking the awkward silence. So she *was* out of town, as I suspected.

"You were away? I didn't even notice," I lie.

"Bree and I went to an influencer event in LA. We got to meet with different clothing and makeup brands. We got back earlier today. She's now gone at Kent's for the weekend." She frowns.

That explains why I hadn't seen Rell home this week. She is coming across as unhappy tonight and not her usual self, and I feel like I should ask her what's on her mind. I also want to know where our photo went.

"Is something going on? You seem down." I ask her tapping her leg. She moves it over for me, and I get closer and more comfortable with her on the swing.

"I think I am just exhausted from being gone all week," she says, still frowning.

"I can see that," I nod. "Want me to leave?"

"No, you can stay."

I get settled in on the swing next to her. I feel good that she doesn't want me to go yet. I still have so much I want to know.

"So…Laura liked me?"

"Oh yes, Jay wanted you to have her number. He said something about shopping this weekend."

"I can message Laura in the morning. I don't have any plans tomorrow."

"So, you still want to do this between us? I noticed the photo was gone," I didn't want to ask her this way, but I wanted to know.

"About that. I'm sorry, but I just thought we wouldn't be trying this anymore since Friday was a disaster. I know I should've talked to you first. It's why it took me a while to respond tonight," she says with her head down.

I knew this might be how she felt. It was a little messy for us, but it worked out in the end. As much as this is such a weird situation with us, I can't hide the fact that it felt good having Rell around me and calling her my fiance. If she wants to hang out with Laura, I think the right thing for us to do is continue this arrangement.

"It's alright. I understand. We started it wrong, but we should keep it up. I think we can both agree that this could help us. I can work better with you next time and try not to be so cranky, as you put it." I tell her, unable to take my eyes off her even though she is trying to avoid eye contact with me.

A slight smile comes across her lips as she lifts her head to look at me. I feel butterflies in my chest. Something I know I shouldn't be feeling at this moment.

"Well, I should probably get going. If you go tomorrow, will you let me know?"

"I will. I should be getting in bed." Rell gets up off the swing at the same time as me, "Thanks for bringing me her number. I'll see you around," she opens the door as I walk down the steps.

"Later," I say, and her back door closes shut.

I jump back over the fence and into the back door of my house. I got the answers I wanted and finally got to see her.

I got the best sleep last night that I had gotten all week. When I woke up this morning, I had a message from Rell saying she was going out with Laura today. Instead of waiting around the house today, I figured I could explore the city. I started at the Golden Gate bridge before biking across and back, which was tiring. The bridge is way bigger than I imagined it to be. Since I was tired of biking, but it was still early, I decided to take the trolley and sightsee some more places. After exploring for the day, I planned to meet Jay at a local brewery for lunch.

Getting to the restaurant before Jay, I ordered a beer while I waited for him to arrive. He messaged me while riding the trolley, and I didn't want to turn him down when he asked me for lunch. I know he wants to meet since the women are out today. I plan to only talk about work and not mention Rell. There are facts about us I could get wrong, and I know I could mess this up.

"How's it going?" Jay says, coming up behind me and taking a seat on the barstool across from me.

"Good," I say. I don't want Jay to know I was exploring the city without Rell this morning, considering that is something we should be doing together.

The waitress comes by, and Jay orders a beer. We both put in our order of appetizers. When the waitress walks away, Jay wastes no time discussing work. "How is the job coming along?"

"Everything seems to be running smoothly right now. I know it won't always be like this, but I'll enjoy it while I can," I laugh. "I like it here so far."

"That is great to hear. Word around the office is everyone was intimidated by you coming here. They say you're a hard worker, always on time, and never getting into anyone else's business."

That was my plan all along. I wanted to come here and prove that I was good at what I did, so maybe this promotion could only go up from here. I like Jay, but I hope to have his job one day. It's why I wanted no distractions, and I got myself into one during the first week here. I will have to put it aside and focus solely on work during the week. I need to remember why I came here, for work and to get away from my life back in Kansas City.

We continue talking about work and the office. The waitress brings out our food, and there are sports on TV. Jay and I cheer for our favorite team while watching a big-screen basketball game. Our conversation then turns over to baseball. I know I'll want to go to a baseball game once the season starts, just like I often did back home.

We manage to have lunch without talking about the women, and once the basketball game on tv ends, we both decide to end our lunch. We get up at the same time to leave, and once we get outside, I tell him. "Thanks for lunch. I'll see you Monday,"

"See you then," he says, walking off. "Oh hey," he spins around, and then I turn to look at him. "Tell Rell congratulations on the new clothing deal. You must be happy for her."

I have no idea what he is talking about, but instead of being confused, I say, "Yeah, I am. Thank you," I wave, and we both take off in opposite directions.

What is he talking about regarding clothing deals? Rell didn't mention anything about this to me. Instead of waiting to get home to speak with Rell about this. I immediately take my phone from my pocket and message her once I get in my truck.

Me- We need to talk now.

I promised her I would be more sociable, so I will try my best to keep that promise to her. I also need to keep my composure and not get "cranky" with her, but I'm a little upset that she didn't tell me anything about this. I know this isn't in agreement, but after last night's conversation, I feel we would share more details.

———————————

Rell

When I got Jansen's text, I knew exactly why he wanted to talk. It wasn't my fault that when I got the long-awaited phone call from the clothing brand about a potential clothing deal, I just happened to be with Laura while she was on the phone with Jay. We'd been out shopping for hours. I bought nothing, but I helped her style some outfits. I could never afford what she purchased, but it was nice being able to shop for top-label brands. Of course, I documented shopping at these places for *The Gram*.

Last week while I was in LA, a famous brand of clothing known among influencers contacted me about potentially getting a line of clothing through them. I was ecstatic but quickly discovered I wasn't the only influencer they had in mind. So, I went through an interview process and showed them the type of clothing I would like to have, and then they were going to decide who they wanted. I was stressing out for the rest of the week. It was a dream of mine to do this one day, and I knew that if I didn't get this now, I probably never would. There was no reason to mention it to Jansen last night because if it didn't work out, then it didn't matter to him, but now that I got it, we have a problem. I'll need to talk to him to determine what will happen between us.

I shoot him a quick response.

Me- Yes. I just got home.

Only five minutes pass, and there is a knock on my front door. I know who it is, exactly.

I open the door, and Jansen walks in without saying anything. I can already tell he's going to get fussy about this. I know he promised last night he would try to do a better job speaking with me, so we will see how this goes.

"Hello to you, too," I say, rolling my eyes.

"Sorry." he takes a seat on the couch. "Hello."

"Look, I didn't get a chance to speak with you first about this because Laura was on the phone with Jay standing next to me when I got the call, okay," I say, taking a seat next to him.

"Congratulations on the clothing line, by the way."

I frown. Whatever this is, it's complicated between us, but I feel bad not being able to tell Jansen. Since Bree has been out with

Kent this weekend, she hasn't been available for me to tell her. It all happened not even an hour ago. Laura's gossip traveled fast.

"Thank you. I'm sorry."

"We aren't in a real relationship or anything, so it's not like I should be the first person you tell. It surprised me when Jay mentioned it, and I knew nothing."

"Well, there's more to this that we need to talk about." I take a deep breath, and he straightens to look at me. "I'm staying in LA for a month to work on the clothing line."

He looked surprised, "You're leaving?"

"They want me there after next week. I'll still be able to come home on the weekends, and then I'll need to be back in LA Monday through Friday. So I can still do this fake relationship deal with you on the weekends. Laura knows about this, so it will work out."

His face falls, and something tells me there's more to this than he's letting on.

"How was lunch?" I ask him to change the subject.

He leans back on the couch, crossing his arms. "It went well. We didn't talk about you, so I didn't have to come up with any lies."

"Good, I didn't talk about you either. I hate lying, so it was good that I didn't have to lie about anything." I sit back and cross my arms, just like him.

It's then that he notices my hand and leans over to me. He takes my hand in his, looking at the ring on my finger. I needed to be still engaged while out with Laura today, so I found the ring I already had.

"Where did you get this?" he asks me.

I pull my hand out of his, "I had it," and then I get up from the couch.

"It doesn't look like the one you wore on Friday, I'll give it back to you, and you can wear that one from now on," he demands.

"This one's fine. Laura probably didn't even notice a difference."

I catch him rolling his eyes at me. He's annoyed for no reason.

I walk into the kitchen to grab boxed water from the fridge, and when I get back to the living room, Jansen is still, arms crossed, sitting on the couch.

"Laura and Jay invited us over tomorrow afternoon. They are hosting a barbeque with some people from the office coming. I told Laura we would be there," I say to Jansen, handing him the water.

"Sounds good," he says.

"Great."

Chapter Seven

Jansen

Another date with Rell before she leaves town, I'll take it. When she dropped the bombshell of not only a clothing line of her own but that she would stay in LA for a month, I was unhappy. Don't get me wrong; I'm happy that she got an opportunity to get herself out there and show people something else about her by getting this clothing line. It's so displeasing that it meant I couldn't see her during the week, but it would be much easier for me to focus at work, knowing where she was when she was not home. There I am, back to no distractions.

Knowing my days with Rell will be over soon once she leaves for LA, I want to spend time with her. While she says she wants to continue helping me, she has yet to ask me for help in return, making me think this little game we are playing won't last much longer. I don't see how she'll want to spend her weekends helping me when she's away from home all week. She has other things I'm sure she would like to do instead. I know she and Laura are becoming friends, Rell has that presence about her, and she makes friends quickly. It's why Rell has one point five million followers on, *The Gram*. I don't care what other people say about her. She's probably the most incredible person I've ever met. There's a chance that this clothing line could mean she makes a move to LA, so I need to enjoy my time with her while she is here.

I walk over to Rell's house to get her before we leave for The Wilsons, wearing jeans and a flannel button-up. The sun shines bright, but the breeze in the air makes me shiver.

I knocked on her door and waited for her to answer. Turning around, I see Margret on the sidewalk with her neighbor friend, Linda. I wave to them and know this will be all they will discuss today.

Rell answers, looking hot as hell. She wears a fitted black sweater, flared jeans, and high-heeled boots. Her long brown hair is down and straight. She's wearing just enough makeup to look natural and jewelry. This is *not* good. Not a single person will believe she is with me at this gathering, considering I'm just an average guy who doesn't talk much, and I'm bringing someone who lights up a room.

She walks out the door and then turns to lock it. I still haven't said a word.

"Hello to you too," she says, "When are you going to quit being so rude?"

I then grab Rell's hand and hold it, giving Margret and Linda precisely the show they wanted to see. We walk down the stairs to the sidewalk, and surprisingly Rell hasn't swatted my hand away yet.

She looks over to see Margret and Linda. She waves at them and realizes we are holding hands, and she yanks her hand away before yelling "Hi" to them.

We get into the truck, "Why are you being weird?"

"Well, why did you have to look so hot?" I blurt out. I'm instantly regretting saying that out loud.

She looks over at me, shaking her head, "I didn't realize we had a dress code for these dates."

"We don't," I say as I start the truck so we can be on our way for another awkward dinner.

Rell and I share some of our favorite things on the way over there in case we get ridiculous questions this time. Her favorite color is pink; she doesn't drink coffee and likes indie music. I didn't know these things, but I don't think we will share this information with anyone else. We need to ask each other better questions, like about our fake relationship, but by the time I think about it, we've already arrived.

She lets me open her door to let her out, and we are already off to a better start than the last time we were here. People walk around the back when we get there, so we follow them. I retake Rell's hand because I like holding it and want people here to know she is mine, even though she isn't. Pretending with Rell can be great, and I need some fun right now. But are we really even faking it?

When we turn the corner of the house, there are way more people from the office than I imagined. I pull Rell closer to me as comfort because even though I see most of these people daily, I don't know them. This is the downfall of wanting only to work when I am at work. I get nervous, and my palms start to get sweaty.

"Rell, there you two are," I hear Laura's voice and follow it to see her and Jay standing on the back deck. Rell pulls me to follow her to Laura. They hug and exchange kisses on the cheek.

"Jay," I say, waving to him.

"Thank you for coming," Laura says to Rell.

"Thank you for inviting us. There are a lot more people than I expected," Rell answers.

Nice to know Rell thinks this is too many people too.

Someone comes up to Laura and Jay, and they turn their attention over to them. I look around to see who all is here and still holding Rell's hand for comfort and show. Mainly comfort. I notice an odd amount of attention from other people looking our way, and I look at Rell to ensure there isn't anything wrong with her. Then it dawns on me that all these people know her.

"Shit Rell, we have to leave," I whisper.

"Language, cranky."

Holding her hand, I drag her down on the lawn with me, away from everyone so no one can hear us. "No, I am serious. I forgot all these people know who you are, and it's going to blow our cover with the Wilsons."

She looks around and notices all the eyes on her.

"Shit." She says.

"Language, hot stuff."

"What are we going to do? Oh my gosh, I've ruined this for you," she puts her hand on her forehead before looking down.

I look around the backyard again and think for a second. We could leave then my day with Rell is over. We could stay and hope no one says anything, or the worst option, we can tell the truth. Honestly, none of these options sound great at this time. I want to stay just as much as she does, so we should stay. We can hope no one says anything. If they do, then we can come up with a story.

"We're staying," I say.

She lifts her head to look at me. "Are you sure?"

"Yes, I am."

She smiles at me, and I pull her in for a hug. Not on our list of rules, but I don't care. She doesn't pull back when I hug her and instead wraps her arms around me and squeezes me before letting go. I know it was for show. I retake her hand and walk back over to the party of people hanging around the back porch. I'm sure Rell wants to keep to herself, so she doesn't slip on who she is. Who knew I would fake dating someone famous?

After we both make plates of food, piling them high with different sides and barbeque meats, we play it safe and sit at the table with Laura and Jay. It's just the four of us at a table. We all stay primarily quiet while we eat, with the women talking about the shopping trip they took yesterday.

Laura yells to everyone when we are all done eating and picking up our mess. "Who's ready for the games?"

There was no mention of games being played today until now. I meet Rell at the trash can as she is throwing away her plate, and she seems to be just as surprised about this as me. Since she was the one who knew about this gathering before me, I figured she would know about this. "What game are we playing?" I ask her.

Before she can answer, someone from the office says, "The newlywed game. We play every year at this couple's gathering. Watch out for Ted and his wife, Nancy. They win every year."

Rell overhears what he just told me and smiles like it's game on. I know three things about Rell, and as much as I love a game, there is no chance we can win this. None.

We all drew numbers out of a bowl to determine what order we would go. Rell and I got the last group, so we had time to ask questions and prepare for our turn. We are both seated next to each other at a table far from the others. She's sitting back, legs crossed, watching everyone play when I lean in to whisper, "Let's ask questions."

She looks over her shoulder at me, "No, I want to see how well we know each other without asking questions."

"Fine, I hope you like losing then."

When it's our turn, we learn we only need a score of five to win. The first and second-round winning couples only earned a score of four. Rell and I took our seats. Our chairs are back to back, so we can't take a peek at each other's questions. I think for a second how much fun it would be to put down the wrong answer even if I knew the honest answer since Rell didn't seem to care to learn more about me before the game. Everyone else playing this game is married. Rell and I only got in on the fun since we are "engaged."

Laura asks, "What is your spouse's favorite color?"

Easy. I write down pink, and Rell should be writing down black. We know this.

Everyone gave their answers, and Rell answered correctly.

Laura asked, "What is your spouse's most prized possession?"

This one is a hard one for both of us. I would say mine's probably my deer. I have no idea what Rell's could be, so I'm left to guess. When it gets to us to answer, Rell says, "His deer hanging above his mantle," as her answer, and I'm impressed. Her answer to the question is her swinging daybed, which was what I had guessed—another point for us. We get the following two questions right again. They ask more fundamental questions about each other. Her drink of choice is a smoothie, while mine is beer. Then we get to the question of their favorite types of music, her indie and mine country. We talked about all this in the car on the way over here, and while I thought they were dumb questions, they came in handy.

We're all tied at four and previous winning couples of this outrageous game. While I feel like there is a chance for us, I already answered the only questions I could about Rell. There is nothing left that I know.

Laura asks us the game's last question: "How many home runs did Mac Milligan score for the San Francisco Seals last season?"

A surprising question. We all seem confused, so Laura explains, "If you love your spouse enough, you watch sports together. Everyone should know this answer."

I know the answer, the San Francisco Seals will be the best in the league this year after making it to the world series last season. I was thrilled to move to a city with an incredible major-league baseball team. While I know the answer, I guarantee Rell knows nothing about sports.

All the other teams' husbands answer correctly, but their wives all answer wrong. Rell and I are the last ones to give our answers. I give my answer, fifty-two. I wince, knowing Rell might give an embarrassing response. I look down at the ground. Rell picks up her dry-erase board with her answer, and I turn around to see what she wrote. She wrote down the correct answer. She knows sports. What the hell? I can't help but wonder how Rell knew the answer.

"You watch sports?" I ask her with a smile.

She shrugs her shoulders, "It was just a lucky guess."

She's lying. That wasn't just a lucky guess. She somehow knew the answer to that question.

We might have won, but there was no prize. The game was played purely for entertainment and to get to know everyone there. While the fun was getting started, I knew it was probably time for me and Rell to leave. We have been able to keep to ourselves all afternoon, and I would like to keep it that way. I don't care if someone spoils Rell's identity after we leave as long as we aren't here when it happens. I know our days together are coming to an end soon, anyways.

Taking Rell by the hand, we walk to Laura and Jay to say our goodbyes before being the first people to leave the party. When we get in the truck, I am still interested in Rell's sports knowledge. I know she must watch sports if she hasn't already stunned me enough.

"Okay, without lying this time. Do you watch sports?"

She is scrolling through her phone and puts it away so she can look at me when she talks. "Caught me. I might have watched some baseball games last season,"

"Do you watch anything besides baseball?"

"I watch college football, went to a few NFL games, and some major league baseball games," she shrugs like it's no big deal.

"It's cute when a woman watches sports," I smile.

"When Bree and I were flight attendants, we went to as many games as possible when traveling. It was what we did to pass the time while visiting different cities. Then when we moved here, we just continued going. So I know a thing or two about sports. I couldn't say it while we were there because people who know me on The Gram know my love for sports."

"See, these are the conversations we should have had all along. You told me so much about yourself that I didn't know."

She rests on the armrest between us and leans closer to me. "I think you forgot that you were the one who didn't want to get to know each other," she said, poking me in the arm with her index finger.

She isn't wrong. Our first date at the Wilson's was a disaster because of me. I didn't want to get to know her then, but now she leaves me so interested in who she is that I want to ask all the questions.

We pull up to my house, and Rell wastes no time getting out of the truck and walking around the back. By the time I am out, she is already almost at her house.

"Where are you going?" I ask her.

She walks toward me and stops at the fence separating our yards. "Home."

"Do you not need my help anymore with content?"

She points her finger at me, "Right, content. I almost forgot."

I pull my phone from my back pocket and simultaneously pull Rell into my arms. I have one arm across her chest, just at her shoulders, and hold the phone out in front of us. I put my face close to Rell's and snap a perfect picture. A new photo for her contact picture.

I slowly let her go, "I'll send that to you."

"Thanks, see you around," she says while walking back to her house.

She is always quick to leave and says, "See you around," which I am starting to hate. It is her way of not committing to seeing me again. If I had known that she wanted to end this time together so quickly, I would have stayed at the party longer than we did. I wave bye to her even though I know she is inside already, and then head inside.

Chapter Eight

Rell

My suitcase is open and lying on my bed. The time to leave for LA has arrived, and I can't wait to start this month-long adventure. It has been a long week of waiting and sharing lots of content. After my day with Jansen a week ago, I shared our photo on, T*he Gram* account. My followers seemed obsessed with the idea of me finally sharing a boyfriend. Too bad it is all pretend, and I'm not sure how long it will last.

Jansen and I got together a couple more times this week, sharing photos of holding hands and lounging on the daybed swing, but our moments together were short and nothing more than the photos taken. The ideas of the content were his, and I thought it was thoughtful of him. We are finally getting along, and my time spent with him has been fun lately. My followers see a side of me they haven't, helping me gain a larger following. I have Jansen to thank because I was on the verge of not wanting to spend time with him or share us anymore. Since Laura and I had gotten close, I knew that meant I still needed to help Jansen. I was going to try to slide by without asking for Jansen's help, but when he mentioned it, I couldn't tell him no.

"Which one do you think?" I ask Bree holding up a black jacket in one hand and a denim one in the other. I'm packing for my trip, and I *need* clothes to impress.

"The black jacket," she says, lying on my bed.

I throw the black jacket in my suitcase and continue flipping through my closet, looking for more clothes to pack. "Are you sure you don't want to come?" I ask her.

Laughing, she says, "Rell, you can do this without me."

"I know."

Bree has Kent coming here to stay with her this week while I am gone. We filmed extra content videos and photos so she would be busy with our account. She wanted to ensure I had nothing on my mind while I was gone, and I'm relieved she thought of that. I'll update her every day while I'm there and not have to worry about our account. As for Jansen, things between us will stay the same while I'm gone. If he needs me for anything with our arrangement, I'll hear from him. I want to come home next weekend and enjoy my birthday, so I hope he doesn't make any plans for us. I think I've had enough pretending for now.

"Are you mad at me that I won't be here this weekend when you get back?" Bree asks.

I frown at her, "Mad, no. Sad, yes. I'm heartbroken that my best friend won't be here to celebrate my birthday."

My birthday is Saturday, and Kent made plans for them to go on an overnight date, so it looks like I'll be spending it alone. I could tell Jansen about my birthday, but I don't feel like I need to, considering we barely know each other. At this point, I'm not even sure what to call us besides neighbors.

I pack the rest of my things with help from Bree, and then she drives me to the airport. This is my first trip without Bree. We give each other hugs and say goodbyes as if I was going away for a long time. Rolling my oversized luggage bag through the airport, I feel the same way I did on my first day as a flight attendant. I feel like this is my first genuine big-girl job on my own. Nervous is an understatement. I'm feeling all sorts of emotions.

Before getting to my gate, I stop at a small store inside the airport to grab a book, gummy worms, and water. My necessities when traveling. I wait for boarding, pulling my phone out of my bag to pass the time. I'm always an early traveler. Something I learned from my flight attendant days. No one wants to be that last passenger everyone stares at while getting on the flight. Embarrassing.

Just when they announce boarding over the intercom, a text comes through my phone.

Jansen- Good Luck this week

I smile just before putting my phone back inside the side pocket of my carry-on bag.

I never did get a goodbye from Jansen before now. Nor has he ever texted me anything that doesn't have to do with our arrangements. This is one message I don't mind sliding outside of our agreement.

I slide my bag on my arm before getting in line with everyone else. *Here it goes.* I'm just under two hours from what I hope is something extraordinary.

After my flight, I book an uber while I wait for my luggage at the baggage claim. I should be going to my hotel first, but I think checking in can wait. I don't want to wait any longer to see the *Threads* office and meet everyone there.

Threads is a women's clothing brand. They will produce a single line of clothing designed by me. Their fashion consists of everyday clothing, and they're a well-known company amongst influencers, and I know this will be a once and lifetime deal for me. For them to choose me over others is quite a big deal. I want to go into this knowing this could be my only shot at getting my clothing line. I'm going to give it my all.

After grabbing my bag from the baggage claim, my uber ride awaited me when I got outside. The friendly woman driver gets out, helps me put my bag in the truck, and we get inside the car. I give her the address to the *Threads* office, and she starts the route.

Los Angeles is seriously so gorgeous. Bree and I frequently visited this place when we were flight attendants. We considered moving here once but ultimately knew that San Francisco felt more like home. We know quite a few influencers who call LA home, and we didn't want to add ourselves to the list. We have always wanted to be different from everyone else.

It takes the driver an hour to get to *Threads*. Thanks to the terrible LA traffic. She pulls up out front and helps me get my bag. I stand out in front of the vast modern black office with the word *Threads* in white across the front. I walk up to the two glass front doors, rolling my luggage behind me. I open the door to find a white counter at the front door and two ladies dressed in Threads clothing standing behind it. "Hello, Welcome to Threads," one of them says.

"Hello, Rell Campbell. I'm here for Stacey Pierce."

"Rell, it's so nice to meet you. We have heard all about you," she holds her hand out for me to shake. "Come this way,"

She's a tall skinny blonde, a model for sure. I follow behind her, still rolling my luggage with me. She takes us down a long hallway with offices on both sides of the hall. "I'm Felicia, by the way," she says, turning her head back to me while we continue down the aisle of offices.

"Nice to meet you, Felicia."

She stops right at the end of the hall at a double door. "This is Stacey's office. She's expecting you, so she should be inside," Felicia says, knocking on the door before opening it.

She opens one of the doors, and Stacey sits behind her desk. Felicia holds the door for me to walk in. "Hello, Stacey."

"Rell," she says before getting up from her desk to greet me at the door. "How was the flight here?"

"It was good, thank you," I say nervously.

"Come in, take a seat." She says, pointing to a chair in her office.

Stacey's office is nice but very basic. She has a couple of green velvet chairs across from her wooden desk. Her walls hold just a couple of framed photos of models wearing Threads clothing.

Stacey sits back at her desk, and Felicia leaves, shutting the door behind her.

"So, are you excited?"

"Yes, I am ready to start," I say, my nerves feeling slightly less tense than when I walked in.

"This week, I'll give you a tour of the design office, show you the fabric studio, and we'll start drawing some ideas you have. Next week, we'll get more into the design aspect and so on."

"Sounds good," I nod.

I might be slightly anxious, but I know that ideas will come to mind once I tour and see the fabrics.

Stacey is older, mid 50's. She has darker long hair back in a hair clip. She's wearing layers of clothing, and I'm sure they are all from Threads. She seemed nice, and we got along well when I met her during my interview process for the clothing line. She hasn't come across as bossy yet and knows clothes better than anyone I've ever met. I know she will greatly help me and what kind of clothing I want to produce.

"Alright, let's go take a quick tour, and then you can check into your hotel for the day,"

She gets up from her cute green velvet desk chair, and I follow her through her office door back down the long hallway. She points to Felicia and another blonde working the front counter. "This is Felicia and Shae. They work the front desk. You will see them every day."

I wave to them and then take off down another long hall on the opposite side of the building. We reach the fabric room first, and when we walk in, my face lights up at all the fabric options to choose from. I don't wear a lot of florals and prints, but there are some in here that I would consider for a skirt or top. I run my fingers down the fabrics on the shelf while looking around. They are so soft, and you can tell they are all made of excellent quality.

Stacey stands at the door and watches me while I look around at all the fabrics. Some ideas are already starting to flow in my brain, and I know this will be one of my life's best experiences.

Once I meet Stacey back at the door, we walk out together. She then leads us to another set of double doors, and when we walk through them, we are in the warehouse. There is clothing covering every wall, shoes lining shelves and boxes. There are people at tables boxing orders and getting them prepped to mail out. "Wow."

"This is where the magic happens. You get to see the stuff you worked so hard on get shipped to someone who loves it,"

"Incredible." I'm astonished.

She gives me a quick tour of the warehouse, then we walk back to her office, where we talk about a few more things regarding what I will be doing during my time here, and then I take my luggage and roll it with me to the front door. I'm done here for the day, and I can't wait to come back tomorrow to get started.

"See you tomorrow!" I say, smiling while opening the front door with my backside.

They both lift their heads, returning the smile, and then wave before I walk out the door.

Chapter Nine

Jansen

They broke ground this week on the condos. I've been working hard for days now, making sure that all the deliveries of supplies are here and that we have everything we need to get these buildings started. It meant I worked some late nights this week in the office without any plans or Rell being home; that was easy for me to do. I have hardly spoken to Jay this week, considering we have both been busy in the office during the day. I don't want to admit it, but I have been trying to avoid him, so we don't make any plans for the weekend.

It's Thursday now, and I deserve a pleasant night's swim after my long week. There's been a few nights this week that I've seen Kent and Bree on the back porch when taking out the trash, but I haven't interacted with them. That's because they're always too busy making out to notice I walked out there. If I see them out there tonight, I'm sure it'll be the same.

I grab a towel from the bathroom before walking out the back door. I'm just wearing a shirt and swimming trunks, and it's cold, giving me goosebumps before jumping into the water. I again take a kid's approach and make a huge splash—water splashing around the pool's edges. When I come up to the surface, I swim over to the side.

Even though I know Rell isn't home this week, I would still like to know how she is doing. She never responded to the text I sent her before flying out to LA. When I get to the side, I look over to see the back porch empty, but the lights are on inside the house. To pass the time, I swim laps around the small pool to get a little workout. It doesn't take many laps before I spot Bree coming out the back door and walking down the stairs. I ignore that I see her even though I secretly want to ask her about Rell. She comes over to the side of the fence while I take one last lap.

"Hey," Bree yells out to me.

I turn around, pretending to be surprised to see her there, "Hey."

"I have been wanting to ask you something," she says.

Swimming over to the other side of the pool, I get out and dry off. I wrap the towel around me before walking up to Bree. If she needed to talk to me, she shouldn't have swapped spit with her boy toy all week when I was outside.

"Yes," I say, stopping right in front of her.

"Rell's thirtieth birthday is Saturday. We are having a surprise birthday party tomorrow night. I was wondering if you would want to come,"

"Of course, I will be there."

"Great, we'll be setting everything up tomorrow in the backyard. We're inviting some of our friends. You can help too if you'd like," She smiles like she needs help decorating, so she wants me to say yes.

"I can help after work."

"Perfect. Rell gets in sometime after seven. Can you be the one to pick her up from the airport? She thinks I'll be out of town with Kent this weekend, and I don't want to spoil the surprise for her. She can't know that you know it is her birthday," she once again shoots me a big smile like she is pleading for me to say yes again.

"I can do that. Do you need anything else from me?"

"Nope. That's all," Bree says, skipping away from the fence and back up the stairs. "Thank you, Jansen. See you tomorrow."

I nod before she walks in the back door. I wouldn't miss Rell's surprise birthday party for anything. I need to figure out if I should show up as the neighbor Jansen or the fake boyfriend, Jansen. Also, her followers will know it's her birthday, and a gift from her boyfriend needs to be shared. I'll need some free time tomorrow to pick up Rell a gift.

I walk over to my back door, taking my semi-wet, cold body back inside with a smile on my face. It isn't until I'm about to get into the shower that I realize I never asked Bree how Rell was doing this week in LA. Luckily she asked me to be the one to get her from the airport, so I will be the first person she sees when she returns.

I didn't care how busy I was today with work. I was leaving early and coming to help Bree. She has me inside on decorating duty. I am hanging streamers, balloons, and whatever else she needs me to do. On my way over, I stopped by the party store to get Rell two giant pink foil balloons. One is a three, and the other is a zero. I tied them to the pink flowers I got her along with a card with her gift inside that I know she will love, hopefully. It didn't take long to figure out what I should get Rell for her birthday.

Bree and Kent are outside, decorating the backyard. They hired a company to set up a large balloon arch with different shades of pink balloons. They also had large white letters that said *RELL 30*, and all lit up with bright bulbs. Everything out back is glamorous, putting my two pink foil balloons to shame, but I don't care. I still think Rell will like my gift for her.

I look over to the clock, knowing I must leave soon to pick up Rell from the airport. The front doorbell rings, and I'm just about to head back to tell Bree I'm going. Looking around, I think, why not answer myself even though I don't live here? It's probably just a friend for the party. Walking to the front door, I open it, and to my surprise, it's a delivery. A man holding a large box is standing there.

"Hello," I say, opening the door wider.

"Delivery for Rell Campbell?" The older man says before handing over the box to me.

"Thanks, I'll get it to her."

"Good day," the man says, walking off the front porch.

I close the door and see a card on top of the large red box. Setting the red box on the counter next to the flowers I got Rell, I looked around the room to see if anyone was around. Then my eyes spot an open envelope taped to the top of the box. I'm interested in what's in the box and from who.

Pulling out a little white card, I open it to read it.

Happy Birthday my Beautiful Rell

I hope your 30th is your best year yet.

I miss you every day.

Love, M.

Who the heck is M? I shake my head, confused because when I asked Rell if she had a boyfriend, she laughed and said no, but this sure as hell looks like it's from a boyfriend. Then again, he said he misses her every day.

Sliding the card back into the envelope, I take the top off the red box on the counter to find at least one hundred perfect red roses nicely lined up inside the red box. When the hell did roses come in a box?

Putting the top back on the box of roses, I try to calm myself down from getting anxious over this delivery. Rell and I are.... I don't even know. I don't understand why something like this is getting me so worked up.

Bree walks in from the back door and notices the box on the counter. She looks at me and then at the box again. It's like she knows who sent them. Maybe it's something this person always sends to Rell on her birthday. What if it's her mother? *Oh my god, I'm so dumb. They are from her mother.*

"We got a delivery?" Bree asks me.

"Yes," I say, not trying to sound suspicious. "Well, I should probably go get Rell now," I tell Bree as I walk backward out of the kitchen, smacking my back on the doorframe.

"You good?" Bree asks me.

"Yep. I'll be right back," I turn around, walking quickly to the front door.

She knows that I opened that box.

Rell

This week spent in LA was the start of something good for me. We didn't do much designing yet, but I met everyone working there and learned about the brand Threads. I made a couple of new friends in Felicia and Shae, and next week they plan to take me out for drinks and to explore some of LA more. I can't wait to come back on Monday and start working on my line.

Since she's out of town, Bree texted me earlier today that a friend would pick me up from the airport. She didn't say what friend but that I would recognize them when I landed. My flight just landed, and I am walking through the airport to the baggage claim to gather my bag. I knew whoever was here to get me would be waiting for me.

I haven't spoken to anyone besides Bree this week, and I was hoping someone would message me about making plans for my birthday, but I never got a message. Jansen doesn't know, and I didn't intend to tell him. We hardly know each other enough for me to spend my special day with him. I don't want to give him that kind of pressure.

In line for the escalator, I glance through my phone to ensure I haven't missed any messages about who was there to pick me up. Bree knows surprises aren't my favorite thing. I get on the escalator, still looking through my phone, and once I come up short, I slide it into the side pocket of my bag. Looking around the airport for anyone I might recognize, I see Jansen standing behind a little old lady with a smile. I can't help but smile in return and feel some tiny butterflies in my stomach. He isn't who I thought would pick me up, but now that I know it is him, I'm not a tiny bit sad about it.

When I get off the escalator, Jansen walks up to me and surprisingly takes my carry-on bag from me. "Thank you. You don't have to do that."

"I don't get a hello? Don't be so rude," he says, smiling.

"Hello," I smile while walking beside him to the baggage claim.

"How was LA?"

"It was good. How is San Francisco?"

"Busy, but I am sure it missed you," I instantly realize that maybe he isn't talking about San Francisco. Perhaps he's talking about him.

We stop feet away from the baggage claim to wait. Jansen looks nice tonight, as if he has plans, or maybe he just got off work. He's wearing jeans, a nice flannel button-up, and boots. While I usually am dressed nice, tonight I opted for a sweatshirt, leggings, and sneakers because I couldn't get out of my skirt, matching top, and heels fast enough once I got through working at *Threads* today. I wanted to be comfy not only for my flight but because I was tired of dressing up every day.

Jansen looks to be waiting for my bag patiently, and I keep looking at him, trying to decide if I should tell him tomorrow is my birthday since he is the one and the only person here this weekend that I could spend it with.

"Something you need to tell me?" keeping his eyes forward.

"Can we stop and get an In-N-Out burger when we leave here? I'm starving."

He shakes his head no and continues to watch for my bag.

"I'm so hungry. I've been eating salads and poke bowls all week, and I want something delicious right now. Please," pouting my lower lip to Jansen.

He huffs, "Fine, but if the line is long, we can't… um…." he looks at me, pointing his finger like he doesn't remember what he was going to say.

I tilt my head at him, confused, "We can't what?"

"We will get the food, and I have strict instructions to take you home."

I shrug, "Bree can be so bossy. What the heck does she need me home for anyways? She's not there."

He gives me a sexy smile before laughing just as the bags start coming in.

Once he grabs my adorable pink luggage bag, we walk to his parked truck outside the exit. He throws all my load in his backseat before we get into the vehicle. He types in his navigation In-N-Out burger and then drives off following the directions. There is only one location, and I know it will be busy, so hopefully, he doesn't change his mind.

When we get closer, his phone goes off with a message, and he responds quickly before putting his phone away in the cupholder. I pretend that I didn't notice that he was texting and driving. His phone goes off again, but this time I grab it. "I can respond for you."

He looks over, snatching the phone quickly from my hands. I didn't even get a chance to see who it was. "You can't see that."

"Well, you shouldn't be texting and driving."

He puts the phone away in his door pocket, and we pull up at the restaurant. It's crowded with cars and people, but the line isn't too bad. Looking over at Jansen, waiting for him to tell me no, he surprisingly pulls into the drive-thru line. He must know that when a girl says she is starving, you feed the woman, and I can appreciate that about him.

"What are you getting?" I ask him.

"Nothing."

I sit straight in my seat, leaning closer to him with my elbow supporting my weight on the armrest, "What. Come on now. You can't let me eat alone."

He leans his head back, resting it on his headrest, and then looks over at the menu.

"Fine. I'll get a double-double with fries."

"Really! That's a good choice. I want the same but animal-style fries. I've been craving those since the last time I was here."

We pull up to the window, and he orders the same order as me. I can already smell the food, and it makes my stomach growl. Jansen looks over at me, laughing.

"Did you eat anything this week?"

"Everyone at Threads barely takes a lunch break, and most days, food got delivered, but it was always salads. Sometimes things I couldn't even tell you what it was. When I got to my hotel every night, it was always too late to order and wait on room service."

We get to the window, and they hand us our food and drinks. My mouth is watering when Jansen sets the food between us. I waste no time opening up the fries container and looking for utensils to eat them. I dig right in once I take the fork out of its wrapper, and we haven't even left the parking lot. I hear Jansen's phone go off again, but he doesn't even look at it this time and instead asks me to open his fries. He must be starving, too, but he doesn't want to admit it. I set my fries down to help him, handing him his with a fork. He takes one huge bite and starts moaning like it is the best thing he has ever eaten.

"Good, right?"

He shakes his head yes as he has another mouthful of fries.

It takes us two minutes to finish our fries, and then we eat our burgers simultaneously. We are just a few minutes from home, and I am so glad I didn't wait till we got there to eat. This meal was everything I wanted right now. Thankfully Jansen didn't let me get hangry, and we finally got to share a meal that wasn't a fancy dinner at the Wilsons.

We pull into Jansen's driveway, and I pick up our trash. Once he notices what I am doing, he tells me to leave it. I guess he wants the smell for tomorrow. When I get out of the truck, he already has his hands full with my bags. I walk over to take them from him, but he pulls them away.

"I'll take them in for you. Also, we need to go in through the back door." Jansen nods in the direction of the back of my house.

"That's ridiculous, come on," I say, taking off for the front door.

"Stop. We are going around the side and into the back. That way, no one sees that you'll be home alone. There could be someone out here watching you."

"Yeah, you are that someone out here watching me," I smirk.

After looking around, clearly evident that we were alone, so I took off toward the back anyway. Jansen follows behind me, and all I can hear is my luggage bag rolling across the concrete. I open the side gate, and once in the back, I hear "Surprise!" before all the lights turn on, including large letters that say *RELL 30*.

I throw my hands up to cover my face. Bree knows surprises make me nervous. I feel Jansens hand on my back give me a little push to walk. So I take my hands down from my face and start greeting everyone. From the corner of my eye, I can see Jansen taking my bags inside the house at the back door. Then, I realize Bree must have asked him for help with this surprise.

Our friends are here, including a few influencers from our area. I give everyone hugs and thank them for coming. Everyone already has drinks in their hand, and I search around, knowing I need to find myself a drink because this has been a long week. Instantly music starts playing as if someone just turned on their music playlist because there isn't a DJ here. I finally spot Bree, and she comes up and gives me a giant squeeze. "Surprised?"

"Yes, I even made Jansen stop for In-N-out burgers before coming here. I had no idea."

"That explains why he didn't respond to my message. I was wondering what was taking so long," Bree says with her finger on her chin.

That explains why he didn't let me see his phone. I wonder why he ignored it once we got food if he knew Bree was wondering where we were.

"Well, go mingle and have some fun. It is your last day in your twenties," she winks.

"*Ha Ha,*" I say to her just before she walks off.

Everyone around the backyard is talking, so I slip away for a minute. I need to find the drinks. Turning around, I take off for the house, knowing I could find a drink inside. When I open the back door, Jansen stands with two drinks in his hand. "Here, I was bringing this to you."

I smile before taking the drink from him. "Thank you," then I tip the cup up to him, "I was looking for this."

"It's white wine. Hopefully, that is your preference because it seems to be all Bree bought," he shrugged.

"It is."

Slipping through the door to head back outside with my drink, thanks to Jansen, and he follows. I take a sip of my wine and start making my way around to people in the backyard. Being around a lot of people usually isn't my thing, but I know this is what Bree would want me to do. I peek back to see Jansen is no longer behind me but socializing among some of my friends. I think it's great for him to meet people, knowing he hasn't met many people here since he moved. This is probably the first time I have been around Jansen that we haven't had to pretend that we are a couple, and it dawns on me that even though these people here are my friends, they think Jansen is my boyfriend, according to *The Gram* account. I will keep my distance for now, but I know we'll need to get cozy if someone says anything.

I find a group of people and make conversation. Most people ask me about being in LA and working with *Threads* for the week. I tell them all about my experiences. Bree ends up hearing me talk about it, and she ends up in our group. Our conversation turns to influence stuff, and Bree gets excited about it. While Bree is talking, I look around once more to see if I can find Jansen, and this time I come up short. Surely, he hasn't left the party yet.

"Excuse me for a minute," I put my hand on Bree's shoulder before walking away.

I don't know why I keep looking for him, but I do. Part of me wants to see what he's doing. I stand on the back porch, looking around the yard, and he's nowhere in sight. Opening the door to walk inside, I find him pouring more wine into his cup. When I walk in, he looks up at me with the sexiest smile, giving me a slight chill.

"Hey," He mutters.

"Hey."

He reaches up and scratches the back of his neck. "There are a lot of people out there I don't know, so I came in to get more drinks," he lifts his cup to me.

"I understand. That is too many people for me," I walk over beside him before noticing two large giant pink 30 balloons tied to flowers.

"I wonder who these are from," I tug on one of the balloons, then lean in to smell the flowers.

"Me," he says, looking up at me while leaning against the counter.

"Jansen, that's sweet. You really shouldn't have."

He sets his drink on the kitchen counter and crosses his arms while looking at me as I admire the flowers and balloons he got me. "I wasn't sure if I was supposed to be neighbor Jansen tonight or boyfriend Jansen, so I went with who I thought I should be, your boyfriend."

I smile at him, "Good choice."

Taking the card with my name on it that's attached to the flowers, I open the envelope and pull out a blank pink card. Opening the card, I pull out two tickets to the season opener game for San Francisco Seals. I look up at him and smile.

"You can take Bree or anyone else you want to take."

"Thank you."

"You're welcome."

Putting the tickets back into the envelope, I slide them into a drawer in the kitchen so no one will find them. When I turn back to the kitchen island, I see a huge red box and look over to Jansen.

"Who is this from?"

Jansen shrugs his shoulders as if he doesn't know.

Taking the card off the box, I quickly realize these look familiar to a gift I had before but were white last year. Skimming the card, I then put it back into the envelope. I don't even open the box, already knowing what's inside. I don't feel like talking about who sent these to Jansen.

"Want to go back outside?" I ask him.

"Sure," he stands back up from leaning against the counter.

I walk out the door first, with him following closely behind me. I'm returning to the group of people Bree's standing with and turning around to see Jansen behind me. When I return to talking to everyone, I feel his hand slide around me, bringing me closer to him. I glance at him, and he gives me his best sensual smile. He's doing the most boyfriend thing he has ever done, and he's not even my boyfriend. *Yet.*

Chapter Ten

Jansen

I've done my best to stay around for the rest of the party. Now that everyone has left, it is time for us to clean up what mess we can for the night. Watching Rell pick up trash, I can tell she's tired, and I don't blame her if she wants to go to bed. She has been gone all week and to come home to a surprise party that has required her to stand and talk all night is exhausting. I didn't even leave for a week and found this party tiring, but I stuck it out for Rell. Bree and Kent are taking down some of the decorations on the other side of the backyard.

"Why don't you go to bed? I can finish up here."

"Okay," she throws away the last bit of trash in her hand and then starts to walk towards the house. She didn't even argue, so I know she's over it for the night.

"Rell," I yell to her before she makes it to the steps.

"Yea," she turns around with tired eyes.

"Happy Birthday."

She smiles before turning back around to walk inside the house.

I get back to cleaning up the backyard. It is past midnight now, and I'm ready for bed myself. My day has gone toward Rell, and while I enjoyed it, I don't know what has gotten into me. This wasn't supposed to happen when I came to San Francisco, but I bought flowers and baseball tickets for a girl because I wanted to. I could've turned her down when she asked to eat before coming home, but I didn't because I wanted that time with her. I wanted to know more about her trip but didn't ask. She's making me feel things inside that I haven't felt in a long time, and I can't just ignore them.

When I throw away the last of the trash, I find Bree and Kent sitting on the stairs holding hands and laughing. They have managed to be the most adorable couple. While I think Kent overpowers Bree, they look like a good couple.

"Thanks for letting me be a part of this. Goodnight, you two," I nod to them before walking off.

"Thanks for the help," Bree says while Kent waves at me.

I jump over the fence before walking into my house through the back door. Instead of showering before bed like I always do, tonight calls for just going straight to sleep. There will be a sleeping-in for me tomorrow, and I need it.

I wake up to the sound of my phone vibrating on the nightstand. It is early; I can feel it. I reach over with my eyes still closed and grab my phone. I don't even look at the screen before answering the call.

"Hello," I say with a raspy morning voice.

"Dude, where were all the pallets of wood out here yesterday? The crew is here to work, and all the supplies are gone."

Sitting straight up in my bed and pinching the bridge of my nose, "Do what now? Everything was out there last night. I don't understand. It would have to have been stolen."

"Hey," he yells to someone, "Jansen thinks someone stole it all."

"Shit. Give me a few minutes, and I'll be out there."

I hang up the phone and throw on the first thing that is appropriate to wear on the job site. Even though I'm just the project manager at the job site, you need a hard hat, which I don't bother grabbing because there won't be construction without supplies.

Getting into my truck, I drove out to the job site to see that it was completely clean of every supply we had out there. *Shit*. This does not look like a good situation for me. When I get out of the truck, I call Jay.

"Hello?"

"Jay, someone stole all the supplies sometime last night. The crew is here to work, and we have nothing."

"I knew something like this could happen. We have had this problem before."

"I will go to the office now and reorder all the supplies. I will get them out here as fast as I can."

"Okay. Let me know if you need any help with anything."

"Alright, will do," I say before hanging up the phone.

Before leaving, I yell at the guys to go and come back on Monday. This is not what I wanted to do today, but I don't have a choice. This job means so much to me, and it got screwed up.

I'm the only person in the office working on Saturday. It takes me hours to get everything back in line and some cameras installed on the property to make sure nothing like this happens again. We're almost out of money in my budget. The worst thing that could happen in my new job here happened, and I know I need to work harder to ensure something like this never happens on my watch again. I don't want to lose this job if it does.

It's almost dark when I get home, and I'm tired from waking up early. I realize I never ate anything today. I could go for precisely what Rell and I had last night. I get why she said she'd been craving those fries since the last time she ate them.

There are no lights on at her place, and I'm sure they're out for her birthday. This is something else I forgot today between all the mess I had to fix.

When I head inside, I take the longest steaming hot shower I've ever taken and get dressed in something comfortable. I look in my cabinets for something to eat, but I haven't been grocery shopping since I moved in, and I don't think I can make anything with what I have on hand. I find a package of beef jerky and eat a couple of pieces left at the bottom of the bag before throwing it away. The trash can full, so I pull the bag out, tie the strings, and take it out the back door.

When I throw it in the can, I see the back porch lights at Rell's house. There she is on her swing, with her book, *alone*. My heart tells me to go over there, but I shouldn't. Walking back to the house, I look over at her *one more time* before opening the door.

"Screw it."

Strolling over, I jump the fence. Rell sits up and looks down at me, smiling, which tells me I did the right thing.

"What are you doing?" she asks me.

"What are you doing?" I retort.

She frowns, "Just reading."

"Are you all alone on your birthday?" I walk up the steps, taking a seat on the swing by her feet.

"I've been alone all day. Bree and Kent went out of town for the night, so I've just been napping and reading all day before I leave again tomorrow."

I frown, looking down at the ground. I feel terrible that Rell has been alone for her birthday. She could've at least messaged Laura to go shopping or for lunch.

"I'm fixing to make something for dinner and film a video."

"You're going to film yourself cooking dinner?" I look up at her.

"It's part of the job," she shrugs.

"I'll get going so you can do that," I get up from the swing.

She puts her arm out to stop me from walking away. "Stay."

Turning around, I look into her pleading eyes. My mind said go; this is already crossing a road I didn't want to travel. My heart says stay; spend time with Rell because you know you want to. I'm all over the place right now but looking her in her eyes makes me want to stay.

"I'll stay."

Rell gets up from the swing, walks into the house with me following her, and closes the door when we get inside. She walks over to the fridge to pull out a bag. A phone stand on the kitchen island with a ring light is ready. It must be what she uses when she films her videos. Next to the phone stand, I see the flowers I got her for her birthday and the balloons still tied to them. The vast box of red roses is gone, and I wonder where they went. *Who were they from?*

Rell interrupts my thoughts, asking me, "Are you hungry?"

I move my eyes from the flowers on the counter to her, "Yes."

She sets the bag on the counter, then sets her phone up on the stand so she can film herself. I walk around to the other side of the kitchen island, taking a seat at one of the barstools to watch her. She smiles at me from the other side of the island while installing her camera.

"It won't take long. You can help me if you want."

I smile in return, "That's okay. I'm sure you can handle this on your own."

Rell brings the bag of food in front of the phone stand. I've seen these meal kits before and have never had one, but I know all the ingredients are in the bag. There's a disposable pan in the bag that tells me this is going to be an easy meal. I watch Rell easily talk into the camera as she assembles a creamy sun-dried tomato pasta dish. She mixes all the ingredients in the pan while continuing to record herself. Rell has a smile on her face the whole time and always looks at me, still smiling. Once she has everything together in the pan the way it should be, she turns off the phone. Then walks over to the stove to put in the oven.

"Done," she throws her hands up.

I laugh.

"I mean the video. I'll take a photo when I put it on a plate. Bree will edit it with our code, and everything will be good to go. People will use our code, and then we get paid, easy."

She opens the fridge to search for something. I watch her from behind, trying not to check her out. She bends down, pulling out a bottle of wine. I spot a tall cake covered in sprinkles on the fridge's top shelf. I wonder if we forgot it last night while we had her party, I never remember Bree mentioning one, and we never got one out for her.

"Where is the cake from?"

She turns back to look at me with the bottle of wine in her hand. "Oh, it was delivered today. It came from everyone at Threads. I haven't touched it yet."

She closes the fridge before setting the bottle of wine on the counter. I don't think I can stomach another glass of white wine, but I will for Rell this last time. She walks over to a shelf by the kitchen sink, grabbing two Solo cups from last night's party. Once she sets the two cups on the counter, she opens the wine bottle and pours some into each glass.

"You know you never did take a photo last night for your birthday," I say to her.

She slides one of the Solo cups over to me, "I thought about that today. Guess I was too busy enjoying someone's company to remember to take one."

"Let's me take one now," I say, getting up from the stool.

She laughs like she is confused. I take her by the arms and walk her over to a stool. I make her sit down right in front of the flowers and balloons. She giggles, "What are you doing?"

"Do you have candles?" I ask her while opening the drawers.

"Second drawer," she points out.

I open the second drawer and find candles for a cake. Before closing it, I take three long pink candles and matches from the drawer. I open the fridge, take out the untouched cake, and set it on the counter. I put the three pink candles on the top and lit them with a match. I walk around to Rell and hand her the cake, spinning her around in her seat and then standing back, ensuring everything is in the photo.

"Okay, make a wish and blow out your candles."

She looks at me, smiling before looking back at the lit candles. I take out my phone from my pocket. She closes her eyes, thinking of a wish. In the camera view is Rell, closing her eyes while holding her cake with the balloons and flowers in the background, a perfect birthday photo of her. I take one shot before she opens her eyes, blowing out her candles while I snap one more picture. I slide my phone back into my pocket. She is still holding the cake while looking at me, so I take it from her before sliding it on the counter.

"What did you wish for?"

She slightly smiles, "I can't tell you."

"I didn't think you would, but I thought I would at least give it a shot."

The timer on the oven goes off. Rell gets up from the stool, and her body brushes against mine before walking to the stove. The movement is enough to get my heart racing for a second. Rell and I have only been close when faking to be with each other but haven't been close when it is just us alone.

"You uh," I pause, forgetting what I was going to ask. "Help. Do you need help?"

She grabs a towel and then opens the oven door. She reaches in and pulls out the food before sitting it on the stovetop.

"I got it."

I should've helped her with all of this. It's her birthday; she's spent most of the day alone. I should've offered to help her with everything when she asked me to stay. I walk over to her and start opening cabinets to look for plates. She reaches up at the cabinet next to her as I do, placing my hand over hers. This time my whole body heats up with a desire to kiss her. I grab her hand and turn my body towards her while keeping her hand in mine. She looks at me, her dark eyes looking into mine, and we never lose contact. When I place her hand at her side, I lose my balance while trying not to get too close and fall right into her. I stop myself with my hands gripping her hips. I push my body up against her—so much for not trying to get too close.

Looking up, I realize she has never stopped looking at me. She licks her bottom lip before biting down on it, telling me she wants the same thing as me. Not wasting any more time, I lean into her with my hands still holding onto her hips and place a kiss on her lips, fully expecting her to stop me. Except she doesn't. She leans into me and parts her lips asking for me, which I give her. Rell's hands glide up my shoulders, then behind my neck, and she pulls on the hair on the back of my neck. While passionately kissing her, I push her back into the cabinets and lift her butt onto the counter. She moans into my mouth, causing me to want more, and thank god I put her on the counter because my erection through these joggers would be shoving right in her. I move my hands from her thighs up to her stomach, sliding my hands under her oversized sweatshirt, touching her bare skin. Before I can go further than her stomach, she stops me with her hands and places her head back on the cabinet door.

Heavily breathing, I say, "I am so sorry." Lying because I'm *not* sorry. Since I met Rell, I've wanted to kiss her. I want so much more with her now that I *have* kissed her. There's something there between us that I've never experienced before. I can't put my finger on what it is, though. While sex was on my mind, Rell isn't the type of person that you have a first kiss and then intercourse on the same day. I respect her way more than that.

Before she says anything, I notice the baby hairs standing on her arms with chill bumps, telling me everything. "Don't," she pauses, trying to catch her breath. "Don't be sorry."

Stepping back from her, I run my hands down my face. As much as we both wanted that to happen, regret began filling my mind. What is going on between Rell and me wasn't supposed to happen. Something I keep telling myself, but I keep coming back for more of her. It has nothing to do with her and everything to do with me. I ran from my problems back home; the last thing I want is a problem here.

Scratching the back of my neck, I say, "I should probably leave."

Rell gets down from the counter and stands right in front of me, "Jansen, you don't have to leave. It's okay. I said don't be sorry. I wanted it just as much as you," she places her hand on my arm, hoping she can stop me from leaving just as she did outside. She tells me to stay with her eyes, but I can't. I need to go before this gets any further than it already did.

"Sorry, Rell," I kiss her goodbye on her forehead. "I'm leaving."

I walk away from her toward the back door and never look back before walking out. Looking back would mean I would want to stay, and staying means I would like more with her. Placing that goodbye kiss on her forehead wasn't just a goodbye for now but maybe longer. I need to get over whatever is going through my head and heart before seeing Rell again. I'll regret making this decision, but I need to do it.

After jumping the fence and heading inside through the back door, I crash onto my bed and pull out my phone. The least I can do is send Rell the photo I took of her tonight blowing out her candles. During our moment, I forgot it was her birthday, and I now feel like a total asshole.

I hit send on the photo, knowing she won't respond, before placing my phone on my chest. I put my hands under my head while looking at the ceiling fan, reciting Rell's words. *"I wanted this just as much as you."*

Rell

Jansen Davis is a total asshole. I stood still, looking at the backdoor, hoping he might walk right back in. He won't, but I want him to. Crossing my arms across my chest, I debate if I want to cry or go to my bedroom. I hear my phone go off on the kitchen island, so I walk over to it and see Jansen's photo of me blowing out my candles just after making a wish. I got what I wished for, but for some reason, I ended it abruptly. Our kiss was everything I wanted it to be. There was a spark between us I knew would be there and a passion that I hadn't felt before, but I stopped it because…. I don't even know why. Maybe I wasn't ready, or perhaps it was too much too soon.

I never expected Jansen to leave afterward. I feel that something was bothering him about what we did just as much as I did when I decided to stop us. If we both wanted it, what stopped us from enjoying it more? I'll admit, I'm not ready for anything serious, but this whole thing with Jansen has me wanting something more with him. Would that even be an option for us, knowing Jansen may not feel the same? It's precisely why our whole relationship is fake. I know we crossed that line that we shouldn't have crossed yet.

With my phone in my hand, I grab the cake from the counter and flip the kitchen light off. I take the cake to my bed. Happy birthday to me.

Chapter Eleven

Rell

I left early this morning for my flight. I didn't wake Bree, knowing she needed to catch up on sleep from her night away with Kent. I also didn't respond to Jansen. At least not through text. I posted the photo he took last night and captioned it with " a night to remember." Knowing he would see it when he checked his *The Gram* account. Jansen may not follow me, but I know he still looks at my post. The photo and the caption are for him, and I hope he knows that when he sees them.

      After devouring almost half my cake by myself, I concluded that what Jansen and I did was out of line, which was why he left. We need to take a step back. I need to focus on this clothing line just as much as he needs to focus on his new job. I've already decided I'm not coming home this weekend and want to stay in LA. I packed products and clothing sent to us for the sponsored ads to film this week, and I can do that from my hotel room in between work days. I'll be sending them to Bree to edit and post while there. I have no intentions of speaking to Jansen, giving him the space I think he needs. We have a deal anyways when it comes to talking to each other.

      Once my flight lands, I feel relaxed, knowing I finally get to work on my clothing line. It will keep me so busy that this ordeal with Jansen will be off my mind by the end of the week. I haven't told Bree yet that I plan to stay, but I know she won't mind. She seems to be so busy with Kent lately since he stays at the house with her.

I call Bree to let her know I landed just as I walk out of the airport looking for my uber driver, "Hey, I landed," I say once I know she answered.

"Great. Have fun. I know you're going to kill it this week. I am so proud of you."

I smile, "Thank you, Bree."

My uber pulls up, "I just want you to know I am staying here this weekend," I roll my bag over to the driver to put it into the back, "I know I should've told you already, but I have everything with me for ads, and I will send them to you once I film them."

"Sounds good. I think it will be good for you to stay and explore LA."

"Love you, Bree. I gotta go," I say as I open the door to slide into the back seat.

"Love you, Rell," she says before hanging up.

I turn my phone on silent before sliding it into my bag. I don't need to go to Threads until tomorrow, but I can't wait any longer to get started, so I have my uber driver take me there now anyways. If I sit in an empty hotel room alone, I know my thoughts will lead me somewhere else, and I don't want diversions this week.

Half an hour later, my uber drops me off outside of *Threads*. I don't know who will be here on Sunday, but I hope someone will be. Rolling my luggage, I walk up to the front door. I pull on it to see if it is locked, and it opens. I walk in the doors knowing Shae and Felicia are off on Sundays, so I say "Hello," to see if anyone is around.

I hear a faint "Hello" coming from the direction of Stacey's office.

I'm dragging my heavy overloaded bag with me as I walk down the long hallway. The light's on, and the door is open to Stacey's office; I know it must be her who responded when I said hello, so I walked through her doorway.

She's sitting at her desk when I walk in. "Rell, I thought that voice was you."

Walking in further, I leave my bag by the door and sit in one of her armchairs. "I know I'm here early. I was overly excited to work on my clothing line, so I'm glad you are here."

"You'll find me here every Sunday. I enjoy coming in here when it's quiet."

"I can leave if you'd like to work alone," I say.

"Oh, I think it's great that you are here today. We can get started, and I can help with some designs if you'd like me to."

"That would be great."

She grabs a sketchbook and pencils from a cabinet behind her desk. When she hands them to me, I open my bag to take out some of the ideas I was able to draw up while home alone yesterday. While here last week, I spent several hours looking at fabrics in the fabric room. I took photos of the ones that stuck out to me the most on my phone, so I could remember every detail while drawing at home. I was able to draw up a few shirt designs and skirts. You could wear those items of clothing with anything. They were versatile, and I knew that was something that Stacey would love.

As we both sit quietly in her office, I work on the designs I have already drawn while she works on her computer. Stacey reminds me of Bree, but Stacey is older. We get along well, and I'll love working with her. She made *Threads* feel like home to me last week and welcomed me. I feel like I fit right into this place, and while I don't know what my business will be with this company when the next few weeks are over, I can only hope to come back here one day.

After finishing all the designs I'd already drawn up, I looked over to see that Stacey wasn't busy. I get up from the armchair and set my design book in front of her so she can check everything. Stacey smiles at me before picking up the book to open it. I watched her flip through all the pages I used, slowly looking at the few designs.

She closes the book and slides it back over in my direction."You have talent, Rell. These designs are lovely. How long have you wanted to do something like this?"

"Um, I guess since college. I went to school for business because I wasn't sure what I wanted to do then. I was a flight attendant out of college with my best friend Bree for something fun, and that is when we started The Gram account. I shared fashion because I was always into it but never pursued it."

"Well, I'm very impressed. The day you interviewed, we saw a passion in you that no one else had. You have this drive about you, and we could tell you got enthusiastic about doing something like this. After interviewing you, we all knew we didn't need to interview anyone else. You were the girl for the job."

I blush, "Thank you."

When she said the word passion, Jansen fell into my mind. Everything else was warming my heart. Knowing that they see me for who I am and that this was something I wanted. It feels so good. It reminds me that all those comments and things people said about me on my Gram account don't matter. I suddenly feel like I'm finally somewhere I need to be.

I worked with Stacey for a few more hours on designs, and we sat in her office afterward, talking about the company. The sun was setting when I walked outside with my luggage rolling behind me to my uber. As much as I wanted to stay longer, I had two weeks in LA to work on anything I needed for my clothing line, so I knew I had plenty of time. As Stacey mentioned, I'm discovering I might have a knack for designing. I never felt more in my element than talking about clothes.

My uber drops me off outside my modern hotel that *Threads* has me staying in while I'm here in Los Angeles. It is the same hotel I stayed in last week, but this time noticing all the bars nearby that I could stop in one night when a drink is needed. Tonight is one of those nights, but fatigue is consuming my body. Last night I got the worst sleep thinking about Jansen. There was even a point during the night I felt like I should go over the fence to wake him from what I'm sure was glorious sleep to talk, but I didn't. It would've just crossed another line considering I probably would've tried to finish what we started. Was I mentally or sexually frustrated? I'll never know.

After opening my hotel room and leaving my bag by the tv stand, I walk over to the massive window to look at the view. All I see are lights from bars, restaurants, and clubs. It's too dark to notice any palm trees. I think about what it would be like to live here and keep up with all the trends of a different city. My life would be different from living in my neighborhood in San Francisco. I love my area of older people and my new neighbor, and Bree calls that place home. If I were ever to come here, she wouldn't go with me, I know it. She has Kent, and well, I have me. While coming here alone sounds so lonely, it may be something I should consider if *Threads* ever asked me. I'm getting ahead of myself thinking of this now, but I want to prepare myself before they even ask.

I put an order on my phone for food delivery and then turn on the tv. I change into my sweats for the night before turning on *How to be Single*, my favorite rom-com and go-to movie when I'm alone. Half an hour later, my food is delivered, burgers and fries. After placing the food on the nightstand, I realized my phone had been in my bag on silent all day. While it was nice not needing it, I knew I should at least check it.

Once I grab it out of the side pocket of my bag, I notice several missed calls and some texts from Bree. I immediately call her back.

"Bree, what's going on?" I say after she answers.

"Where have you been? Are you okay?"

"I'm fine. I just wanted some time to myself while at Threads today. I'm now in my sweats with a burger and fries in my hotel room. Is everything okay?"

"Rell… Kent proposed to me today! We're getting married!" she says excitedly.

"AHHHH….That's wonderful, Bree. I want details. How did he ask you?"

I say it like I'm happy, but my best friend will officially be going to the next step in her life, and I don't know what that means for us. She'll do all the things now that everyone our age is doing. Something I should be ready for, but I'm not. I frown, thinking about what this could mean for our business. I love them together and should be happy for them now, but Bree and I have only had each other for so many years, and I don't know what I'd do without her.

"He asked me on the porch swing today. He just pulled the ring out of his pocket and asked me. He said he wanted to do it while we were gone this weekend but left the ring at his place, so he asked me today."

I love the porch swing, dang it. It was mine. Now Bree and Kent are going to want that when she leaves. My personal life is turning into a mess at the moment. There's a chance of losing my fake boyfriend, best friend, and probably my porch swing from my life soon. When I return, I'll need to read every book on that swing on my TBR (to be read) list. It's not like I have better plans anyways.

"How sweet," I say because I wouldn't mind getting proposed to on that swing. "I'm so happy for you. I can't wait to hear all the plans you two will have made when I get back next weekend."

"I have that news already," Bree squeals.

Shocked, I stand from the bed and pace the room. "You do?"

"Yes, we want to get married next month."

"Wow, Bree, that's great," I lie because we're too far apart to tell her the truth, and well, I don't need another person mad at me for something I said or did.

"I miss you, Rell," she says. Almost like she can sense that I'm indifferent about this. She knows me better than anyone. I also know she wishes I was there when he asked her. Dang, Kent, for forgetting the ring and me stopping something with Jansen. This weekend could've turned out to be one for the books.

"I miss you too."

I haven't had a chance to tell Bree about what happened last night with Jansen, and I don't think now is the time to say it to her.

"Oh, your boyfriend is out here."

I stop pacing, "He is!" I say a little too loud. So whispering, I continued, "what is he doing?" I wanted to know. I needed to know.

"Swimming. You want me to let Jansen know I am on the phone with you?"

"NO," I say, louder again, and shake my head. Get it together, Rell.

"Don't tell him I am on the phone. We might have had, um…."

"Sex?" she questions me.

"No, god, no," That's what I wanted, though.

"We just….I don't know."

It's right now that I wish I weren't already in sweats for the night so I could go out for that drink I should've gone out for earlier.

"Oh, that must be why he asked about you then."

I smack myself in the face. This conversation about Jansen has gone on far enough, and while I want to know what he asked about me, I shouldn't. It'll leave my mind wondering and thinking about him.

"Tell him I'm fine. I'm going to go. Congratulations to you, Bree. I love you."

I hang up. I already know our routine of phone conversations.

Bree loves me too.

Jansen

Sitting in my office for the fourth day in a row, thumbing over Rell's text thread, knowing if I text her, she won't respond, but I want to know how she's doing. I want to talk about the other night, tell her I'm sorry for kissing her. We shouldn't have done it. This week has been shit. I spend hours in the office working on stuff for my condo project. Then go to the job site to check on the progress. I come home, eat a lousy dinner, and then go for a swim. Rell may not be home, but Bree and Kent are there, and they talk. I ask them about

Rell, knowing Bree has spoken to her. She's told me every day this week that Rell is fine. It's hard to believe that is all she can say about Rell. It's almost as if Rell was telling her to say that.

Setting my phone down after deciding not to text her again, I open my computer to my *The Gram* account. It's been tempting all week to look at her account. Every day this week, I have gone to the website but changed my mind and closed out of it. Today I'm opening her page, and I don't care. I need to see her.

When I open her account, the first thing I see is the photo I took of her on her birthday, the night that could've ended better than it did. I scroll down to see the caption, "*a night to remember.*" Ouch. That was a message for me to see. What does she mean by it, though? Remember, it was good because kissing her was everything, or remember because I left. I'm leaning towards the good because it was more than reasonable. Kissing Rell was something I remember. It has been on my mind every day since.

I open up Rell's stories to watch her try on many outfits and put on makeup, boring shit, but I can't stop watching her videos repeatedly because I can tell she's happy. My heart drops when I realize she's happy because she's there and doing something she loves. I haven't thought about it since I found out she got this clothing deal, but it comes back to me. There's that chance Rell will stay there and never come back here. There would be no reason for her to stay. I suddenly start feeling nauseated. It's not supposed to be this way; I didn't intend on actual feelings forming.

I close out of *The Gram* and shut down my computer for the day. Before leaving, I grab anything I need in my office to take home. Walking by Jay's office before leaving, I wave goodbye to him. I haven't been able to talk to him lately because I don't want him asking me about Rell, so I always keep it short by waving instead of talking.

"Hey," he yells out as I keep walking by.

I wince before turning around.

"Laura hasn't been able to get in touch with Rell. We know she's busy, and this is the first time I've talked to you, but we are having dinner on Saturday. Can we expect you and Rell there?"

"Of course. We will be there." I nod.

"Great, I'll email you with all the details later," he says before walking back into his office.

This dinner is just what Rell and I need to get us back into our fake dating relationship. All I will need to do is talk to her when she gets into town so I can apologize for what happened between us. It's also a reason to text her, and now I wish I had talked to him sooner.

When I get to my truck, I message Rell.

Me- Laura and Jay invited us to something Saturday. I was hoping we could make it there. Together. I would also like to talk if you are okay with that when you return.

I toss my phone in the door before making my way home.

When I pull up my drive, I can see lights on at Rell and Bree's house, meaning Bree and Kent are there. I'll do my routine for the night, and hopefully, they'll be back when I head out for a swim. There's something I would like to ask Bree.

When I take my phone out of the door, I notice there still isn't a reply. As much as I want to hear from Rell, I know we crossed a line that we shouldn't have. I want her to go with me Saturday, but I know there is a chance that our deal is over for good. And if so, I'll have to let this, whatever I feel for Rell, go.

After a quick shower and dinner, I walk out in my everyday joggers and tee. I suddenly don't feel like swimming tonight. When I look over to Rell's house, I spot Bree and Kent on Rell's swing like I have every night this week.

Bree sees me first and waves.

I wave back, "How is Rell?"

"She's doing great."

That was a new answer for the week, and I can't help but think Rell told her to say that because she noticed I watched her stories today and saw the birthday photo. I know she's doing great. She's happy where she is.

"That's good. I have a question."

Bree gets up from the swing and comes down the stairs. "What's up?" She asked me right when she met me at the fence.

"Can I get Rell from the airport tomorrow night? I want to talk to her about something."

Bree frowns, "She didn't tell you? She's not coming home this weekend. She is staying in LA."

My pulse picks up, and my heart sinks once again. Rell is staying there. My mind knew this would happen, but I didn't want to believe it.

"She didn't tell me and won't talk to me."

"Have you tried texting her?"

"Yes, and nothing."

"You two need to work out your problems," Bree laughs.

"I'm trying….Wait? You know something's going on between us."

Bree shrugs her shoulders and then starts to walk away. I wasn't supposed to know that Bree knew something, and she wasn't supposed to talk to me about it.

"Bree, come on. Help me out here."

Bree doesn't turn back and continues walking up the stairs, and I watch her. She gets on the back porch before yelling, "Jansen, just give her time."

Right, time. I need my fake fiance tomorrow, and she's in LA. Who knows if and when she will ever be back?

Chapter Twelve

Rell

"Isn't this place great?" Shae asks me loudly.

  This place is something else. We're in a large dark room with leather seating all around. Felicia and Shae got us into the most sought-after bar right when we left *Threads* today. They said if we didn't get here early, then we wouldn't be able to get in. I was hesitant to get to the bar early, knowing I would wear down fast and want to go to the hotel before dark, but I wanted to experience something fun this weekend.

  "It's pretty cool," I tell her.

  Felicia stands across from us while we sit on the white leather sofa. She's ordering drinks for all of us while talking to the waitress. I scan the room, and while it seems busy, I can't imagine what this place will look like in an hour or two. They swore up and down before dragging me here that a famous person would walk into this bar tonight. If it's going to be Ryan Gosling, I'm here for it. He may be married with kids now, but I could at least stare at him.

  When the waitress walks to the bar to get our drinks, Felicia sits across from us. The couch has a couple of arguing already to her left, which I'm sure Jansen and I would be doing right now if he was here. Then right on cue, as if his ears were burning, my phone on my lap lights up with a message from him. He knows the rules, so this has to be about Laura and Jay. I picked it up to read his text.

J- Laura and Jay invited us to something Saturday. I was hoping we could make it there. Together. I would also like to talk if you are okay with that when you return.

Just as I finish reading it, Shae snatches my phone from my hand.

"We're putting this away for the night," she slips it into her small black purse and closes it. "You don't need him on your mind all night while we are out having fun."

She isn't wrong; I shouldn't have him on my mind all night, considering he's all I seemed to talk about this week when hanging with Shae and Felicia at *Threads*. They asked me if I was seeing anyone, and while I told them no, I couldn't leave out that I was a fake fiance for Jansen to impress his boss. They couldn't believe it since you only read about it in books. They wanted all the details of this fake relationship, so I spilled it all for them, including my special birthday kiss. They seemed so into the story, like I was reading them a book, only to be disappointed when I told him he'd left.

Instead of being mad that I didn't get to respond, I tell Shae, "Thanks," even though I feel a tiny flip in my stomach that I should be home this weekend for him. When I chose to stay here, I wasn't thinking about my deal with him. I was thinking about myself and how I wanted to forget something between us that wasn't bad but something good. We broke the rules, but I didn't hate it. Jansen broke some of our regulations on night one of our deals.

The waitress brings a tray full of drinks. She sets down three espresso martinis on the table in front of us. "Felicia, you know I don't drink coffee."

She laughs, "These are all the rage right now. Try one."

I pick up the martini glass and lift it in the air dissecting it from every angle before finally trying a sip. I'm a social media expert. I should at least try the trends. It feels foamy on my lips, but it doesn't taste that bad once I swallow my sip before taking another drink, which tastes a little better than the first.

"So, what else do you two like to do for fun here in LA?" I yell out since this bar has not only many people in it, but their music is just as loud.

"This is about it, besides hanging by the pool at our condo. Quite a few nice-looking guys live in our building and meet us down there sometimes. Right Shae?" she winks at her.

"Hey, let's not mention what happened last summer at the pool. That was so last year," Shae answers.

I'm officially interested in their story, "Oh, I'm going to need to hear this."

Felicia leans in closer to the table to tell us the story. I match her by leaning in, but Shae sits back, not wanting any part of this conversation.

"Last summer, Shae got pretty flirty with one guy who always met up with us at the pool. One night they got pretty hot and heavy in the pool, leading to more action when he whisked her off to his condo." She laughs, looking at Shae, who now has her head down, embarrassed. "Anyways, Shae slept with him that night. Then the next week, his girlfriend started joining us. The guy was a sleaze bag, and Shae hasn't slept with anyone since."

"Do things like that happen quite a bit around here? Guys using girls for what they want, even when they have a girlfriend?" I ask.

"Oh yeah, don't come here expecting to find the one. Men here are players. They get into this mindset that they live here and can get anyone, anytime they want. Men don't settle. Shae and I have considered leaving here before, but our job at Threads is just too good. They pay us well, and we wouldn't be able to find a better place to work."

Interesting information. I'm starting to feel like I'm living in an episode of *The Hills*. I could be the new Lauren Conrad with my new friends here. Fashion and then going out to different exclusive clubs that Felicia and Shae can get us in. While at twenty, that would have been the time of my life. I just turned thirty and need to think about my future and more than just the clothing line. I need to figure out who and what Rell wants to be. My life here could be wonderful. Would I still even want to run *The Gram* account without Bree? If there's that chance of a job and life here. I could always hand it over to Bree for her to run, or she could come with me. She could be my assistant. Still, we could do this together.

I down the rest of my espresso martini just as Shae and Felicia finish theirs. Felicia waves to the waitress to bring us three more. I get up from the sofa and take a second to use the restroom. "I'll be back."

The bathroom is at the back of the bar. I have to push people out of my way to reach the door. There are bars back in San Francisco that Bree and I could go to for fun like this, but we never have because, honestly, that isn't our thing. Here I feel like that is what you do to mingle and meet people. I finally open the door to find a line of people waiting, so I wait. I wish I had my phone; I would message Jansen back and tell him I won't be able to make it. But then I think about it. I mean, I could get a flight in the morning. It's only an hour and a half flight. I could be there in time. I like Laura a lot, and we get along together. Jansen asked to talk, though, and I know he will say sorry. I know he's sorry. I don't want to let him down yet by telling him we can't let something like that happen again, even though I know we both enjoyed it. We made a deal. He probably doesn't even want something like that to happen again anyways.

I use the bathroom and leave after washing my hands. While walking back to meet the girls on the sofa so we can drink another trendy drink while waiting around, I feel like someone is looking at me. It's then I spot a dark-haired guy giving me a look sitting on the couch next to our area. I flash him a quick smile before taking my seat with the girls. Sitting down, I noticed the arguing couple had left, leaving Felicia alone on the sofa. I pick up the new espresso martini and catch Shae on her phone.

"Hey, that's not fair. Give me mine back."

She slides hers into her purse before closing it, "No way. Do you two want to go somewhere else? This bar is dreary tonight. Lame."

"I like lame sometimes," I wink.

"Let's stay another hour, and then we can leave if nothing happens," Felicia says.

It was almost like the guy behind us was listening to our conversation because he sat right next to Felicia. He has two friends with him, bringing Felicia and Shae to straighten up in their seats, smiling. I give them no reaction.

"Hey, I'm Cameron," he leans towards me and holds his hand out.

"Rell," I shake his hand. "These are my friends Felicia and Shae."

He's not a bad-looking guy. Now that he is closer to me, he's sort of attractive. He has dark hair, blue eyes, sun-tanned skin, a fitted white shirt, and joggers. It seems he follows influencers because he's wearing that brand all the women share with their husbands. Now see why they share it.

"I know who you are," he smiles. I'm flush-faced because his smile makes me nervous, or maybe it's that stupid trendy drink I am drinking. It makes me feel guilty for talking to him—a feeling that makes no sense because I'm single, but then again, I'm unavailable.

"Let me guess, The Gram?" I ask, knowing that is where he knows me.

"Correct."

"So tell me, Cameron, what are you doing?"

"I'm talking to the one and only Rell Campbell, the gorgeous influencer."

Charming, but I'm not falling for it since my earlier conversation with the girls is starting to make sense. He knows me, knows my image, and I know what he wants. If he follows me, he should already know I'm not single.

"Cute, is that what you tell all the ladies you meet here,"

"No, just you. You want to get out of here?" he asks me.

I look over to Felicia and then back to Shae. Their looks tell me I should do it, but I know I shouldn't. I finish my drink before setting it down on the table. I was ready to go since we hadn't seen a famous person in the hours we had been here.

"Walk me to my hotel?" I ask him.

I'm not really going to let him walk me to my hotel but the one before mine. I don't know who this guy is; he doesn't need to know where I am staying. Also, if I leave, I can get my phone back from Shae. She would not let me go without knowing I had safely made it to my hotel. I need it to not only text her and Felicia but to text Jansen. That flight home in the morning is starting to sound good right now.

"Sure," he answers.

Promising the girls I would text them when I got to my hotel after Shae handed my phone back to me. Cameron gets up to leave and holds his hand out to help me up off the sofa. He seems sweet, but what do I know? I've only known him for precisely five minutes. I let go of his hand while we walked through the bar and out the front doors. I instantly felt the fresh air I needed on my face.

"What brings you here?" he asks me.

Squinting my eyes, I try to remember what *The Gram* account tells everyone so I can keep my information with him short. "Work. I'm leaving in the morning."

I check my phone for new messages before checking my airline app to see the first flight out of LA tomorrow.

"Going back to San Francisco to see that boyfriend of yours? You know you made all the guys following you jealous when you posted you had a boyfriend."

Yep, just as I thought. Cameron knows.

"Yes, I am. I didn't know guys were following me, so that's news. I guess you could say I don't keep up with that." I'm still looking down at my phone and booking a flight. Cameron doesn't seem to mind that I'm on my phone, so I open my texts with Jansen.

Me- Yes. I just booked a flight for nine am. See you at the airport tomorrow?

"Instead of taking you to your hotel, you want to get a coffee or something?"

I looked up and realized he had been watching me on my phone.

"So…" I slid my phone into the back pocket of my jeans. I didn't dress like I was going out tonight. I dressed for *Threads* in something appropriate for working there. Designing clothes requires lots of drawing and then trips to the fabric room. I move around a lot, and something like a skirt and jacket are uncomfortable after two days.

Looking around, he says, "You're mistaken if you think I am trying to get you into bed. I have followed you for a while, and when I saw you tonight, I just thought I could get a chance to get to know you a little bit."

"Um, sure. I don't drink coffee, but we can go to a coffee shop if you want."

"You weren't just drinking espresso martinis?" he laughed.

"Don't ask," I say, waving my hand.

We end up at a coffee shop just across the street from my hotel. It must have been the martinis talking, but I ordered a coffee. I realized after a few drinks that coffee wasn't what I thought it was. While I feel guilty being here with Cameron, someone I just met, I feel better knowing I'll see Jansen again tomorrow.

Chapter Thirteen

Jansen

I'm standing in the airport waiting for Rell in the same spot I stood last weekend when I picked her up. She texted me late last night, but I didn't read or respond until I woke up. I could barely contain my excitement, knowing that she was coming home. I know I asked to talk, but maybe we shouldn't discuss what happened after much consideration. It would make things awkward between us again, and I want to return to what we were before that night. I want to act as if everything's okay and nothing has changed between us and our deal. I want to hear about her trip to LA and how her clothing line is coming along. I want to talk about Rell with Rell.

It doesn't take long after her flight to land that I see her coming down the escalator, wearing a bright smile. She looks almost relieved to see me. I want to think it's because she missed me, but I fold that thought in my mind and place it away. She's wearing my favorite, an oversized sweatshirt and leggings with a bag of sour gummy worms in her hand, a travel snack I always pick for myself.

"Hello," I smile as I reach for her bags while she steps off the escalator. If I don't say hello, she will say I am cranky, and today I'm not.

"Hi."

I don't want to ask about Los Angeles now because she'll keep it short, and I want to know how it went, so I'm waiting till we get to the car to ask.

"Candy for breakfast?" I ask her as we walk over to the baggage claim.

"A little coffee, too, before I boarded my flight." she grins.

"I thought you drink smoothies," I stop and wait with my arms crossed. Rell stops next to me and stands by me closely, our arms touching.

She doesn't answer me, telling me maybe she wants to say something, but she's waiting. So instead of bringing something up to talk about, we both wait for her luggage quietly. I pick up Rell's bag and roll it beside me as we walk out to the truck. Once we both get in, I realize I never asked her. "Does Bree know you are here?"

"She doesn't. I've only talked to her about The Gram since she surprised me with her news."

"What news?" I back out of my parking spot and start driving toward my house.

"Kent and Bree got engaged Sunday. She called me to tell me over the phone since I missed it. He asked her on the porch swing since he forgot the ring at home while they were gone," Rell says as she leans over on the console between us.

"Wow, that explains all the make-out sessions they had on the porch swing this week while you were gone."

I look at Rell to see her frowning, knowing what's bothering her. "You want me to buy you a new porch swing? Maybe I could put one on my back porch for you to use."

She smiles just slightly and then frowns again while looking down.

"They are getting married next month."

Bree and Kent are adorable and seem like the perfect fit, but I know they have only been dating not even a year and next month seems quick for getting married. Rell's probably upset because she's afraid she'll lose her best friend after she gets married. Also, Bree's not only her best friend but her business partner. Rell seems to have a lot on her mind right now. She didn't come home just for me. She's home because she wants answers to where her life is heading.

"So, tell me all about LA? I want to hear everything," I finally ask because I want to know and see a smile on her face.

"It was good," is all she says, and I'm not taking that as the answer. I watched her videos, and she was happy.

"Rell, I'm serious. I want to know, how was it?"

"My clothing line is going better than I could have ever imagined. Stacey, my boss, said she saw so much passion in me when she interviewed me that she knew I was the one they wanted to hire for the job. She said she was impressed with my designs. I've made some friends, Felicia and Shae. They work the front counter at Threads. We all went out last night for drinks at some exclusive place and…" she pauses.

"That's all great, Rell, it is. But what's the and?"

"Someone who follows me saw me while we were out. He asked me out for coffee, so I went."

"He?"

"His name is Cameron. He lives in LA, but when he saw me at the bar, he hoped to meet me and get to know me a little. So, we walked to a coffee shop by my hotel and talked briefly."

A guy. She met a guy who knew who she was. Someone who has known who she is for who knows how long. He probably knew what he needed to do and say to her. The thought of them maybe kissing or something else runs through my mind, and I suddenly feel like an idiot. A sick idiot because this information is not sitting well with me. I feel like I'm riding a rollercoaster, and it just hit a significant drop, that empty stomach feeling.

Rell reaches over, placing her hand on my arm. "I wanted to tell you because I felt guilty the whole time I was with him. While he was nice, I felt I shouldn't have been there. He knows about you. He asked about my boyfriend before I went to coffee with him."

"But I'm not your boyfriend. You're allowed to do whatever you want and when you want. Our relationship is not real, and while I know it looks like it's real to people who follow you, that doesn't mean you have to act like it is when you are there. I don't want it to hold you back from doing something you want to do."

Rell lets go of my arm and then turns to face the window to look out. I shouldn't have said what I said, but it's true. We aren't in anything that needs to tie her down from doing things. I hate saying it, but she can do what she wants.

"What's the plan for today?" she asks, and I'm happy she's changing the subject because I didn't want to tell her anything else I didn't want to say to her.

"Jay and Laura have another dinner at their house. The email says it's indoors, and a chef is coming to cook dinner with beer and wine available to drink. It's another get-to-know-you thing with no games this time. It said four other couples are coming, but they are their friends and not people I work with," I pause to look over at her as she continues to look out the window, "You can wear whatever you want," I tell her knowing she will ask what she needs to wear.

We pull up the driveway at my house, and instead of a typical hurry out of the car, Rell takes her time to get out. I have her bags in both hands before she even opens the door. I stand at the back end of the truck waiting for her but notice her walking toward my front door.

"What are you doing?"

She places a strand of hair behind her ear before saying, "Can I hang out with you?"

"Yeah, of course," I say, slightly smiling.

I unlock the front door to my house, let Rell walk in first, and follow behind her with her bags. She sits on my living room sofa, and I take her bags into the dining room and lay them on the table before joining her. Taking a seat on the loveseat next to the couch, I notice Rell has already made herself comfortable, laying her head back on the cushion.

"What time is dinner?" she asks.

"It's not until seven."

Looking at my watch, I see it's almost lunchtime. Rell mentioned having coffee and candy, but that's not even considered real food. I'm sure she's starving if it's just like the last time I picked her up.

"You want something for lunch?"

"I'm fine, thank you."

I'm starting to realize that she's looking more and more tired. Rell was out late last night and up early this morning for her flight on top of what hours she worked at *Threads* this week, also making videos and working on content for *The Gram*.

"How about this? You can nap here while I run out to get us something to eat. I know just the place to get us something; it could take an hour."

She yawns, putting her hand over her mouth, and then says, "Sounds good."

I don't even get up from the loveseat before she pulls down a blanket from the back of the couch to cover up.

Walking back out the front door, I see Bree grabbing the mail. I pretend that I don't notice her and hurry into the truck. She looks over in my direction after hearing me shut my door. She then walks to my vehicle, so I roll down my window, "Yes?"

"You wouldn't happen to have heard from Rell, have you?"

"No, sorry, I haven't," I lie.

"If you do, let me know. I've only been able to reach Rell through text since last Sunday."

I'm not exactly sure why Rell doesn't want to see Bree, but my only assumption is that Rell isn't ready to talk to Bree about her engagement. I've had an intuition that Rell was once engaged, which may have something to do with it.

"Sure thing. Later, Bree."

She walks back into her house, and I back out of the driveway. I'm going to Rell's favorite place for lunch, and while last time we went there, I was hoping for a short line, this time, I wouldn't mind the long line to wait in for burgers and fries. It would give Rell time to sleep.

It took me under an hour to get food and return home. Rell looked to be sleeping peacefully, so I stuck her food in the microwave while letting her nap. I flipped the tv on a basketball game. March Madness started, and we have a brackets competition going on at work. The winner gets a nice size cash bonus. I don't stand a chance at winning since the whole office has submitted brackets, so I haven't even thought about what I would do with the money if I did win. I chose Kansas to win the whole thing, precisely the team playing in the game that I just turned on the tv.

Turning the game on mute so I don't wake Rell from her beauty sleep, I open up my food to eat while I watch the game. It's been a while since I had a woman sleeping on my couch while watching basketball on tv, a hot one at that. Rell isn't just anyone, though. She's different from anyone I've ever been with, and I know it has to do with how our relationship works. There is no relationship when we are apart, but when we are together and putting on our fake show, it all just seems natural. She seems to feel the same about the rules besides our little mishap that we have yet to discuss, and I don't want to talk about it. We have only been together a short time today, and it already feels like the kiss is a thing of the past for us.

After eating, the game was at halftime, so I got into the shower.

When I woke up to Rell's text message this morning, I had little time to get ready before I needed to leave for the airport, so I skipped taking one. Most of that was because she was coming home when I needed her. I needed her for the relationship or comfort; I wasn't sure yet.

I dry off, then wrap the towel around my waist. I hear a sound coming from the kitchen, knowing it has to be Rell. She must have woken up while I was showering. Rell has seen me in a towel, maybe not naked underneath but close, so I walk into the kitchen to check on her.

She takes her food out of the microwave when I get to the kitchen. Her eyes go right to the nice-sized bulge under the towel and then up to my chest, and I get a little déjà vu from when she checked me out after I ran in front of her place. She quickly moves her eyes to my face and holds up the food bag, "Thanks."

"For the view or the food?" I laugh.

"Both," she says, walking away to the living room.

I follow behind her to the living room. She already has a chick flick movie on my tv instead of basketball. She sits in the spot I was sitting in and opens up her food. Once it is all out, she notices I'm in the room with her. Her eyes go back to where they were staring.

"Bree was wondering if I had talked to you and I had to lie. How come you don't want to go home, Rell?"

Rell shook her head no while she tried to swallow a bite of her burger. Once she finally gets it down, she turns to look me in the face this time. "I'll go. Just not now, maybe later."

"Does it have anything to do with Bree getting engaged, maybe?" I ask.

She shakes her head, "Uh…. No. I have a lot on my plate now, and I figured I could relax until tonight. I'm exhausted from working on the clothing line and traveling here and back there, plus what happened between the two of us has been keeping me up at night." she throws her hands up, "My life went from this perfect little bubble to a bunch of tiny bubbles floating everywhere."

"Forget about what happened between us."

"I don't want to forget it."

"Don't you think we need to forget it if we want to continue this fake relationship without being uncomfortable?" I ask.

"I guess so."

I leave the living room because I don't want to talk about it anymore. I need to put some clothes on before I make another rash decision by taking this towel off me in front of Rell. Not only did she not want to forget our kiss, but she also had her eyes all over me while talking in the living room, and it took everything in me not to pounce on her, stripping her down to nothing with me. It's been way too long since the last time I was inside a woman, and while Rell looks at me like she wants it, I don't want to cross that boundary with her yet. I'll stick to the shower strokes until then.

Barely getting pants on, Rell appears at my bedroom door and knocks on it even though it is open, and I see her standing there. "Care if I take a quick shower?"

"Here? You want to shower here when you have a house next door."

She pretends she doesn't hear me, walks on by with toiletries in her hand, and goes into my bathroom as if it were hers. She shuts the doors behind her but not all the way. After slipping on my shirt, I look over at the cracked door, catching a glimpse of Rell getting undressed. She's playing a little game with me. Since I gave her a little show by walking around in a towel, she provided me with one too. I regret thinking it would be rude to jerk off in the shower with Rell in my house. I should've done it. I could stand here and finish the show she is giving me, or I could join her in crossing that boundary that now doesn't sound so bad since just the glimpse of her naked body makes me hot.

Sadly I choose to ignore the ever-growing erection in my pants but bottle up the glimpse of Rell's perfect breast in my mind. I walk over to my dresser and pull out the ring she wore the first night we started this relationship. She'll fight, but she's wearing the damn thing tonight. It's much smaller and more believable than the one she has. I still need to figure out where that thing came from; no woman has a large ring without someone gifting it to her.

I hear Rell in the shower, so I open the door, "Do you even have anything to wear tonight?"

"There are extra clothes in my bag I can wear," she says behind the shower curtain.

Leaving the door open, I walk down the hallway. When I pass the dining room, I notice Rell's luggage is open wide with clothes lying around the table. I left the living room for five minutes, and she had moved in. I walk into the living room to check the scores of the basketball games and hear a sound coming from the laundry room. She's washing her laundry.

I walk back down the hallway. When I enter my room, Rell is standing there, a towel wrapped around her, and her hair is messy. I want to lose my shit on her right now for not going home, but there's something about how she is standing there looking like literal perfection, fresh out of the shower.

"You're doing a whole ass load of laundry?"

"Don't be an ass."

"Oh, I can be."

I take the ring off the dresser and hold it out to her. "You have to wear this."

"Again, with the ring?"

"Well, you could walk over to your house to get the huge one you own. Your choice. This one or that one because you're not going over there without one."

She rolls her eyes at me, annoyed, before taking the ring from my hand.

Chapter Fourteen

Rell

Cranky Jansen wasn't the one who picked me up from the airport today, so when I decided I didn't want to go home while on the airplane, I knew Jansen wouldn't turn me down. He needs me this weekend, so he can go along with what I want. While I love Bree very much, I'm not ready to face the fact that she is engaged. I need a little more time to process all the information. I know it has more to do with me being jealous that she's doing things that I should be doing too. While I had my chance long ago, it wasn't with the right person.

  I was not expecting a half-naked Jansen walking around his own house while I was there. He might have been wearing a towel, but I could outline every detail of what it covered. Let's say I wasn't disappointed. There needed to be payback in the form of my naked body; from the looks of it, it worked. Jansen peeped for just a few seconds through the cracked door, and it was all I wanted to give him anyway. I only wanted him to see enough that maybe he would like to see more one day. Kissing Jansen was good, so I can only imagine what more would be like if we ever got there.

  He was nice enough to help me fold and pack it back into my bag for someone so irritable at me for doing laundry. Luckily I brought extras I never wore, so I will have plenty of outfits for next week when I return tomorrow.

Jansen and I got ready, and he even let us coordinate outfits for the night. He chose a black flannel button-up, jeans, and boots. I wore a long-sleeved black bodysuit, dark-wash skinny jeans, and high boots. He barely touched his touseled hair and facial scruff while I chose to curl my hair into waves and added a nice dark lip for the night. He must have liked what I chose; instead of his "Why did you have to dress so hot," I got a smack on the butt while walking out the door to leave. He had no self-control at the moment, I guess.

We're on our way to Laura and Jay for the night. This time makes me nervous since we are having dinner with some of their friends we don't know. We almost got caught during the last gathering. I've been on high alert for any signs of someone knowing who I am. I don't want to be the one to ruin this for him.

I twirl the ring on my finger while Jansen has his eyes locked on the road. This is the perfect moment to ask what I have always wanted to know. "What's the story with the ring?"

"You seriously want to know?" Jansen asks.

"I wouldn't have asked if I didn't."

He hesitates for a second, "Her name was Natalie, and we were together for two years. I wasn't ready to get married, but she insisted it was time or she was leaving me. I came here last summer to meet Jay and apply for my job. I mentioned to him I was getting engaged. I was scared to come here alone if I got the job, so I bought the ring, and when I got back home, I found her in our apartment with my best friend."

"Yikes, I'm so sorry."

"At the moment, I was livid. He was my best friend years before I was with her. I found out later that they had been sleeping with each other during the last year of our relationship. They're now married and have a kid on the way. That isn't something I see myself doing yet. So, honestly, it turned out for the best for me. I kept the ring because I never gave it to her, so it's not hers, and she never even knew about it."

"I guess that's good then if you think so."

He turns to me, smiling, "My life now is much better," he clears his throat. "It's only fair, I ask. Where did your ring come from?"

I didn't think about Jansen reciprocating that question.

Since he was honest with me, I know I should be truthful too. I can't look at him while telling him, so I look out the front window of his truck, "I was engaged," keeping it short.

"That's obvious, Rell. I want the story."

Hesitating just a bit, I finally say, "I didn't want to live in his shadows. He didn't like what I did and encouraged me to quit before we married. I found myself forcing my love for him. I wasn't who I am now when I was with him, and I still had dreams of being something more. He took me breaking it off with him hard since we were together for a couple of years. It was also kind of a secret like us but different. I never shared him on *The Gram*, and he never shared me. Our relationship was very private. Last I checked, he is still single."

"I don't understand how someone wouldn't want to share that they were with you?" he asks me, concerned.

"I know," I say, keeping this short once again.

"He was the one who sent the flowers for your birthday?"

"Yes."

It didn't surprise me that Jansen asked about the flowers. I had this feeling he knew that had to come from a guy since it was a box full of red roses. Those roses now belong to Margret across the street. Not only did I not want them, but there was also no place for them at my house. Jansen's flowers were perfect enough.

Pulling up outside Laura and Jay's house, I feel a sense of relief since talking about my past relationship is something I wouldn't say I like talking about with Jansen. The past is the past, and I have moved on from it.

Just like clockwork, Jansen takes my hand in his once we get out of the truck. We seem to be the last ones to arrive with the number of cars parked out front. After Jansen rings the doorbell, he pulls me closer to him while we wait for them to open the door.

"You look hot, by the way," he smiles.

I glance over at him, blushing. I knew that was coming sometime tonight.

He laughs, then the front door opens.

"There you two are," Jay says.

We walk inside, and Jansen grips my hand harder. I always take it as a sign of comfort that he doesn't want me to let go. Jay introduces us to four other couples, and I immediately forget their names. Then he introduces us to Kelsey, a good friend of Laura's who came by herself tonight. She's gorgeous, with her long dark hair and petite frame. She's wearing black dress pants and a white silk top. She looks around the same age as Laura, making her just a few years older than me. Kelsey has had some work done to herself, her breasts, and her lips.

"Nice to meet you," she holds her hand out to Jansen. She shakes his hand before placing it back at her side, ignoring my presence. I flash her a fake smile. She's already giving me a bad vibe.

We all enter the dining room, where dinner is ready to be served. Jansen pulls my chair out, letting me take a seat before him. Once he sits next to me, I notice Kelsey sitting in the chair across from him and giving him a flirty smile. I choose to ignore it, thinking maybe that is just the type of person she is.

Once we've all taken our seats, everyone around the table continues with their conversations. Since Jansen and I showed up late, we are both sitting there just listening to everyone else talk. Other times we have been here, I've been comfortable, but I feel like we're out of place this time. Almost like we shouldn't be here. We barely know Jay and Laura, and everyone here knows them well.

Our food, which is things on a plate I know nothing about, is served before me. Luckily it all smells great. My plate looks like it was in a magazine, and I almost don't want to touch whatever it is. I was barely listening when the chef was describing the plate. I notice everyone at the table, including Jansen, starts eating. I place my napkin in my lap and then pick up my fork to join them.

The conversation slows down at the table while everyone eats. I notice Kelsey's eyes on Jansen like she wants to ask him a question, but she's waiting for the right moment. Since we sat at the table, I haven't touched Jansen, but Kelsey's looks at him make me wish I was sitting on his lap. Once we finish eating the main course, dessert is brought out to us, which is something I know: cheesecake.

We make it through dinner, thank goodness. I've said maybe two words since we got here, but Jansen was able to talk amongst the men at dinner about work. Laura's friends seem to be taking all her attention, so I haven't been able to speak to her. All the men wander off to the movie theater room to watch one of the basketball games on tv. Laura walks us women out to the balcony to watch the sunset. The fresh air is just what I need after that dinner.

"Rell has her clothing line coming out soon," Laura mentions.

"Laura," I flash her a smile, "We don't have to talk about that."

Sweet of Laura to bring this up, but it's not something I feel comfortable talking about, considering they haven't approved them yet.

"That's impressive," Kelsey says, holding a wine glass and flipping her hair behind her shoulder.

There was wine with dinner, but I didn't choose to drink any since I felt uncomfortable. Jansen hadn't had anything to drink either, but everyone else did.

"Thank you. It's nothing special yet. Threads could easily choose not to make or sell my designs."

"I bet they look wonderful," Laura says.

"I think they'll be perfect, but I'm a little biased," I let out a slight laugh.

Laura and her friends sit on the outdoor furniture on the patio while I choose to stay standing. I notice Kelsey lasted not even two minutes with us and has already taken off for what I suppose is the bathroom, with as much wine as she drank.

I take in the views of the bay area and bridge while the women mingle and wish the men and women didn't split so I could spend some time with Jansen. I like Laura, but her friends treat her like a queen. I began to wonder how we got invited. I came here for Jansen, but I wish I were home now.

While taking in the scenic views, I think about what Bree's doing. I haven't spoken to her since I got here today, and this party is making me miss her. There will be a time in my life that I wish I had spent more time with her. Tonight is one of those nights. I made a mistake today.

Coming home for Jansen today only complicates my life more than I thought it would. There is something about being with him all day today. It is the most time we spent with each other outside of dinners and my party, and it's a closeness I know I'll miss when I return to LA tomorrow.

"I'll be right back, ladies," I tell them before walking inside.

When I was here for the first time, Laura and Jay gave us a tour of their house, so I knew exactly where the movie theater was. Walking down the hallway, I could hear some of the men cheering, and before I got to the doorway, I overheard a woman's laugh. I walk into the room and see Kelsey sitting in the chair next to Jansen, leaning over and her hand on his chest as she laughs at something he said.

Kelsey stops laughing when she sees me walk in and clears her throat. Jansen looks over at me before getting up from the chair. I turn around and walk right out of the room.

"Rell," Jansen calls out.

I turn around, stopping in the middle of the hallway, rubbing my forehead with my hand, "Jansen, I want to go home."

When he catches up, he wraps his arm around me, pulling me into his chest. "Rell, I'm sorry."

"Can we leave?"

Letting me out of his hold, he lifts my chin with his hand to look up at him, "Stay with me. We will stay a few minutes longer, and then we can go home, okay?"

I don't say a word but shake my head, yes.

As much as I want to leave, I get that we are here for him, and as long as he stays with me for the rest of the time we're here, then I should be fine. This night wasn't what I expected, and I let my problems get to me. One of those problems was Laura's friend Kelsey. I knew she wouldn't be pleasant when I walked through the door.

Jansen takes my hand while we walk back to the movie room. I follow behind him, and he pulls me on his lap when he takes his seat next to Kelsey. *Take that, Kelsey.* I could feel her eyes on us while sitting next to her; maybe she was learning a lesson. Then I notice the rather large diamond ring on her finger and realize perhaps I was exaggerating her touches and advances towards Jansen. It shouldn't have mattered what she was doing, but it did. It bothered me more than I wanted.

Jansen rests one of his hands on my thigh while my legs are over his, and his other hand rubs my lower back. My mind had been all over the place since we walked in here, but now it seems nothing matters anymore, as Jansen comforts me.

"Kelsey, not sure you have met my fiance yet? This is Rell," Jansen says to Kelsey as she takes another sip of her wine, trying to ignore the fact I was there.

I want to laugh because I am glad Jansen noticed when we walked in that she only introduced herself to him, not me.

"I did. I heard all about Rell's clothing line. You must be so pleased," she takes another sip.

Jansen smiles before looking at me, "I couldn't be more proud of her."

I blush before returning a smile.

Kelsey pretends to watch the game on TV before finally leaving the room. When she goes, Jansen doesn't stop his attention on me while watching the game. This whole night has been a bust for me, but now that Kelsey has left, it isn't so bad. I would've liked to get to know Laura and her friends, but I never got the chance. They all seem to be inseparable, and it just makes me miss Bree.

When the game finishes, we all leave the movie room and head back to the front of the house. When we get to the living room, I see all the women have congregated here.

"Thanks for having us, but I think Rell and I are going to go," Jansen announces while taking my hand.

"Thank you two for coming," Laura says, getting up from the couch.

We say our goodbyes to everyone and then walk to the front door. Laura and Jay meet us there, and Jay opens the door. "We will see you two again soon. Thanks for coming," we wave, and the door shuts behind us. I take a deep breath.

"You good?" Jansen asks when we get in the truck.

"Yeah. I want to go home for the night."

Jansen doesn't say anything but instead drives us home. We both stay quiet on the drive, and it's late when I look at the clock. Exhaustion from the week and traveling is setting in, and even though Jansen let me nap today, it wasn't enough to catch up on sleep. When I finish my trips to LA, I need to take one full day of rest and movie-watching.

When we pull into the driveway, I notice all the lights off at my house, and the only car in the driveway is mine. Bree must be staying at Kent's for the night. Jansen turns the truck off and then relaxes his head back on the headrest, looking over at me. "Did I do something wrong?"

"No, Jansen, you didn't. Tonight was just different than I thought it would be," I pause, and he reaches over to take my hand. "You were right, and I should've gone home today. That dinner party just made me miss Bree."

He lets my hand go, and we get out of the truck. Jansen unlocks his front door, and I walk in before him, flipping the switch to turn the living room lamp on for us. I walk into the dining room to get my bag from the table. Before I take it off the table, Jansen stops me with his hand on mine. "Stay. It didn't look like anyone was at your place,"

"Jansen."

"You don't have to go. I know I told you earlier to go but....don't."

I put my bag back on the table and take my hand off it. A grin appears across Jansen's face, and I hope I make the right choice. If I go home, I'll be alone, and my mind will still be all over the place.

"I'll stay."

Jansen

I woke up to Rell; her hair was all laid across her pillow. She looked so beautiful sleeping while the sun rose in the window behind her. I brushed my hand across her face and placed a kiss right on her cheek. It was a view I could get used to waking to every day.

I roll over, and my eyes open; I'm in the living room. *Damn it*. My dream of waking up to Rell in my bed was only a dream. Last night when Rell finally decided to stay here, we got ready for bed in my room. She was already asleep on my bed when I came out of the bathroom. I covered her up for the night and then went to the couch. I don't think she would have been fond of waking up next to me.

I hear a noise coming down the hallway, meaning Rell's already up for the day. She must be an early riser. Stripping the blanket off, I sit on the couch, reminding myself I never want to sleep there again. My back is killing me, and my age of thirty-two is starting to show. I get up to check on Rell and find her walking down the hallway toward me, dressed for the day.

"Morning," I tell her. She looks so goddamn beautiful this morning. Just like she did in my dream.

"I have to go," She walks past me.

"Already?"

"Stacey called me this morning, and they want to see my designs first thing in the morning. I need to get to LA and put the finishing touches on them, so I moved my flight up. It leaves in an hour."

"Let me throw some clothes on. I'll take you," I say, wearing boxers and realizing that neither of us minded what I was wearing.

"It's okay. I can drive there."

She walks into the dining room, taking her bag off the table. She slips her carry-on bag on her shoulder. Walking over to me, as I stand against the wall in the hallway, she quickly kisses my cheek with her baby-soft lips before walking towards the front door. I follow her.

"What was that for?"

"Comforting me last night and letting me stay," She opens the front door.

"I'll see you around, Jansen," then she walks out.

Chapter Fifteen

Rell

Running through the airport to make my flight with one minute to spare, I board my flight out of breath. When flying, I always sit next to the window, my favorite chair. When I woke up to my phone vibrating on Jansen's nightstand, I answered it immediately when I saw it was Stacey. Even though I hadn't washed my hair in days, I got up and threw on some clothes to get out the door. This clothing line is my top priority in my life right now, and I want to ensure that they are perfect when I show them my designs tomorrow.

Thankfully I have extra gummy worms in my bag since I skipped breakfast this morning. My diet is all over the place, and I can't wait to return to those meal deliveries every night again.

I hated to rush from Jansen's this morning, we didn't get a chance to talk about last night, and I wanted to tell him sorry for wanting to leave Jay and Laura's. I wasn't myself.

Pulling my phone out of my bag, I text Stacey that I am on my way.

Getting this clothing line accepted would be everything to me right now. It would mean all my dreams would come true. I could continue my job as an influencer, but I could cut back, knowing it isn't the only source of income. I know that I would have to move, and while right now that sounds difficult, it is something I could deal with when it comes to that time. I don't want to leave a place I've called home for years and the people I love, but maybe there's a chance Bree would like to come too. We've been inseparable for so long. I know she's getting married, but maybe there's a chance this could be good for her, too, and they could move to LA. Coming here alone is scary, but I know a few people already.

  When I land in LA, I have an uber driver take me straight to *Threads*. Stacey is already in her office when I arrive. I set my bags by the door and joined her at her desk.

  She slides the designs over to me. "I made a few notes on some things we could change, but honestly, Rell, these designs are amazing."

  "Thank you, I'm nervous about tomorrow," I take the designs and open them to look at the notes she made. She made tiny notes about little things I had already thought about changing.

  "Don't be nervous. You're going to do great."

  Erasing some of the designs' details, I drew out what looked better. Then I walk down to the fabric room. I need to cut small samples of the fabrics for each design. I am going to need to make boards. Each board will contain my design and fabric samples attached to the sides. Along the bottom of the board, I would like to feature other designs I made that can be matched or layered for a look. It's not even the afternoon yet, so I have plenty of time to finish these today.

  Getting right to cutting the samples, I put them all to the side and began to check out if there were more that I would like to use. I still had some ideas for tops and was hoping to squeeze in drawing at least one more design before the day ended. Something about being in this room inspires me to do more. Designing my fabrics one day would be fun, but I will stick to their collection now.

  I haven't spoken to Bree and meant to call her after last night's dinner. So I pull out my phone and put it on speaker while I continue in the fabric room.

"Rell, I've missed you," she answers.

"You have no idea how much I've missed you."

"Margret told me that she saw you were leaving Jansen's house this morning, and I told her there was no way because you were in LA. Then I thought there's no way Jansen was seeing someone besides you because of the deal you two have…." Oh, Margret. I didn't think of her this weekend while staying at Jansen's. I should've known.

"Bree," I interrupted her. "It was me. Look, I am sorry, but Friday night, he messaged me about another dinner for Saturday. I came home yesterday for him but stayed at his place. I shouldn't have done it, Bree. I'm sorry."

"But, Why?"

"Well, to be honest, I haven't been dealing well with this whole engagement thing. It has nothing to do with you and everything to do with me, Bree. You're going to be leaving me and moving on. You will be doing things I should be doing, but I am just not there yet. Some part of me is jealous, and the other part is hurting that I will lose you," I stop looking around the room and take a seat by my phone. This conversation is putting me in a gloomy mood now.

"Rell, I would never leave you. I may not live with you, but I will always be your best friend and there for you. If you're worried about me leaving you as a partner for influencing, you're crazy. Working with you is my dream job. I understand there is a lot of unknown in your life because of this clothing line, but I promise you that figuring out where your life will go will happen soon."

"Bree, can you come to LA? They want me to present my designs tomorrow morning, and I'm so nervous. You are the only person who can get me through this."

"Tomorrow? I thought you didn't have to present them for another week or so?"

"They are ready, and so is Stacey. So it looks like this process is moving faster than I thought."

"Let me see what I can do. I want to be there for you. If I can get a flight, I'll text you."

"Thanks, Bree."

Once I hang up from our conversation, I pick up my designs and fabric to take down to Stacey's office. When I walked into her office, she was working behind her desk on something, then she turned to see me, hands full, and ran over to help me. Grabbing some of the things I'm holding, we both stop in the doorway.

"I put some boards in the empty office down the hall if you'd like to work there."

"Uh, yeah. That sounds great."

Working in an empty office alone is what I need.

We walk a couple of doors down from Stacey's office. Stacey opens the door to an office with just a white desk and a black office chair. The desk is a significant size, so I can place a few boards down to work on them at once.

"Thanks."

We place all the design drawings and fabric on the desk, and Stacey walks back to the door. "If you need anything, just let me know. There should be some supplies inside the desk,"

I nod before she walks out.

As I start laying everything around, my phone goes off with a text message.

Bree- The flight leaves in two hours. See you soon!

I feel relief knowing she will be here soon to help me finish these boards and help with my presentation for tomorrow.

It's late when I finally place all the boards along the office wall that Stacey let me use for the day. Bree showed up hours ago to help me set everything on the boards. Stacey helped for a while but left a few hours ago. Bree and Stacey are impressed with my clothing line designs and how I put the panels together. This is my first time doing anything like this, and I would say I *killed* it. I must practice some of my presentations with Bree before bed, and I should be good.

Bree and I hadn't seen each other in a week, and we picked up right where we had left off. Having her here for this means the world to me. I wouldn't be here if it weren't for her. She is my better half and the backbone of *The Gram* account. I couldn't do anything without her, which is why all this engagement news was bittersweet.

As we walk out of the office, confident that we have finished everything, Bree and I close up *Threads* with Stacey's key. This company has been the greatest to me since I walked in.

We both have our bags, and thankfully Stacey set us up with the hotel just across the street for this trip, so we don't have to go far. As we walk across the street to our hotel, Bree mentions something I completely forgot.

"Did you eat anything today?"

"Just some chips from the breakroom," I laugh. "Let's get room service and chat. You have so much to catch me up on."

As we walk into the hotel, she nudges me with her arm, "You have so much to catch me up on. I mean, come on, you stayed at Jansen's last night."

I clench my teeth and shake my head, "It's not what you think."

After checking in, we take the elevator and walk down the hallway to our third-floor two-queen-bed suite. Threads have taken care of all my hotel rooms and flights for my trips, and it has been nothing short of excellent. They put me in the best rooms that I would never reserve for myself.

Once we enter the door and drop our bags, Bree and I fall back on a bed, making us giggle.

"How was Kent with you coming here?"

"He knew I missed you, so he didn't have a problem with it. Does Jansen know I'm here with you? We could use him to watch the house while we are gone."

"No, we don't talk unless it concerns our agreement. Plus, Margret will do a great job noticing we aren't home. She's got it." I laugh.

We lay quietly for a moment. Neither of us knows what to talk about, but I know there's much to say. Bree is the first to break the silence.

"So, what happened last night?"

I get up from my bed and walk over to the bed Bree is on beside her. "The dinner was mostly their friends. Laura's friends are, well, they like her attention, so I felt left out. She has a friend, Kelsey, who came alone and flirted with Jansen all night. I caught her hand on him when I was trying to find Jansen. I was ready to leave, but he wanted to stay. He took me back into the theatre room, where they were watching the game, and sat me on his lap. Then he introduced me as his fiance to Kelsey."

"Isn't it weird to you that he calls you that? I mean, it's weird to me."

"It's strange to hear it when he says it. It's *how* he says it, as though it doesn't bother him. I missed you so much while I was there. Just seeing Laura with her friends and then me coming to town and not telling you. It was a tough night for me. I wanted to go home, but Jansen asked me to stay since you weren't home, so I did. I fell asleep and left as soon as I got Stacey's call this morning. I haven't talked to him since."

"So what? You won't talk to him until he needs you to be his fiance again?" Bree says, and it sounds like our situation may be a little messed up.

"Yep," I flip over on my stomach so I can look at Bree when I talk to her, "Tell me about the wedding and everything?"

"Kent wants a short engagement, and I don't mind. We are getting older, so why waste time when we know we want to be together? We'll have a small wedding or maybe elope. We haven't talked much about it, but we know we want to get married next month."

"I'm happy for you, I really am. I know my actions from this last week don't make it look like I am, but I have a hard time thinking about you moving forward without me. Jansen begged me to go home and talk to you yesterday. I just wasn't ready yet. I can't thank you enough for coming here for me when I was not a good friend to you."

She flips over to her stomach and wraps an arm around me for a half hug. Bree is the best and also so very forgiving. Wrapping my arm around her shoulder, I bring her into a side hug.

"I'm also sorry for the way I told you about the engagement. I wanted to tell you in person but just got so excited."

Smiling at her, "It's okay."

"That Jansen seems like a good guy," she winks.

I let out a little laugh. "He is."

Bree and I needed this conversation, even though it was something I should have opened up about last week, but it was hard to talk about while I was away. No matter what we go through next in our lives, I know what friendship Bree and I have. We will always be there for each other, no matter what.

We spend the next couple of hours eating room service while she helps rehearse some lines for tomorrow's big day. My stomach is in knots, knowing tomorrow could be a life-changing moment for me and, hopefully, Bree. Whatever the outcome is, though, I'm ready for it.

I hold Bree's hand as we walk into *Threads*. Instead of going to the *Threads* CEO's office for this meeting, the big guys are coming here. This is huge, and deep down, I feel like I'm going to throw up. I practiced everything I was going to say while lying in bed last night, which meant I got zero sleep. I put on my best dress paired with a blazer. I want to look professional, as if I know what I'm doing even though I don't.

"You got this," Bree squeezes my hand tightly before letting it go. We just got through the door, and Felicia and Shae give me a big grin when they see me walking in.

"RELL!" Felicia yells excitedly. *Gosh, I love her*.

Bree and I walk up to them, standing at the front counter. I notice a large clear vase full of white roses sitting on the counter between them.

"These are for you," Shae points to them, "They are gorgeous, aren't they?"

"Awe, you two shouldn't have," I say, taking the card off them.

"Oh, these are not from us," Felicia says with a huge smile. She definitely read the card.

I give them both a glare before opening the card.

I'm proud of you. Don't worry, Rell.

I know you're going to do great.

Jansen

A goofy grin comes across my face before putting the card back into the envelope. When I look up, everyone looks at me, wondering who sent the roses, including Stacey.

"So, sweet. Did your fiance send them?" Stacey looks at the ring on my finger before looking at me.

It didn't phase me until now that I was still wearing Jansen's ring from Saturday. I've been twirling this thing on my hand for days without even a care in the world.

"Uh," all the girls giggle while still staring at me, "Yes. Sweet, isn't it," I say.

Bree, Felicia, and Shae all put their hands over their mouths. They each know my story; I don't think I have ever admitted to having a fiance until now. He's only been a boyfriend this whole time. *I am facepalming myself mentally.*

"Ready to go?" Stacey asks me.

"As ready as I'll ever be."

Bree stays with Felicia and Shae while I walk to the empty office with Stacey, with all my boards on the wall. I stacked them along the border nicely before leaving with Bree last night, and they're in the order that I want to present them. Stacey helps me gather them before we make our way to the conference room.

"You're going to do great," Stacey says as we continue walking together, "I haven't told you this before, but Rell, we not only wanted to hire you because of your passion and drive. We wanted you to help Threads as a company. Your designs are unlike anything we have done, and I know they'll love them. We *need* someone like you here."

Do what now? I feel a faint feeling coming over me. I'm here to *help* Threads as if I wasn't already nervous. No big deal Rell, right?

Stopping outside the conference room door, I'm almost positive my face was white, as if all the blood had rushed out of my body. I close my eyes, and the first thing I see is Jansen's face, telling me I got this. I feel warm all over suddenly and almost as if Jansen was here giving me a tight hand squeeze. I opened my eyes to Stacey sadly. She's staring at me, wondering what the heck is going through my mind. I haven't spoken one word on this walk to the conference room.

"Rell, you okay?"

Taking a deep breath before spitting out, "I got this."

"Yes, now get in there. They're waiting for you," Stacey opens the door and then pushes me in. This is it. This is my moment to shine.

Chapter Sixteen

Jansen

It's raining in San Francisco on this murky Tuesday. Yesterday I spent most of my day at the job site of the condos for work, and it helped keep me busy, so my mind wasn't pondering about Rell. I wanted to know how she did with her presentation and if she liked the roses I sent, but I never heard a word from her. A part of me thought her kiss on Sunday was a goodbye kiss. She said her famous goodbye words of "see you around," I don't want to see Rell around whenever. I'm finding myself wanting to see her every day. The weekend with her wasn't long enough. I wanted more time, just us.

Arms crossed, sitting back in the desk chair, watching the rain hit my office window, I hear a knock on my door. I kick my feet, turning my chair around to see Laura standing in my doorway.

"Hey, come in."

I've never had a one-on-one conversation with Laura outside of her home. I wonder what she's doing here. She takes a seat in the chair across from my desk. I sense some worry in her actions.

"I want to apologize for Saturday night. I didn't get much time with Rell at the dinner. I know she must have felt out of place while hanging out with my friends and me on the balcony. Then I found out yesterday that Kelsey acted out of line toward you. I know Rell must have had a terrible time, and I am so sorry."

That explains so much. Rell seemed upset, and I thought it was all my fault. Kelsey was out of line, and I hated that it had to be toward me. I'll never forget the look on Rell's face when she wanted to leave. The hurt. I thought that was the only reason Rell was upset. I tried to comfort her, and she thanked me for it yesterday.

"Thank you, Laura. I am sure Rell will accept your apology."

"How is she? I've felt so bad about how Saturday went that I haven't tried contacting her yet."

"She's…" I wish I knew the answer to that question. "Good," I'm telling myself, at least.

Laura looks at me, confused by my answer. I know it didn't sound believable. I should know more than I do. So I can at least tell her something I do know about Rell to cover my tracks.

"She's busy in LA right now. She presented her clothing line yesterday, and I know she is just waiting for what's next. I'll tell her you came by and have her contact you if you want me to."

"That would be great, but honestly, I'm sure she would rather hear an apology from me, so I'll call her later."

"Sounds good," I say, wishing I was around for that phone call.

Laura gets up from the chair to leave my office and stops before walking out. She turns to me one last time, "Jay and I adore you and Rell," smiling, then she walks away.

I adore Rell myself, but us together is something that needs some explanation right now. I want more with Rell every day, but there's a deal between us. There's also a lot of unknown as to what Rell's future holds.

Once Laura is out of sight, I get back to working like I should've been doing hours ago, but I find it hard to concentrate. It could be because this weather is making me feel like shit. It reminds me of the day I met Rell. She didn't even know me then but walked out in the pouring rain to invite me into her home.

I look down at the time on my computer. The workday is almost over, so I could leave for the day. I shut down my laptop to put it away. I should be taking it home, but I don't feel like doing any work. I turn off all the lights in my office before walking out.

When I get home, I see that no one looks to be home over at Bree and Rell's. Rell left town two days ago, and I haven't seen Bree show up there once since. No sign of Kent either. Bree didn't know that Rell stayed with me Saturday, and if she found out, I'm sure it would mean they weren't on good terms with each other. They have a strong friendship, though, and I can only hope they are both the type to move on quickly from anything happening between them.

I get out of the truck, and the rain picks up to a downpour. I rush to the front door and unlock it quickly. I'm soaking wet when I make it inside the door. I would have been showering tonight anyway, but I make it my priority when I walk in the door. There are some basketball games on that I could watch. The championship game's this weekend, and I haven't been keeping up with my bracket well enough to know how I'm doing.

I strip out of my wet clothes and toss them in the laundry room before walking down the hall to my bedroom. I'm fully naked when I enter the bathroom to turn on the shower. Right before I can pull back the shower curtain to get in the shower, I hear my phone ringing from the bathroom counter. I look over to see the picture of Rell on her birthday light up on my screen.

Rell has never once called me, and mixed excitement and nervousness come over me, wondering why she is calling me. Naked still, I grab my phone off the counter, not even worried about slipping a towel around my waist.

"Hello," I answered

"Hey, are you busy?" she says, and the background is so loud that I can barely hear her. I turn around to turn off the shower, making it quiet.

"No, not at all. How are you?" I ask as I stare at my naked body in the mirror while talking on the phone to her. I reach my arm back, grabbing a towel off the towel hook while keeping the phone between my shoulder and ear. I wrap it around my waist.

"I'm sorry I haven't been able to thank you for the roses yesterday. Things around here have just been crazy," the noise in the background is finally getting quiet.

"It's okay. How did it go?"

"It went well. Jansen, they want to make them all. So, Threads by Rell will be launching very soon."

"Rell, that's great," I say, smiling while walking out of the bathroom and taking a seat on the side of my bed.

"The girls insisted we celebrate, so we just got to a bar here in LA. Bree flew in on Sunday, so she is here and..." she paused, and we both stayed quiet. "Sorry, I don't know why I am telling you all this."

"You can tell me anything."

"I'll be home tomorrow. I get a break from LA while they work on making my designs. I was hoping we could, I don't know..." she pauses again.

"See each other?" I ask, guessing.

"Maybe."

Beaming, I fall back onto the bed. Rell wants to see me outside our agreement, and honestly, I couldn't be happier this minute. "I want to."

"Would it be alright if we hung out… Rell," someone in the background says her name, interrupting her talking. Then I start hearing more people talking in the background. "I should probably go, Jansen. Can we talk later?"

"Yeah, I'll let you get back to celebrating."

"Bye, Jansen."

The phone goes silent.

It doesn't bother me that she got off the phone. What's bothering me is I want to be there to celebrate this massive accomplishment with her, and I was here. I don't want to think about what will happen if she moves there. I only want to think about my time with her here.

Getting up off the bed, I start the shower again, but this time in a much more pleasant mood than I was earlier. Will I hear from Rell again tonight? I hope so. I know I will see her when she returns home, and it excites me for tomorrow.

The one day I want work to be over with as soon as possible, everything goes wrong. The first problem was someone getting hurt on the job site, so I rushed into the office to get all the paperwork and everything to fix that situation. Thankfully, the man wasn't hurt too seriously but got a broken arm, meaning they would be down a man for some time. The second problem came when a shipment of supplies didn't get delivered today like it was supposed to, so I had to leave the office building to head to the condo site. There were more issues when I discovered more things were wrong at the condos. I was just out here on Monday, and everything seemed fine, but I guess the rain yesterday messed some of the projects up, and now they have to redo some of the construction. I'm so frustrated. Today of all days.

Rell texted me when she got to her hotel room last night, asking if we could hang out at her place after I got off work today. I knew she missed home, so it doesn't bother me that is where she wants to hang out tonight. I'm just anxious as to how this is going to go.

It's way later than I would typically leave work, but this day has been a catastrophe. I haven't even had time to message Rell to tell her I was running late. I haven't heard from her since she told me her flight landed hours ago.

Rell's car is the only one I see in her driveway when I get home. She may be the only person home, and that's what I was hoping. After a quick change into something more comfortable, I open the back door of my house, knowing exactly where to find Rell, and I'm right.

She's covered with a blanket on the back porch swing, reading when I jump over the fence. When I see her there, first-date nerves come over me, except I've been out with Rell. I shouldn't be nervous. She sits up smiling when she sees me coming.

"Hey," she says nervously.

"Hey."

I make it to the top of the steps and stand at the foot of the swing like always. She scoots over, holding the blanket up for me to lay next to her, so I do. Trying not to get too close yet but close enough to her that we touch, I lie on my back, and our shoulders are touching.

"What are you reading?"

She lifts her book, "Romance, because I like reading about other people's love lives even if they aren't real. How was work?"

"A disaster. Sorry, I'm late."

"I didn't know we had a set time for this...." she waves, thinking what to say.

"Date?"

She laughs, "Hangout, a date is something more than this. Almost like what we've already been doing, but different. We're doing things backward, and I feel we haven't just got to know each other."

She couldn't be more right. We have a complicated relationship. Most days, I don't even know what we are or what to tell people we are. My fiance has been the easiest to call her, but that's not even what she is.

I roll over on my side to face her and place my hand over her stomach. I'm surprised when she doesn't move away.

"What do you call us when you are around people?"

"Well, most days, you are just Jansen. To my followers, you are my boyfriend, but I haven't told them your name. Bree, Felicia, and Shae know about our deal, and then my new boss thinks you're my fiance," she holds up her hand, the ring still on her finger. "Then Margret across the street thinks we are sleeping together,"

"You haven't taken that off?"

"No."

"Wear it as long as you want."

"Laura called me today to apologize for Saturday," she frowns.

"She came by my office yesterday. Why didn't you tell me what was going on?"

I scoot closer to her, using my arm to hold my head up, still looking at Rell. She lays her head closer to my chest and looks down at her hand, playing with the blanket.

"I don't even know what was going on. The dinner felt off. Laura's friends took all her attention, and then Kelsey. Seeing her with her friends made me miss Bree, and I just felt like I wanted to be home. It could have been me feeling that way since I have a lot going on now. Being with you at the end of the night was comforting. I appreciated it," I see a slight grin when she mentions me comforting her.

Rell then rolls to her side and snuggles into my chest. So I wrap my arms around her, rubbing my hand up and down her back. All this closeness between us right now feels so right. It feels good to do these things with her and not be putting on a show for anyone. It's just us, and I will enjoy it while I can.

"Did Kelsey make you a little jealous?"

I can't see Rell's face for a reaction, but I can feel her smiling into my chest.

"You didn't see Bree and Kent, you know, having sex on my swing last week, did you?"

"Changing the subject?" I smile. "They were making out on it almost every day. I would say that probably led to some things."

Laying there quiet for a few minutes, neither one of us knows what to talk about, just holding each other. I slide my hand up Rell's back to play with her hair, closing my eyes, not knowing how long this feeling will last—feeling as if I've known Rell for years. She's been my comfort lately.

"Rell, what are we? What are we doing?"

She holds on to me, her face still against my chest. "I don't know. I spent a whole day with you, received roses, and when I went into my presentation, it was like you were there to get me through it.

I like the time I spend with you, Jansen. Boyfriend, fiance, neighbor, or friend. I don't want to put a permanent title to us considering we are every one of those titles already,"

"Do you want to spend more time together?"

She lifts her head to look at me, "Is that okay?"

"Of course," I say, brushing her hair back from her face.

"Now, tell me more about your presentation."

She puts her head back against my chest, and I can feel her smiling again—a feeling I want to get used to.

Rell and I spend hours on the back porch swing, talking. Something that we haven't done since we've known each other. We were comfortable, ending the night with a simple hug goodbye.

───────────

It's Friday, and there are no new issues on the condos, but I'm working out the kinks in our problems, and it's been a nightmare. I'm somehow starting to blame myself for the diversions in my life. While the distraction of Rell has been good lately, I'm trying not to get too carried away thinking about her while I am at work.

Today I decided to work at the job site of the condos. The men need some help, and I could use this time to catch them up on most of the problems we are behind on. It's been a day of hard labor, and it isn't something I'm used to but needs doing. I haven't spoken with Jay about the issues from the other day, and I know my time will be coming soon when he wants to know why I'm having problems.

I should stay out here all day, but I can't. There are still things I need to work on in my office. I haven't spoken to Rell much since our night together a couple of nights ago. She's been busy getting content back in order on her influencing with Bree, and I'm stuck working overtime. We don't have plans to see each other this weekend, but I hope we can try at some point.

By the time I make it into the office, most people have gone home for the day. Almost everyone in the office has families and wives to get home to, and since I don't, it doesn't bother me to work as long as I need to so I can get stuff done.

I take a seat at my computer, all the lights are off in everyone's office, and the sun is starting to set. I open some emails I've ignored all day and respond to them. I missed quite a few since I wasn't around my computer all day. I hear a quick knock on my office door, and someone walks in to take a seat. I look up from my laptop to see Jay.

"Hey, I didn't know you were still here," I say.

"I was waiting around for you. I had some things to do, and Laura is away this weekend, so I was going to stay late anyways," he sits back and crosses his arms.

"Look, if this is about everything going wrong with the condos, I take full blame…."

"That's why I'm here. I understand you're new, so I expected this might happen at some point. You're doing well, and I won't judge the way you work because of what has been going on, but if more things go wrong, I can't guarantee that you can keep this job,"

I nod, "I'm sorry. I love this job and promise to do better."

He leans forward, resting his elbows on his knees, "I like you, Jansen, and Laura loves Rell, but it's more than just a relationship outside the office. I need you to step it up, take responsibility, and fix things quickly. I understand you are new here, and Rell has been gone, but your mind needs to be on this job when you are in this office."

"I understand."

He stands from the chair, "Good. I want you to succeed, Jansen."

"Thanks, Jay."

"See you soon."

I nod before he walks away.

This conversation was coming, and I knew it. I need to do better. I have to. This job means more to me than anything else. If I lose this, it will be back to Kansas City for me, and I don't want that. I would leave a place I am starting to love and Rell. Someone I can't say goodbye to even though I have known her for such a short time.

I spend another hour finishing up emails and sorting out some issues with my job before leaving. I close up my laptop and go for the day. Even if Rell was home, I don't think tonight would be a good night to see her. I need to figure out a way to separate my work and personal life. It has been a while since I have had to separate the two, and while it was easy before coming here since my personal life was nonexistent, now there's something there that shouldn't be, and I don't want it to go away, either.

Chapter Seventeen

Rell

There are several stacks of packages lined up in the workroom. Bree and I are sitting on the floor, opening them all and then setting the contents to the side. We have been breaking down boxes and opening packages for hours. It's Sunday, and we have been putting these packages off so we can film the content for *The Gram* that we already had scheduled.

    I don't know how long I can stay home before heading back to LA, so we have been working for days to catch up. That means even after our talk the other night to solidify that we will see each other more, I haven't seen Jansen, nor have I spoken to him. It went hot for a night, and now it seems cold. He knows I'm busy, and I assume it's the same for him. I would like to see him before heading back since I know there's a chance I may be there for a bit longer this time.

    "What are we going to do with all this stuff?" Bree asked.

    "I guess we can donate products once we post or film them. We don't need all this."

    "Donate this?" She holds up a tube of organic coconut oil lube.

    I shake my head while laughing at her, "You keep that. I don't need it."

She tosses the tube over her head and returns to opening boxes. These boxes are full of products, clothing, jewelry, etc. When I got the clothing line with *Threads*, I shared it on *The Gram* so all of our followers and everyone knew. We started seeing more packages arriving, and companies who sponsor us sent us bouquets and sweets deliveries. It was a fun few days, feeling all the love from people who supported us.

"So, have you heard anything from Jansen?"

"No," I say, breaking down another box.

"If you two said you wanted to see each other more, why haven't you?"

"I think we agree that work comes first for both of us, and we've been busy. Jansen was having issues at work. We don't exclusively see each other, and no plans have to do with our fake relationship, so it's fine," I say it like it's no big deal, but I wonder what he has been doing.

Bree looks at me like she's not convinced.

"I'll message him."

She smiles, and then we get back to cleaning out boxes.

Once we could get rid of every box, we organized what was inside. We store the ones we want to keep on the shelves, and the ones we want to donate, we keep on the floor. Our job may always look easy to everyone on the internet, but honestly, it requires a lot of work behind the scenes, and some days, I dream of having an everyday life when I'm home. I could be spending this Sunday catching up on reading or watching a new tv show I've been dying to see. I enjoyed my one day of freedom last weekend at Jansen's house.

Kent shows up an hour after finishing the workroom projects and whisks Bree away for lunch and an outing. This is the perfect time to see what Jansen has been doing this weekend.

I pick up my phone off the coffee table.

Me- Are you alive?

A text message comes through before I can set my phone down.

J- I'm alive and well

Me- Well? I beg to differ. I haven't seen you leave your house once this weekend.

J- Stalking me now, that's hot.

Me- You seem to think everything I do is hot

J- Only speaking the truth

Me- Where did cranky Jansen go? He was sexy

J- I can be cranky anytime you want me to be

Me- If I saw you today, which one would I get?

J- It depends on what you're wearing

What I'm wearing? Huh. I look down at myself and then back at my phone.

Me- Sweatshirt and leggings, because I haven't left my house today

I put my hand over my eyes so I wouldn't see his response. These messages are getting me a little turned on, and I was only supposed to find out what Jansen was doing today.

I open my eyes.

J- my favorite

What? A sweatshirt and leggings are something I would find Margret wearing while on the sidewalk watching her neighbors leave each other's houses. It couldn't possibly be his favorite.

Me- You sure? It wasn't the towel I was wearing while in your room

J- No, because next time you're in my room. I want you in nothing.

I gulp.

Jansen wants to get laid.

I'm suddenly shaky and hot.

I need to get laid. It's been far too long.

Me- why are we still texting?

J- why aren't you here?

He has me right where he wants me—feeling all hot and bothered before coming over.

J- Come over, leave on what you're wearing

Pushy, and I like it.

I wonder why now, though, since we haven't seen each other in a few days. Has Jansen been waiting on me all weekend to assure him that what we are doing is okay?

I want to leave him waiting, so I don't respond. I check myself in the bathroom mirror to ensure I look decent in my comfy clothes. I throw my hair up in a ponytail and then spritz myself with a body spray before grabbing my things to leave.

Jansen may jump the fence when coming over, but I like using his front door. Margret is out front per usual, so I wave, and she smiles at me once she sees me walk up the few steps on Jansens front porch. I want her to keep thinking we are sleeping together because, who knows, maybe it'll come true soon. I knock and then wait.

Jansen opens the door without a word and holds it open while I walk inside.

"Hey," I say, walking past him.

He shuts the front door, and once I hear it click closed, I feel Jansen's hand on my arm, and he pulls me back up. He pushes me up against the back of the door with his hands on my hips. He looks at me like he wants to take me right here, but he wouldn't.

"You didn't say you were coming right now."

"Cranky, I like it." I smile, starting to feel all hot and bothered again.

He smiles, "That's what you wanted."

"Oh, I want more than that," I bite my lip. "just not right now, Jansen."

He places a kiss on my cheek before letting go of me.

Pushing me up against the door would've led to all kinds of things if I had let it, but I think Jansen wants confirmation from me on what I want first. I want him, and I have since the kiss on my birthday, but not now. We just started whatever is going on between us.

"Where have you been?" he asks me before taking a seat on his couch. I sit next to him and notice that the March Madness finals are playing on the tv.

"Home, You?"

"You know I've been here. Why did you wait all weekend to text me?" He looks over at me when asking.

"I didn't want to bother you, and things have been busy at home."

"Work?"

"You guessed it. Same for you?"

"Yeah," he says it like it's depressing.

We sit in silence together, watching the game. I don't know who Jansen picked to win this finale, but my bet is on Kansas.

I like being here in the comfort of Jansen's home, but part of me wishes that Jansen would sometimes ask me on an actual date. We've been on a few fake dates, and we always seem to be around other people besides the other night when I got back. I want some time with him that doesn't have to be fake or uncomfortable.

The baseball tickets Jansen got me for my birthday are for the game next weekend, and I know he told me to invite whoever, but I want to invite him. The problem is that it would be considered me asking him on a date, and that is something I have never done before.

"What is your plan for the rest of today?" I ask him.

He looks down at his watch and then back to the game. "You."

I giggle, "No, your real plans?"

He puts his arm over the couch behind me, bringing me closer to him. "Nothing."

He's frustrating. I haven't heard from him or seen him in days, but he's picking up right where we left off with each other. We're giving this a go with no strings attached, like our fake relationship. I can't be mad because I told him I didn't want a title, and I still don't. There has to be more to this for a title.

"How about I make us dinner?"

He laughs, "Remember what happened last time you made us dinner?"

"Neither of us ate it?"

"That too, but you know what I'm talking about."

"I know what you're talking about," I blush.

The kiss, I know.

"I don't have any groceries," he says.

"I just got some new meal kits in. I can go get one of those."

I say it, but still, I hope he will say we can go to dinner.

"Okay."

Annoyed, I get up from the couch. The game's almost over, so I could get Jansen's full attention, but I don't feel like waiting anymore.

I get to his front door, "I'll cook at home. Just come when the game's over."

He turns to me, confused. I open the door and close it before he says anything.

Margret's still standing across the street when I walk out, and I know what she must be thinking, "that was a quickie." Oh, it was Margret; it was a quick minute of me being frustrated with a man. That is precisely what a quickie is. I wave at her and pretend to adjust my clothing as if I just put it back on. I watch her as she puts her hand over her mouth. She just got the best information from people on the street.

I walk into my house and make my way to the kitchen. Opening the fridge, I scan all my meals; none sound that great, but I think about what Jansen would want and pick a chicken and potatoes meal. Unless Jansen decides to shower and wank before coming over, he should be here soon. The game only had a minute left, and Kansas had the win.

Luckily, the meal I chose had a pan already in it, so I had to assemble it before throwing it into the oven. I walk into the living room to turn on the TV and pick up where I left off on *One Tree Hill*. Jansen will be so not into it that maybe our conversation will be about a potential date, perhaps a kiss that is not on the cheek. I regret turning down more when he pinned me behind the door. Maybe the frustration I'm feeling is sexual frustration. It's been over a year since I've been with someone. Even sexually frustrated, I want at least one date before doing the deed.

I'm sitting on the edge of our couch when I hear the back door open. Jansen always comes in through the back unless he picks me up for a date.

"Why'd you leave?" he asks me when he enters the living room.

"Because I think I put on a good enough show for Margret entering and leaving your house, so I thought we could make dinner here."

He walks by me and takes the seat next to me. He looks up at the television and then at me, patting my back. "This is a nice date. You're cooking me dinner. Watching Nathan Scott shoot his shot. Look at you just killing it tonight."

I roll my eyes, annoyed because I am no longer angry with him. "This is not a date," I pick up the remote and turn the basketball games back on. "And we are *not* watching that show together."

The timer on the stove goes off, so Jansen drops his hand from my back, and when I get up, he follows me to the kitchen.

I take the food out of the oven and set it down on the stovetop. Jansen gets plates from the cabinet next to me and sits them beside the food. He starts plating food when I hear my phone going off. I pick it up on the counter and see it is Laura calling.

"Hello," I answered.

"Rell, how are you?"

"Good, how are you?" I say while taking a seat at one of the bar stools.

"I was wondering if you were available for lunch and shopping tomorrow. I know it is a Monday, but I want to make it up to you for last weekend."

Jansens sits my plate in front of me and mouths, "Who is that?"

I mouth "Laura" back, and his face falls a bit. He turns to the fridge, grabs two water boxes, and sits one by my plate and another beside me.

"Yes, I can get out of here tomorrow."

Jansen makes his plate and then sits down by me.

"Great. We can meet for lunch at the cafe down from the shopping mall."

"Sounds good. See you tomorrow Laura," I hang up.

Jansen's eyes get big when he hears me say tomorrow.

I set my phone down between Jansen and me. He has already started eating, so I join him. His expression during that phone call tells me something is going on.

"What did she want?" he asks me.

"She wants to go shopping and have lunch tomorrow."

He doesn't ask about anything else and continues to eat.

"Is that okay?"

"I told you, you can do whatever you want."

"Then why did it seem like it bothered you?"

He sets his fork down and shifts himself in my direction. "Jay and I had a conversation in my office on Friday. I've been running into trouble with the condos. I've spent all week trying to get everything back together. Jay told me I would have to go if I had more issues with my job. Sadly, that means I'll have to return to

Kansas City. I have been working on things from home all weekend because this job means everything to me."

I reach for his hand to hold, then rest them in my lap. "I'm so sorry. I knew the other night you said things were a disaster. I didn't realize it was this bad. I know you will do your best never to let this happen again. You're so good at what you do, and I know most of these issues aren't on you."

"They are. That is the problem. I think I let myself get distracted."

I knew what he meant when the word distracted was said. It pointed to me and everything we've been doing these last few weeks. I'm not sure he meant to say he got distracted.

Instead of saying anything, I turn back to eating my food, and he does the same. I understand why I never heard from him this weekend, and maybe moving forward with seeing each other more isn't such a great idea if it's causing problems. Honestly, it would also be easier for me if we didn't. Then if I get an offer for more designs from Threads, it would make my move there much more manageable. The last thing I need is another broken heart.

———————————

I pull up to the parking lot for the café. Laura texted me not long ago that she was running late, so I was waiting for her to arrive in my car. I not only want to get some information about her friend Kelsey while hanging out with her today. I want to know if she heard anything from Jay about Jansen. She probably wouldn't tell me if she did, considering I'm Jansen's *fiance*.

After our short conversation while eating dinner last night, I think Jansen could sense something was off with me. We cuddled up on the couch to watch some tv before he left. We didn't talk much more, and I don't know if it was because he said it and regretted saying it or he didn't know what to say, but things got awkward with us.

I see Laura's car pull up, so I get out. She gets out wearing jeans and a nice shirt, which I have never seen her wear. Thankfully I toned down my look today for this occasion, wearing jeans and a cute top. Laura has money, and almost all the times I have been around her, you can tell from what she wears and how she looks.

"Rell, it is so good to see you," she walks up to me, giving me a quick hug.

"You, too. How have you been?"

We walked into the café, side by side.

"Great, I was gone with some friends all weekend for a girl's trip in LA."

We get seated at a booth, and both pick up our menus to see what we want to order. It's weird to be with my fake fiance's boss's wife at lunch.

The waitress comes by, and we both put in our orders. Laura checks her phone one last time before sticking it into her purse.

"So, who all went to LA for the girl's trip?"

"Kelsey and I. We have friends there, so we met up with them."

I give her a simple nod. Laura has already called me to apologize for her actions.

"She's married, you know."

"I noticed. I'm not worried about Kelsey, Laura."

The truth is there's nothing to be worried about with Kelsey. Jansen's free to do what he wants, just like I am. We aren't together. I would think a married woman is not his thing.

"So, how is the clothing line going?"

"Good. I should return to Threads sometime soon to see them bring the designs to life. We'll have a launch party when they're ready to go. The clothing line is for spring and summer, so I expect them to be ready to go soon."

"That's so exciting, Rell."

"It's exciting and terrifying. What if people don't like them?"

"Oh, Rell, people will love them."

There's an awkward silence before Laura asks.

"How are things with you and Jansen lately? Jay said he was having some issues with his condos at work. He thought maybe something was going on between the two of you?"

It seems like Laura wanted to talk about the same thing I wanted today. I'm glad I didn't have to fish all this information out of her. The problem is I don't know how to answer her question because I don't even know what's going on with us.

"Um, we're good. I think some of the work issues just come with the new job. Jansen worked hard this weekend on getting things back together, so hopefully, there are no more issues. This job means more to him than anything else, and I know he doesn't want to screw this up."

I need to stand up for Jansen instead of discussing our nonexisting relationship. Jansen's a hard worker, and I know this job means more to him than anything else, or he wouldn't have asked me to be his fake fiancé for his boss.

The waitress brings our food, and while we eat, we talk about other things than Kelsey and Jansen. Once we finish eating our lunch, we stroll to the shopping mall. This mall isn't the typical one that only has the expensive brands that Laura and I once shopped for, making me happy. This is a time that I might buy something.

"When we finish here, I need to stop by the office to see Jay. Would you want to go with me?" Laura asks.

"Yeah, sure," I agree.

Chapter Eighteen

Jansen

I spent all weekend sorting my work life out and figuring out how to prioritize it with my personal life. That meant spending my weekend working out the kinks with my job so that if anything came up with Rell, I could focus on her. It worked, only for me to screw up significantly by dropping the distraction bombshell on her last night. I wasn't going to say anything, but it came out, and she knew what I meant when I said it. The thing is, Rell isn't just any distraction. She is a good distraction that I *want* to have.

      I was trying to come up with the right words to apologize and explain last night, but I came up with nothing. Things just got awkward with us, and I need to figure out how I can make it up to her. There is no sense in calling her or texting her; it's going to have to be something more significant than that. She was weird about something yesterday when she came over. Not sure if it was the fact that I pinned her to the door to take her, and she wasn't ready. The only thing I could come up with as I lay awake most of the night was that she wanted something from me, and I think she wanted something more than just flirty text and hanging out. I can almost always read Rell, but I couldn't yesterday for some reason.

      Since I got the condo situation back to normal, I have been working in the office for the entire day. Rell's out with Laura, and I want to know how it's been going. I knew there was a chance that Laura could've brought up my conversation with Jay to Rell, which is why I needed to tell her about it last night. I didn't want Rell to be surprised if Laura said anything.

I skipped leaving for lunch today and opted to bring my lunch, storing it in the breakroom. It's way after lunchtime, but I realize I haven't eaten yet. Walking down to the breakroom, I pass Jay's office and see him sitting at his desk on the computer. I nod and wave when he looks over at me. I continue to the breakroom, grabbing the leftovers Rell sent me home with last night. I pop them in the microwave to warm up and then get water from the fridge. When the microwave goes off, I take it to eat in my office.

When I pass Jay's office on my way back, his door's closed, and I can see Laura through the glass window standing by his desk. I thought she would still be with Rell, but maybe they ended their day together early. I picked up the pace back to my office to message Rell even though I told myself I couldn't until work was over. I round the corner, and when I walk into my office, there's Rell. She is standing behind my desk, looking out the window and waiting.

"Rell," I say, and she turns around smiling.

"You have a great view."

I walk over to my desk, setting my lunch down before leaning in to give Rell a soft kiss on her cheek.

"Sorry, if I'm not supposed to be here, I can go."

I stand by her while she continues looking out the window.

"No, you can stay."

This is such a pleasant surprise, having her here. I would usually be stressed seeing a woman in my workspace, but Rell can sit at my desk, keeping me company all day.

"Laura wanted to see Jay and asked me if I would want to come by here."

"Well, this is my office," I turn around and hold my arm out.

Rell turns around and looks around the room. "I like it."

I start noticing all the others in their offices around mine looking through the windows. There isn't much privacy, and they have never seen a woman in my office.

"Your office is kind of bare."

She isn't wrong; there's nothing special about my office. I used all the existing furniture. I didn't bring any pictures of anything, and there are no walls to hang photos. Honestly, I am the only new thing in the office.

Rell sits on the edge of my desk instead of sitting in an armchair. I stand back, but now that she's in my office, I want to kiss her. It could be all the eyes looking over at us or the fact that she came here to see me.

"What are your plans tonight?"

I walk over and stand right in front of her between her legs, resting my hands on her thighs. "Nothing."

She frowns, "Oh."

Looking around the office, I can see everyone has piqued their interest in what is happening. Some people know who Rell is and think she is well out of my league. I know she is. She is far more than everyone I have ever been with or wanted.

"Why so disappointed?" I turn my attention back to her.

She looks at my hands on her and shrugs her shoulders. She doesn't want to tell me what she's thinking. I wish I had a slight idea of what has been on her mind these last few days. We are navigating this, spending more time together the wrong way.

I slide my index finger under her chin and lift her face to me. "Rell. Talk to me."

"I've just been waiting for…" she pauses. "Nevermind, it's ridiculous," she looks around and starts noticing all the eyes on us. "I should probably go. I don't want to distract you or get you in trouble."

She moves to get up, and I push her legs back down to sit on the desk. Taking her face into my hands, I inch closer and place my lips on hers. She doesn't reciprocate at first but then slides her hands up my arms before giving me more access to her mouth—our tongues dance for just a second before she pulls back from me.

"Jansen, we.." I put my finger over her mouth.

"We're okay, and I'm not letting you stop us this time," I lean back into her and give her a soft kiss over and over again. "I've wanted to do that since my lips met yours."

I rest my forehead against hers. It's almost as if a lightbulb went off when I kissed Rell. I know what she wants. "Rell, will you go on a date with me?"

She smiles, our faces close still while our foreheads touch, "Yes, finally."

I give her one more kiss on the lips, this one a little longer than the last one.

It's never phased me; that is what she wanted, considering all the dating we have practically been doing when we are faking our relationship. Our fake relationship was the only one we were supposed to have, but I want to give this a shot of being more than that, even with what I know could happen to us.

I wrap my arms around Rell before letting her jump off the desk. Everyone else's eyes have turned away from us now that they got what they wanted. I feel lucky at the moment; not only is Rell my fake girlfriend, but this could potentially be a real relationship between us soon.

I want that.

And I want that with her.

I don't even know who I am since this wasn't something I wanted when I got here, but Rell changed that. She has changed it all.

"I'll call you when I get off, okay?" I tell Rell after we walk to the door.

Suddenly I didn't want her to go just yet, but I wouldn't be able to finish this work day with her here.

She turns around to me, "Okay."

I slip my hand behind her neck and run my fingers through her hair. I give her one more kiss as if I haven't gotten enough while she has been here.

She smiles against my lips before pulling her head back. "Talk to you soon."

Then she leaves me, walking towards Jay's office to meet with Laura.

Watching her walk away this time, knowing I will be able to see her later tonight without any rules at all, feels so good. It is almost like she is mine already.

───────────────

Flipping through the clothes in my closet, I land on a flannel button-up again. Taking it off the hanger, I put it on and buttoned it up. Tonight is the night that I get to take Rell out. I have been looking forward to this night since asking Rell on a date. Rell and I haven't seen each other since she left my office, but we did talk on the phone every night this week. We are starting to get into the habit of calling when I get off and then sending her a goodnight text message before we go to bed. I never thought we would be at this point, but here we are, and I don't want it to change either.

This night is different from the past times I took Rell out; not only is this for real, but I want it to be a perfect night with her. I planned the whole evening for us, with the help of some co-workers, because I don't know what the hell there is here in San Francisco that's romantic. So what's more romantic than a night cruise at the bay, watching the sunset? Apparently, it is something Tim took his wife Nancy on once, and she loved it.

I took off early today to watch the sunset with Rell, and I don't even know who I am anymore. Rell has turned me into a different version of myself.

Running some pomade through my tousled hair, I look at myself in the mirror, knowing that it doesn't matter that I'm putting this stuff in my hair. It will look like shit once the boat ride is over.

On the way out the door, I grab a beanie and coat since tonight on the boat will get cold. I walk over to Rell's house, feeling anxious. I'm eager to see her and finally be able to kiss her when I want to.

After walking up the steps, I knocked on her door before turning around to wait. Margret looks to be standing on her front porch this evening and watching over, so I wave. I find it intriguing that she seems interested in other people's businesses.

When I hear the door opening, I see Rell wearing my favorite sweatshirt, leggings, and ponytail. The same thing she wore the night I asked her to be my fake girlfriend, and the outfit I think she looks simply beautiful in.

"Hey," I say to her before she can even say it herself.

She smiles, "Hey."

She grabs a jacket and blanket folded up on the couch. When she turns to me to leave, I lean into her and give her a soft kiss. She dips her head down nervously and smiles.

I lift her head with my hand to look at me. "You're going to have to get used to that. I can kiss you whenever I want, and I won't be holding back."

"And I'll happily accept them," she blushes.

We walk out the front door, and she locks it behind us. It seems like Bree and Kent are away for the weekend, so I may not be able to leave Rell home alone after this date.

Margret is still sitting on her front porch, so I put my arm around Rell and bring her closer as we walk to my truck. This time I walk her to her side before I get in, even opening the door for her. Tonight I am going to be a proper gentleman for her.

The car ride down to the bay is a typical conversation of our week. Rell has been busy catching up with Bree on their influencing content. She'll be heading back to LA soon, and this time when she leaves, it will be more complicated for me than the last.

When we pull up to the dock, I notice we are the only people boarding the boat for the night, making this even more romantic. I suspected there would be others, but I wanted it to be only us. Not many people book a sunset cruise on a cold night.

Once I help Rell out of the truck, we walk down the dock and step onto the boat. There's a cold chill in the air. I know there will be so much snuggling on this boat with Rell, and I'm not mad about it.

We get settled together on the boat's bow, and it doesn't take long before it takes off from the dock. Rell is positioned right between my legs, and my arms are wrapped tightly around her. She unfolds the blanket and covers us with it, bringing it up to her chest.

"Well, this is nice, Jansen. I never would've guessed you to be a romantic," she laughs.

"Nothing about me is romantic, so consider yourself lucky."

"I feel like we should set some rules for this evening."

"No way. I've been following too many rules with you already, and I'm ruled out," I squeeze her tightly.

She laughs, "Not those kinda rules. I mean setting rules on what we can talk about, like I don't want to talk about LA or work, and no exes. I want to talk about us."

Nestling my chin into her neck, I pull her closer by wrapping my arms tighter around her, "Talk away then."

I can tell she's thinking for a moment as we watch the Golden Gate Bridge get more prominent. The sun is close to setting, but it's still pretty light outside. This ride is just under two hours long, and I'm not sure if that's enough time with Rell for the evening. I need to think about something to do next.

"What is it about me?" she asks. She already wants to get deep.

"I like you, " I keep it short and straightforward.

"I can't help but think maybe you haven't met enough people yet. I mean, I'm your neighbor. There's plenty of women in San Francisco that you haven't met."

"I've met plenty of people in my lifetime, Rell, and none of them have ever interested me as much as you have in the short time I've known you. I don't want to meet anyone else," I place a kiss on her temple.

"What made you ask me to be your fake fiancé?"

"Honestly, that day was when Jay asked me about dinner, and well, you just happened to stare at me this certain way when I was in the pool, and it came across my mind. It was never my intention to ask you, but now that I think about it, I made the best choice by choosing you that night. I mean, I wouldn't have asked anyone else. I would've told him the truth,"

"So, why not tell him the truth now that this is more?"

"Because now I don't have to fake it with you, not that I was doing much acting before. You pretty much had me wrapped around your finger from night one. We both asked each other for a favor, but I can't help but think we needed each other for more than a favor."

Rell lays her head back against my chest as we drift under the bridge, the breeze in the air is starting to give me a chill, or maybe it's just the feeling of being with her. Even though this is something I wasn't looking for or want, I don't want this to end. This sort of feeling I've never felt with someone in my arms.

The sun is finally starting to set, and the most beautiful view of it in the distance has left me and Rell speechless. Where there were shudders, they have now turned into goosebumps. This moment was everything I wanted it to be tonight. Feelings and emotions start stirring in my chest as I don't want to let go of Rell.

"Thank you," I whisper in her ear.

Her face against my chest, now looking up at me. "For what?"

"For wanting more and giving me the best moment of my life," I say before kissing her.

Chapter Nineteen

Rell

Oh, Jansen Davis. Someone who can be such a cranky man can also be the most romantic. How that is possible, I don't even know. I've been on dates, but none have come close to how great tonight is. We shared space while watching the most beautiful sunset. His arms made me feel safe, and his kisses made me feel like I was the only girl he would ever want.

After watching the sunset on the boat wrapped in Jansen's arms, we're now getting off the ship at the dock. I don't know where we are going next, but it doesn't matter if I get to spend tonight with him.

Jansen takes my hand in his, ensuring I don't trip while stepping down. Once my feet are safely on the dock, he intertwines our fingers, kissing me, "We can do anything you want to do now."

"Did you have anything in mind? It doesn't matter to me."

He smiles, "Rell, I can spend the rest of tonight anywhere as long as I'm with you."

Grinning, I say, "We can go to my place or yours."

We get to Jansen's truck, and once inside, I shiver. Tonight has been cold, and not being wrapped in his arms has left me feeling colder than I have felt all night. He must have seen me tremble. He turns up the heat, tossing me the blanket he was carrying.

"Thanks," I say, wrapping the blanket over my legs.

"Anything for you."

Once we drive out of the marina, Jansens seems to be heading toward home. I'm unsure which house we will go to for the rest of the night. Bree is gone for the night with Kent, so my house will be empty.

Jansen reaches over the console of his truck, taking my hand in his. It doesn't feel different from when Jansen and I were faking this. It feels more special now, and the comfortable feeling for us is still very much there.

When we pull up to his house, we both get out together. I walk around expecting us to go to my house for the night. Once I get to the back, Jansen pulls me into him. "You're going the wrong way."

Spinning me around in his arms, he puts me in the direction of his house. I walk in front of him up the steps, and he reaches his arm around me to unlock the door for us. Walking in, I flip on the lamp on the side table. Then slip off my coat and place it on the back of the couch.

"When are you going to take that thing down?" I ask him, nodding to the deer's head above the fireplace mantle.

"Never. I got you, so your little comment about being unable to get a woman failed. Miserably," he laughs.

Jansen walks into the kitchen, "You want anything?"

"I'm okay. Thank you," I say, taking a seat.

Jansen comes back into the living room with two boxes of water in his hand and hands one of them to me.

"Thanks."

He sits next to me on the couch and places his arm around me, bringing me closer to him. I rest my head against his chest as we relax on the sofa.

"You want to come with me tomorrow?" I ask him.

"Where are you going?"

Glancing up at him, "The baseball game is tomorrow. Did you forget about the tickets?"

"It slipped my mind, but I would love to go with you. Are you sure you don't want Bree or someone else to go?"

"No, just you," I look back down, placing my hand on his chest.

He puts his hand over mine, "So, it's a date. You know what happens on a second date?"

"You get to second base?" I grin while rolling my eyes.

"Precisely that," he kisses the top of my head.

There has been sexual chemistry between Jansen and me since we met. I know I want to go to the next step, but it makes me nervous about actually taking that step with him. More than kissing and holding hands mean more to me, which scares me more. I try not to think about the future, but it is hard to shove it into the back of my mind when I am around him.

I wake up to the sound of a door slamming shut. Sitting up quickly in my bed, I flip the sheet before me. Bree must be home from

Kent's house. Sliding the covers off of me, I get up from my bed to see what the commotion is.

When I reach the living room, I see Bree's overnight bag on the couch and her purse. It's early, and it is unusual for her to be back already from his house. The bathroom door is closed, but I can see the light from under it, so I knock on it.

"Bree?"

"Sorry, I didn't mean to wake you," she says, and I can tell she's been crying for some time.

"Open up. What happened?"

She opens the door, and yesterday's mascara is running down her face. Without asking questions, I open my arms and wrap them around her. She loses it when she is tightly in my arms, and tears flow hysterically.

"Oh, stop, you're going to make me cry, and I don't even know what happened."

It takes her a second to say, "I broke it off with Kent."

"Bree. I am so sorry," I rub my hand up and down her back and frown at myself in the mirror when I see how miserable she looks.

They seemed so solid and in love. I can't possibly understand what went wrong. They're engaged, and Bree has been ready for something more with him for a long time.

"How about we move this pity party to your room? You can get sleep to try to clear your mind."

She sniffles, "Okay."

I have my arm around her shoulders while we walk to her bedroom. She climbs onto her bed, and I slide her white comforter over her. Brushing her hair back from her face, "We can talk about this later, okay?"

She shakes her head no before quickly closing her eyes.

I leave her room, cracking the door to hear her. I then rush across the house, go into my room and take my phone off the nightstand.

Me- Mayday! Bree and Kent split. It's not good over here.

Hitting send, knowing it is early, Jansen is probably still sleeping, but a response comes through quickly.

J- Need anything? I can bring something for her.

I smile. That is so nice of Jansen.

Me- That is sweet of you, but I think she will be alright now. I just got her into bed to clear her mind. Hopefully, she will tell me everything when she wakes.

J- Are we still good for tonight?

Me- We are still good.

At least, I hope we are still good for tonight. Bree should understand me leaving for the game. I hope she will be alright by herself when I go.

J- I can't wait

I can't wait, either. Jansen and I finished our date last night, cuddling on the couch until we both got tired. He walked me home, and we ended the night with a kiss—a simple ending to such a fantastic date. Once I settled into bed last night, I missed Jansen and wished I'd asked him to at least stay for the night.

Since I'm up for the day, I decide to go ahead and shower while Bree is napping. That way, when she wakes, she can have my full attention when she wants to talk about what happened between her and Kent.

Once out of the shower, I dry off, put on my silk robe, and wrap my hair in a towel. I walk to Bree's bedroom door to see that she's still sleeping, so I head to the work room to dry my hair. I haven't even taken a seat at the vanity when I hear a knock at the back door.

Looking down at myself, I tighten my robe, knowing it has to be Jansen at the back door. Before I open the door, I take my towel off and shake my head so my hair falls nicely over my shoulders. I take a deep breath before opening the door.

Jansen is standing there holding a bottle of wine and a brown paper bag. He smiles when I come into his view and holds up the bottle of wine.

"You shouldn't have."

He walks into the door, placing a kiss on my lips. "Well, I want Bree to be alright before you leave her tonight."

After setting the bag on the counter, he pulls out all kinds of chocolates and a small flower bouquet.

"Jansen, you're so sweet."

"Oh, these are for you," he hands me the bouquet before taking my face into his hands and kissing me passionately up against the kitchen counter. I'm beginning to think Jansen has something for me when I am in the kitchen.

"This," he stops kissing me, tugging on the front of my robe, "Does things to me."

"Would you rather I take it off?" I tease.

He puts his forehead to mine, "Yes, but not now. Bree's here."

"Right, don't think she would appreciate waking up to someone moaning while going through a breakup."

"You moan?" He asks me with a smirk on his face.

"Guess you'll have to find out," I wink.

He grabs my face again and kisses me with more tongue than before, and I tangle my tongue with him, putting my hands behind his head to bring him closer to me.

He stops and places his forehead on mine again. "If we don't stop...."

"Then we won't be going to the game?" I interrupt.

"Exactly, then no second base."

"We're already there," I giggle.

"I don't want to, but I need to go shower. Give those flowers to Bree, and call me when you're ready to go."

Before I can say anything else, he is out the back door. My heart flutters, and my body aches for more of what Jansen offers.

When I check on Bree before going back into the workroom to get ready for the day, she's awake and sitting on her phone in her bed. She didn't sleep long, but how can one sleep when going through something?

Opening the door, "Need someone to talk to?"

She looks up from her phone and then flashes me a smile.

Walking into her room, I go to the other side, taking a seat on her bed. "What happened?"

"I think we are just taking things too fast," she says before lying back down.

"You've been together for months. You fell hard, fast for Kent, but maybe that means it meant to be for the two of you," I lay my head on hers.

"We got into an argument about something so stupid, and I thought maybe we aren't supposed to be together if we fight over little stuff sometimes."

"Fighting is a good thing. Couples are supposed to fight. It's what makes the relationship healthy. Could you imagine never fighting, just giving him what he wants, and never thinking about yourself? I think the two of you can work this out. You love him. If you love him more than anything else, that is all you need."

I don't know where these words come from, but something has changed inside me. Maybe Jansen is bringing out another side of me I didn't think I had. Jansen and I fought on our first date, and look where we are. In past relationships, I never argued and let them walk all over me, which has never worked out for me.

"Should I call him and talk to him?" she lifts her head to look up at me.

Smiling, "Definitely."

"Thank you, Rell."

I get up from the bed before walking to her doorway, "Anytime. Now fix this. I want to see my happy Bree."

She beams at me.

"Oh, and Jansen brought you chocolate and flowers. They're on the kitchen counter."

I walk away to leave Bree so she can call Kent.

"Rell," she yells out.

My eyes go to her when I step back into her room, "Yes?"

"I hope this relationship with Jansen works for you. I wanted to see my happy Rell again, and I have these past few weeks," she grins.

"Me too, Bree, me too."

With that, I walk out and finally get ready for second base, maybe third.

Jansen and I are walking into the baseball stadium, holding hands. We are early for the game today since the situation at home turned out okay and left us plenty of time to prepare. Bree called Kent, and he came over to talk, so I showed up at Jansen's house early. After a short makeout session, we were on our way here.

I gave Jansen our tickets at his house, so I have no idea where we are seated. I should have looked at them before coming.

Taking the tickets out of his pocket, he looks over them while still holding my hand to find out where we are going. "This way," he says, nodding toward where we should go.

We get to our section and start walking down the stairs together. We walk towards the seats behind the dugout. "Um, what row are we going to?" I ask nervously.

"Row two."

I clench my teeth. I should've looked.

The San Francisco Seals players are warming up on the field, and just when I think, I may be in the clear. There he is, Mac Milligan. My ex.

Chapter Twenty

Jansen

I find our seats, and as we make our way down the steps, Rell squeezes my hand tight before letting go. Turning around, I see her wearing her navy blue SF Seals hat and pulling it down to cover her face. I reach my hand back out to her, and she takes it. When I bought her the tickets, I got to the seats behind the dugout, the section I knew would be the best. When we make it down to our row, I let her walk down the aisle before me.

I sit next to her and place my arm on the back of her chair. With a kiss on her cheek, I ask, "Are you okay?" I look at her, but she has her eyes set on the field, so I follow her gaze, not seeing anything.

"I wasn't expecting our seats to be so close."

"These are the best seats, so of course, that's where I would get you tickets."

She turns to me and smiles. "Thank you again."

Leaning into her, I kiss her. "I'm happy you wanted me to come with you."

She props her feet on the back of the chair in front of her and relaxes back. I place my hand on her leg while we watch the teams warm up. I can't think of a better place to be now: my girl and I at a baseball game.

Rell seems nervous, and it dawns on me that it may be because of all the second base talk we've mentioned. She shouldn't be anxious about where tonight may go and mean for us.

When the team heads into the dugout, I notice Mac Milligan waving in our direction. We're the only people in our area. That's when I look over to see Rell waving back. What the hell?

"You know him?" I whisper into her ear, taking my hand off her leg.

She purses her lips together, not wanting to answer.

"You want to tell me?" I ask.

She pinches the bridge of her nose and closes her eyes. "There's something I need to tell you."

It hits me like a ton of bricks when I realize what she needs to tell me. "Mac is M, isn't he? He's the roses, the ring, and the one that misses you. He's how you knew the answer to the question that night."

She nods.

"Damn it, Rell. Why didn't you tell me this before coming here?"

"I didn't want to talk about it. I wasn't expecting our seats to be where Mac could see us."

I sit back and cross my arms over my chest. I should've known this the night she knew how many home runs he hit, but all she said was that she watches sports, so that's all I thought. I've always been a Mac fan until right this minute. She was engaged to him. It had to be someone like him of all the people she was with before me. The jealousy I'm feeling is making me very unwell.

"Rell," He yells out, motioning for her to come down.

Oh, hell.

Rell gets up from her seat, and before she takes a step, I stop her with my hand on her wrist. "You have your ring on?"

She holds her hand out, and there it is.

"You're my fiancé, right?"

"But...."

"Right?"

"Chill, I was going to tell him," she says.

She walks down to Mac just a row before us. I'll wait here and see what happens, but if he tries to touch her, I will lose my shit.

Finding out Mac is her ex will not stop me from wanting Rell, not one bit, but it does make me wonder why me, though. She had him and could've shared their relationship on her account. She could've been so much more if she had been with him.

Then I remember when she said she didn't want to live in his shadows, and now it makes so much sense. She didn't want to be a player's wife. She had dreams of being better and making something of herself. She could've used her relationship with him to get her where she is today, and she didn't. She took the more complicated route. I can't be upset about her not telling me about him. I'm starting to feel a sense of pride instead.

Rell is standing in front of Mac at the wall between the field and seating. He seems enthralled by her while talking, and Rell appears to be acting herself. I would tell the asshole to get in line like all the other guys, but he had his chance. There won't be another chance for him or anyone else.

I notice Rell holding her hand out and showing him her ring. I want to tell him to fuck off; she's off the market, but the real problem is she isn't.

Rell yells out for me and motions me to come down there. Great.

Getting up from my seat, where I'm comfortable watching them talk from a distance, I now have to speak to him. I'll try to keep my composure and act as if I love Rell with everything I have. I want to show him what he missed out on with her, but he's freakin Mac Milligan.

My heart starts beating a million times a minute before I finally stand right behind Rell. I wrap my arm around her, and she smiles. "Mac, this is my fiancé Jansen. Jansen, Mac," she motions her hand between us.

"Mac," I reached my hand out to shake his.

Mac is intimidating. He is tall and muscular, with sandy blonde hair and tattoos on his arms. He would for sure kill me in a fight. I would like to know what sweet little Rell saw in him when they were together.

"I was wondering who the lucky guy was," he shakes my hand.

"That would be me. Rell's way out of my league," I pull her into my chest, kissing her on the temple.

"You better keep an eye on this one. She's a runner."

I'm not an idiot to know what he means when he says that. There was a reason she left him.

I stir up my face. "Weird. I don't think I have ever seen Rell run once since I met her."

Mac laughs.

"Anyways, I should probably get back. It was really good seeing you again, Rell. It was nice meeting you... umm."

"Jansen," I say.

"Right," he backs up his steps. "Later, you two."

Then he walks off into the dugout. I let Rell walk first back to our seats and follow behind her. Once we are both seated, neither of us knows what to say, and I know there are probably things she wants to tell me right now, but honestly, I don't want to hear it yet. I'm still trying to process the fact that she was engaged to Mac Milligan.

"Shit. I need a beer," I say, getting up to start walking down the aisle.

"Jansen Davis!"

"Right, sorry," I turn around, "Did you want a beer too?"

Shaking her no, she then ignores me.

I walk up the steps to the concession stand line.

Okay, maybe I'm a little shocked right now, but I need to remember that I was excited to be here with Rell on a date before all this happened. Right, a date. I shouldn't be letting this information ruin my night with Rell. We just took steps forward, and if I don't get my shit together, we will take steps back.

Once I get to the front of the line, I order two beers—one for me and one for her. I'm not sure if Rell will drink it, but we could use a drink right now.

After taking the two beers, I walk back down the steps to our seats. Rell is still sitting the way she was when I left. I hand her one of the beers, and she accepts it and takes a sip instantly.

Once seated, I lean over to her. "I'm sorry."

"No, I'm sorry. I should have told you a long time ago, but we barely knew each other that night, and I should've told you before coming. Mac and I have been over for a long time, and I haven't spoken to him since our break up."

"Rell, you don't have to explain anything. I get it," I take her hand in mine. "We are here to have a good time, and I shouldn't let this ruin our night. Okay?"

A faint smile comes across her face, and I lean, kissing her. It is just a soft, quick kiss to reassure her that I am not angry with her. She squeezes my hand in return.

―――――――――

We walk out to the truck once the game ends, holding hands. The game ended up being so much fun with Rell. She does take her sports very seriously. She did great rooting for everyone but Mac, knowing that shit would piss me off. Mac hit two home runs, which ticked me off because it was like he was trying to show off.

Rell had exactly three beers and two hot dogs. Thankfully the hot dogs were enough to soak up the beer, so she wasn't drunk. I have plans for us, and it doesn't include talking about her ex or drinking any more alcohol.

I open Rell's door for the passenger side, and she climbs inside the truck before walking around to my side to get in. We are on our way to my house when Rell finally speaks some words since leaving the field.

"He cheated, you know."

"Sorry….But what?"

She gets comfortable, resting her arm on the console, "And I stayed with him."

"Rell, we are not talking about this."

"He told me he had too many drinks one night after a win, and some girls followed them back to their hotel room. He didn't mean for it to happen. Since there was no sign of a girlfriend on his social, they thought he was available."

"Rell, stop. You don't have to tell me this stuff."

Maybe it's the beer, or she thinks she needs to tell me all this, but I'm not enjoying it.

She holds her hand up to me when I turn to face her. "Let me finish."

I shake my head at her, "Finish."

"I stayed with him for another year after that. He tried everything he could, so he wouldn't lose me. He gave me tickets to his games, so I didn't have to buy my own, and he showered me with gifts and attention. It was six months after he cheated that he proposed, and then after six months of being engaged, I finally got the courage to leave. The hurt outweighed my love for him. I haven't seen anyone else since him. That was over a year ago," she frowns while looking out the window.

I take her hand in mine and bring her hand to my lips. I kiss her knuckles and rest our hands on my lap. "Rell, you are better than what he gave and did to you. You didn't deserve it."

"Which is why I left. I didn't want the life he wanted to give me. I look back now and wonder why I stayed, and I think I just wanted the comfort of someone. I don't know."

"You're better than being with a man who has meaningless sex with a fan and then showers you with unnecessary things to make up for it."

I didn't want to talk about this, but I'm glad Rell finished the conversation. She wanted me to know the hurt she felt, and I wouldn't say I liked that I shook his hand and met him. I don't deserve Rell, honestly. She's a force, a strong person to go through that and be where she is today.

Rell takes her hand out of mine and pulls her vibrating phone from the back pocket of her jeans. She takes a quick look at the screen before answering.

"Hey, Stacey."

I turn down the radio so Rell can talk and hope I can listen to their conversation. I know what this call means, and now I feel unsettled. She's leaving.

"Tomorrow?" she says.

Not tomorrow. Never would be my wish.

"Okay, I'll be there as soon as I can," she smiles while talking on the phone, and my heart wants to break right now. We made up and took those three steps forward in our relationship tonight, and now taking those three steps back.

"See you tomorrow," she says before hanging up the phone.

I don't say anything after she gets off the phone because I don't want her to think I was listening in on their conversation or show that I'm sad about her leaving.

We pull up in the driveway, and Rell still hasn't said anything about the phone call. I hope it's because she feels the same as me. Neither of us wants to prepare for what's going to happen next for us. I won't let it stop me because I want this with Rell more than anything right now.

"You staying?" I ask, shutting the truck off.

"Staying?"

"Sorry, let me try that again. Will you stay with me tonight?" I smile.

"Yes." she returns a smile before kissing me.

We get out, and I meet her at the front door of my home. Wrapping my arms around her, I kiss her like I haven't all night as I want her *forever*. She slides her hands from my shoulders to my neck, opening her mouth to give me more. She's kissing me like she has been waiting for this moment all night.

I don't want to let go of this kiss, so I unlock the front door with one hand while my other hand is in Rell's hair at the back of her head. Once I hear the lock click, I twist the doorknob and swing open the front door. I let out our kiss, but only to grab her by the butt, pick her up, and wrap her legs around me. Once inside, I kick the door closed with my foot before dropping Rell on the couch. Hovering over the top of her with my legs between hers, I take her in, smiling. This is the closest we have ever been with each other.

"Jansen," her deep brown eyes look into mine, cheeks flush.

I brush back a piece of hair from her forehead, "Yea?"

"I want this. I'm scared because I don't know what this is between us, but I like you. I know there's some...."

I stop her by putting my finger to her mouth, "Don't. I want this too, and that's all that matters right now."

She grins, and I dip my head down to kiss her soft lips once.

"Can we go to the bedroom? She asks.

"You mean you want to stay, stay with me? Sleeping in the same bed?" I point to my chest.

She grins and nods. "Please."

Getting up off the couch, I bend down and scoop Rell up in my arms. Carrying her down the hall and into my room, I slowly lay her on the bed. Then I walk over to my dresser to look for a different shirt, leaving her lonely.

"You don't need anything from home?" I ask before taking my shirt off and throwing it into the laundry basket by the closet.

Rell props herself up with her elbows on the bed, looking at me with dark eyes and glare.

"What?" I laugh.

"Stop looking for clothes, and come here."

Shirtless, I crawl onto the bed and hang over her. She drops her head on the mattress and runs her hands up my chest. Her hands are warm with her touch sending chills up my spine. She slides her hands up to my face, pulling me down for a kiss. "I want you," she says, looking me in the eyes like I'm the only person she has ever wanted.

"If we do this, Rell, it means more to me, which means you can't be anyone else's."

"I don't want to be anyone else's. I want to be yours, Jansen."

Placing small kisses on Rell's neck, up to her jawline, I slide my hand up her shirt, slowly sliding right over her stomach, and cup her breast. Her head falls back, and she closes her eyes as if she has longed for that touch. My lips wander from her neck to her mouth, and she instantly opens her mouth, giving and taking more from me. I uncup her breast with my hand, pulling it out of her bra. I'm trying to steady my pace by touching her in places I've wanted to touch her, but I'm anxious. I've wanted her for far too long.

Grabbing at the hem of her shirt, I glide it up, pulling her shirt over her head. I take the view of her breasts, covered in a black lace bra, as if she prepared for something like this to happen between us.

She places her hand on my chest, "You said second base, but I want…."

Throwing her shirt onto the floor before my mouth falls back onto hers, I whisper against her lips, "You're getting all the bases."

She laughs nervously before grabbing my face and kissing me with everything she has. The effect this woman has on me is something I haven't once experienced in my life. There's no turning back after this. There is only going to be moving forward in my life with Rell.

Detaching my lips from Rell's, I slowly move them down her body, giving her tiny touches on my way down. Once I get to her breast, I pull down the lace of her bra just over her nipple. I slowly lick her nipple before gently biting down on it. My eyes look up at her as she closes her eyes and a small moan leaves her mouth. Her hands find their way through my hair before gripping my head, ensuring I stay in place.

I reach down, unbuttoning Rell's jeans before unzipping them. She lifts her ass, insinuating me to slide them off of her. Standing up from the bed, I slide them off her to see that she isn't wearing anything underneath. I know *for sure* that she wants this.

"Fuck's sake, Rell," I can't help myself. I've wanted this day to come, and now that I see her perfect body, almost entirely naked, on my bed, it is almost like I am dreaming.

My words get her attention. She opens her eyes and looks at me with a grin. Then her body shivers as if she is anxious for me.

Unbuttoning my jeans, I slide them off, my erection falling forward. Taking a few steps to the nightstand, I open the top drawer and pull out a condom. Once I open the wrapper, I slide it over myself before crawling back on the bed. I watch Rell as she sits up to undo her bra, sliding the strap down her arms and throwing it on the floor.

I kiss the inside of each of her thighs, "If I touch you right here, what is it going to tell me," I say, barely touching her spot, leaving her wanting more.

"Jansen," she says, shivering once again.

"Patience, baby. Patience."

I slide not one but two fingers up her sex; it's wet, precisely the answer I wanted. I know she's ready, but once I'm inside her, there's no going back, and there's a chance this won't last long for me.

Starting just above her sex, I place lingering touches on my way up her body until I get to her mouth. She wraps her hands around the back of my head, and our mouths collide. Using my hand, I grab myself before slowly sliding my length into her entrance. With every movement, I add more of myself inside her.

Rell glides her hands from the back of my head to my back, gripping me hard when I pick up our pace. My mouth moves from hers to her neck. Before I know it, I'm breathing heavily into her.

More moans come from her mouth, and it takes everything in me not to let myself go. If she didn't come before me, she would never want to do this again, but this between us feels more amazing than I ever thought it would.

I lift my head to see Rell's eyes closed, head back, and mouth open. I kiss her cheek softly before sitting on the bed on my knees, sliding myself out of her.

The movement causes her to open her eyes, "Don't stop."

"Baby, I'm not stopping. I want to give you more."

I pull on her legs, pulling her to the edge of the bed. She laughs, propping herself up on her elbows. "Lose that thing."

"This?" I say, tugging on the condom.

She shakes her head yes, with a grin. "It's fine. You don't have to worry about anything. I promise I'm on the pill."

I let out a deep breath before pulling it off. I don't like them. I've always worn one, but this with her is different from other times, and we are just getting started.

After tossing the condom on the floor, I slid myself back into Rell's sex. S*hit,* this wasn't a good idea. She feels so good that I think I'll lose myself in her after a few movements.

Wrapping Rell's legs around my waist, still standing, I use my thumb to rub against her sex, pacing myself with her. She moans louder as if she is going to come any minute. She mentioned being a moaner, but I wasn't expecting her to, and it's so fucking sexy. She's almost right where I want her to be when I pick up the pace with my thumb over her sex and pound into her harder. She mouths out, "Jansen," before squeezing herself around my length, and that's when I feel the end for me. I lean forward, hands on both sides of her hips, and lose myself in her.

Falling onto her chest, both of us trying to steady our breathing, she runs her hands through my hair as my head lays on her chest.

We lay there for minutes. Both of us take in everything that just happened between us. There is no other way to describe it than using the word *incredible*. What we just did was not typical fucking. I felt something else.

Looking up at her, "You're so amazing, you know that?"

She smiles before kissing my forehead.

"I'm serious, Rell. You've done something to me from the moment I met you."

Lifting my head off her chest, "Come. Let's shower."

Holding my hand out for her after getting up from the bed, she takes it.

"If anyone is doing anything, it's you that's doing something to me," she says before lifting on her toes to kiss me.

Chapter Twenty-one

Rell

Once again, running through the airport to my flight late, I board the plane with seconds to spare. I couldn't get an early flight considering I didn't get to book a flight until this morning. It's good that Stacey only wanted me to fly in today so I could be at *Threads* first thing Monday morning.

    I woke up this morning tangled in Jansen's sheets with him watching me sleep. Last night was incredible and only something I could've dreamed of. No man has ever given me that kind of attention. It was then that I realized I had to leave today, and I'm not sure for how long. I booked my flight after leaving Jansen's house this morning. I wanted to stay there forever, with him, but it wasn't in my cards. Bree needed me before leaving town, and I had to prepare for what could be a long time away.

    Bree and Kent made up after my talk with Bree yesterday. He was at the house this morning when I arrived, and they seemed to be back to what they were. While I was getting ready in the workroom this afternoon, Bree came in to talk to me about their relationship and that the wedding would still happen. Time got away from me; before I knew it, I needed to leave, and there wasn't a chance to tell Bree about my night with Jansen.

    I had plans to drive myself to the airport, but when I walked out to Jansen standing by my car with a package of gummy worms and an offer to take me, I couldn't resist him. We stood outside the airport, not ready to say goodbye.

"Rell, I'm going to miss you," he says, with his arms holding me tight.

"I'll miss you," I say, holding on to him tighter.

He kissed my forehead, and I pulled out of his arms. I reached his lips and gave him one last goodbye before finally walking away. We were out there for a least twenty minutes, so I ran to my gate with only seconds to spare before my flight left without me. Some of me wanted to miss it so I could spend more time with Jansen, but this clothing line is my dream. If I let this go, I'm letting go of everything I worked for and wanted to be.

Once my flight lands in Los Angeles, I roll my overstuffed luggage out to my uber driver. Instead of going to *Threads* as I would typically do when arriving here, I go straight to the hotel. Felicia and Shae got word I was coming back into town, and when I landed, there was a message asking me if I wanted to go out for drinks.

There was no way I could turn them down, considering they probably wanted to hear the next chapter of my story, and I was dying to tell someone about it. Even though I wish it were Bree first. I wanted to be there for her this morning, not talking about how good Jansen is in bed or that there's a slight chance I might be falling for my fake fiancé.

After checking into the hotel, I went to my room for a nap because there was hardly any sleeping going on last night, and if I wanted to keep up with the girls tonight, I'd need to rest. We all decided on a bar not far from my hotel, so I could walk back if we stayed out too late. Hopefully, we don't since tomorrow will be a big day at *Threads*.

When I show up, I look around the bar and find Felicia and Shae sitting on a couch, waiting for me in the corner. Felicia spots me first and waves.

"Hey, sorry I was running late."

"We haven't been here long. How are you?" Felicia says.

"Good," I say, taking a seat.

A waitress drops three drinks on the table in front of us, and it looks like they ordered all the same drinks, a margarita of some sort.

"Spicy Margaritas," Felicia says when she sees me look at the drink.

"What's with you two and trendy drinks?" I smirk.

They both look at each other and laugh.

Shae leans forward toward me so that I can hear what she says. "Rell, your mind will be blown tomorrow, by the way. They have some of your pieces ready, and wow, Rell, they're some of the greatest work to ever come from Threads."

"They're done?" I say quickly. "There's no way they are the greatest work."

Felicia smiles at me, "Really, Rell, they are. I have already claimed most of the ready pieces. We want first dibs. When your stuff goes live, it will sell out quickly. I can already tell you now, prepare this week. They're going to ask you to stay and work at Threads."

I shake my head no, "No way."

My mind didn't know what to think when she said the word *stay*. I knew there was a possibility but never knew it might come true. It's something I should consider with how my life is going back home. I could do this one line of clothing and still be happy, right?

Could I possibly leave San Francisco now, leaving behind Jansen? Why am I even thinking this since we are just beginning something?

"Please tell us you will stay here, right? We could use someone like you at Threads full-time." Felicia begs.

I frown before taking a sip of my drink.

"Please don't tell me you want to stay in San Francisco because of your fake fiancé?" Shae ask.

I clench my teeth. "Maybe," I throw my hands up.

"Rell," Felicia says.

"This last week while I was home, we got close, and well…."

"No way!" Shae yells out, knowing what happened.

I smile. "Do you want the next chapter of this story?"

They both lean into the table and nod their heads.

I start by telling them about the date on the boat. The most magical date, in my opinion, because I don't think there will ever be a date to compare to that one. Then I tell them about the baseball game and how Mac Milligan is my ex-fiancé. They can't believe what they are hearing. Even though they were impressed that I was with him once, I had to let them down and tell them what kind of relationship we had, including his cheating. The best part of the conversation was telling them about last night.

"So wait, he whispers you're getting all the bases?" Felicia asks.

"Yes, and then he gave me *all the bases*. I just wanted to be closer to him. Gosh, you guys, it was so good and different from any other time I've slept with someone. It was like…." I put my finger up to my chin, thinking.

"You fell in love with him?" Shae asks.

"I don't know, maybe a little," I take a sip. "This is all crazy, right?"

"If you move here and that is where your book ends, I'm going to be pissed that that is the ending. That is not the ending this story deserves." Felicia says.

"What ending does it deserve?" I ask.

"I mean, can't he just come here with you? He has to be falling in love with you too. If he stays behind, there is no way this relationship would work between work and traveling?"

"See, that's what is running through my mind. Let's say I don't stay here and turn down the Threads job. I stay in San Francisco and continue my relationship with Jansen and The Gram account. My dream has always been more. This clothing line is more. Then I leave someone I love back home for my dream," I shrug my shoulders. "He can't come here, his dream is the job he has now, and he won't leave that."

"Sounds like shit's about to hit the fan," Felicia says.

"My life is getting complicated," I pick up my drink to finish it.

This conversation has me feeling like crap. I don't want to figure my life out, but I know it will come down to making a choice soon. I'm going to have to look both ways before making a decision. I wanted nothing more than to live my dream and be in love. I have them both now, and sadly it will come down to me being able to choose only one.

When I walk into *Threads* on Monday morning, I no longer get the nervous feeling I always feel when walking in. I'm excited, which is scary. Knowing I'm about to see what I have been working on coming to life is something I want to remember forever. After sharing quick greetings with Felicia and Shae at the front counter, I walk down to Stacey's office. When I enter the door frame, she looks up from her computer with a smile.

"Are you ready for this?" She asks me.

"I'm so ready," I say excitedly.

Stacey gets up from her desk chair, meeting me at the door.

"Let's go down to the warehouse but first, I want to show you something."

We walk a couple of doors down. Stacey stops right in front of the office I once used. She turns the handle and flips the light switch on when she opens it up. When I look inside, the once-empty office now has photos of *Threads* clothing on the walls and supplies on the desk. All the desktop accessories are pink. "This is your new office while you're here,"

I walk into the office, looking around, " Oh, Stacey. Thank you, I love it."

"You will need a place to work because, after this line releases, we would love for you to stay and work on another line for us."

"Really?" I turn around to see her standing at the door.

"Yes, we would love to have you here full-time. We know that it may take time for you to do that, but soon, we would love to have you here and let you call this place your home. Your designs are going to be a hit and help this company."

After talking to Felica and Shae last night, I knew this was coming, but hearing the words from Stacey's mouth was different, and they hit me. I don't even know what to say. I used to want this more than anything.

"Stacey, I would love to, but can I think about it before saying yes? Something like this would change my life tremendously."

"Absolutely," she nods.

"Can we go down to the warehouse now?" I ask.

"Yes."

We walk out of the office, and instead of closing the door and turning off the light, Stacey leaves it open, knowing I'll be returning to work.

We reach the warehouse, and Stacey walks through the double doors before me, and once we both make it in, she says, "Ta-da," throwing her arms out in front of her and pointing to a few mannequins in the middle of the warehouse.

"Oh my gosh," I say, throwing my hands over my mouth. "These are mine," Tears well up in my eyes, and then slowly, a tear falls down my cheek.

"Amazing. Rell, these are something special. Everyone here has been trying to steal these off the mannequins all week. If we all like them, then we know everyone else is going to love them," Stacey says, patting me on the back.

"I'm speechless," I wipe a tear off my cheek, "These are like a dream. I imagined them in my head, drew them, and they still seem like a dream to me."

I pull my phone from my pocket and instantly realize I did because the only thing I want to do now is to call Jansen. He is working on the job site today, and I know he won't be able to answer, so I will take photos of the clothing to send to him later.

"Is this ok?" I ask Stacey to make sure she doesn't mind me taking photos.

She nods her head at me, smiling. "No, go ahead. They are yours."

I take a few photos of the clothing on the mannequins before slipping my phone back into my pocket. I wipe the last tear away from my cheek before putting a piece of hair behind my ear.

We quietly walk back out of the warehouse and to my new office. Once inside, I walk around and take a seat at my desk. Stacey sits in a chair across from me. "The plan is for you to stay here until the launch party next weekend. We have a photo shoot this week and will need your help with styling. Next week we have a local runway show on the schedule for you to show everything off. Then the launch party is next weekend. You'll be able to go back home after the launch party."

I nod. There are so many extra things I didn't realize happened with promoting a clothing line. It all seems like a lot, but I am looking forward to it all. "That sounds great."

"Now, what is next is up to you. If you decide to stay with us, we will work on a fall clothing line when we finish all this. If you decide this isn't the life you want- because I understand it is a lot- having this job means you are devoting your life to it, then we are done here, and we say goodbye."

"Stacey, thank you for all this and for giving me this opportunity. I've loved every second of being here and working with you. I need some time to think about this. While this has been a dream of mine for years, it's also essential that I make the right decision. Moving here would mean leaving behind some important things in my life."

She leans forward, "Take your time to think about things, but Rell, you are one of a kind, and we would love to have you here," she gets up from her chair.

"Thank you, Stacey."

Once she leaves, I look around the office. Still not believing that this space is now mine. I haven't been in Los Angeles for twenty-four hours, and my life is already changing. Changes I knew were coming, yet I didn't prepare myself for this.

Pulling my phone out again because the only person I want to talk to might be busy, but I want to hear his voice. I hit call on Jansen's name. While the phone rings, I close the office door so no one can listen to me before sitting back down at my desk.

"Hey," he answers, and a smile draws across my face.

"Are you too busy to talk? I can call you later."

"No, I'm never too busy for you. Is everything okay?"

I sit back in my chair and pivot it to the side. "Um yeah, a lot of new stuff going on here. They gave me an office, and all my supplies are pink."

"Wow, your own office there," he says, shocked.

I know what he is thinking by the tone of his voice.

"I have a full schedule, and I won't be able to come back home until after next weekend," I say, playing with the hem of the s.

"Rell, we both knew this was going to happen," he pauses. "I do have something to tell you."

"What is it?" I ask, worried it would just be more to add to my plate.

"I won the basketball bracket at the office," he exclaimed.

"What, no way," I say excitedly.

"Yea. I want to use some of the money to come see you," Jansen says, and I can tell he is smiling by the sweet tone of his voice.

"Jansen."

"Two weeks, Rell, is going to be too long," he says, and I can tell by the sound of his voice he wants to see me.

"Next weekend is the launch party for my line. I want you to come."

"I'll be there for you."

"I miss you already," I tell him, shocking myself with my words.

"You have no idea how much I miss you. This last weekend was everything for me."

I go silent. I never expected Jansen ever to say those words.

"I should probably get back to work. Will you call me later when you get to your hotel room?"

"Yes. I'll call you later. Bye, Jansen."

"Bye, Rell."

I hang up the phone and sit it down on my desk.

Spinning my chair around, stopping it right in front of my computer, I wonder if this is what my life could look like if I say yes, to this company and continue my relationship with Jansen. We're both so busy with work during the week that we wouldn't see each other much if I stayed in San Francisco. Could we make the relationship work by seeing each other on the weekends?

Jansen

Setting my phone down on my desk, I spin my chair around, my hands on my head to look out the window. I knew when she said they gave her her office. They asked her to stay. I mean - why wouldn't they? This relationship with Rell could work. We could do the distance. I'm pretty sure that's what she felt after our conversation and the weekend. This could work.

    I woke up yesterday morning to my dreams of Rell coming true. I watched her sleep while tangled up in my sheets, her hair sprawled across the pillow, and the sun coming up in the window behind her. I waited for that day for weeks, and it finally happened. I meant it when I told her this last weekend was everything to me because it was. It meant that I was genuinely ready to be with Rell and whatever I needed to do to be with her. If that means making this work once the distance is a factor in our relationship, then I'm ready to make it work. I will travel any distance to be with her. I've never felt anything like I feel when I'm with her. She's worth it.

    These next two weeks will be long without her, but I think it is the ultimate test for us to know if this is something we want with each other.

Chapter Twenty-two

Jansen

Friday. Some call it the best day of the week because you are that much closer to the weekend. However, this day is like the other shitty days this week. I may be closer to seeing Rell, but I have also spent many days without her. She's been busy since I talked to her on Monday, which means we haven't been able to talk much. We've had quick calls to each other here and there, but we are repeating ourselves with "Miss you" and "Talk later." All I want to do is see her, but a trip to Los Angeles this weekend would be useless, considering she has a photo shoot to attend tomorrow.

Luckily, my job hasn't been giving me crap, and I've been able to stay out of trouble with Jay. I want to say it's because my life has been straightened out but hasn't precisely yet. Rell may be out of town, so there isn't that distraction at work, but she isn't specifically a distraction. Rell is a *priority*. So basically, I think my job is running smoothly because of luck. It doesn't have anything to do with Rell.

Looking out the window of my office, leaving for the day soon, I hear a knock at my door. When I turn around, Jay is standing there. "Hey, come in. Have a seat," I point to the armchair.

Jay sits in the chair across my desk, so I retake a seat behind my desk.

"How are you?" he asks me.

I cross my arms over my chest and sit back. "Good."

I'm lying because I precisely feel like shit without Rell here.

"Good. I don't think I've seen you around much, and you didn't respond to the email I sent, but there's a family event next weekend with everyone from the office. We rent out a spot in the park, and families come to enjoy games and food. I wasn't sure if it were something I would see you and Rell at."

I saw the email, and he's right; I have been ignoring him this week. I didn't want plans made when Rell returned to town because I wanted her all to myself when she got home. Sadly, if Rell found out we missed this from Laura, she wouldn't be happy with me. She knows work is essential to me—this one not so much, though.

"I'm sorry, I must have missed the email. I've been so busy, but I'll look into it. We may be able to make it. Rell is out of town but should be back by then."

She'll be back in town but only for a few hours before this event, and I don't want her more overloaded with shit to do than she already is. We can easily skip this work event even though we are in an actual relationship for this one if we attend. Then again, being in a real relationship in front of people we've been faking for weeks sounds exciting.

"We would love for you two to make it if you can, but understand that life has been busy for Rell lately."

"I'll talk to Rell. Thank you for stopping by."

"No problem."

Jay gets up from the armchair and walks towards the door to leave. He turns around quickly like he forgot to say something. "Keep up the good work. This job is looking good."

"Thanks," I say, waving my hand at him as he walks away.

Guess I'll be calling Rell about this tonight, or maybe I can hold off until I see her next weekend in Los Angeles. She already has so much on her plate. Dare I add more nonsense?

I finish up at the office for the day before heading home. Bree and Kent must've worked things out since they have been hanging outside on the swing this week. The place I usually find them when Rell is out of town, and I know Rell will eventually want another swing to replace the one they have christened. We need a swing of our own.

When I pull into the driveway, I see Bree loading a luggage bag into her car. There's only one place she could be going, to see Rell.

I get out, shutting the truck door. "Hey, where are you going?" I shout to her before she gets into her car to leave. When she turns to look at me, a frown instantly comes across her face.

"Rell needs help, so I'm going to LA."

I shake my head at her, then turn away.

"Jansen."

I walk up the steps and then turn around. "Yeah."

"If you could be there for her this weekend, I know she would want you there, but I'm sorry. They told her she could get an assistant for the shoot and the show next week, so I'm going to help. She misses you."

I wave my hand to her, "Thank you, Bree."

She gets into her car as I walk inside my house.

I don't know why I bothered to ask Bree, knowing where she was heading. I guess I need the reassurance that I was, in fact, right about where she was going, and it stings a bit knowing she can go there and I can't. I'm aware I could buy a plane ticket and go, but it would be pointless because Rell is too busy to even spend time with me. We barely can get on a phone call, yet somehow I still feel like this relationship will work with the distance. It won't always be like this.

Stripping down, I get into the shower because it's the only thing calming me down from everything happening inside me since Rell left. A shower reminds me of the night before she left. It was this very shower that Rell gave me more of her, but I let her control what she wanted the second time. It wasn't just sex between us that night, it was more, and I'm afraid to say that I am falling more for her every day. The more is what is making this whole distance thing hard for me. I know my heart will beat right out of my chest when I see her.

―――――――――

Rell

The only person left in the *Threads* building, I'm ensuring everything is ready for tomorrow's photo shoot. Thankfully it got pushed back to tomorrow because I wasn't prepared for this yet. I feel like they sprung this on me and left me to do most things alone. There was only one person I could trust to help me with this: Bree. Her flight landed not long ago, and I'm waiting for her to show up soon so we can finish getting ready for this together.

I've hardly had any time to think about Jansen this week or talk to him, and I'm starting to feel guilty about it. I miss him, but this life here in LA is always a rush, and there is never enough time in the day to think.

I fall asleep when I get into my hotel room every night. Then wake up to do the same thing the next day. Life before Jansen, I wouldn't mind this type of life.

"Hello," I hear a voice yell out.

When I walk out into the hallway, I see Bree walking towards me. "Thank goodness you're here." I hug her when she reaches me, and then we walk into my office.

The clothing line is hanging on the rack in the middle of the office. Bree sets her bag down on the floor and crosses her arms while looking at everything hanging.

"What?" I ask her.

"I want to cry, Rell. My best friend, these designed clothes."

"Oh, stop it." I pat her back. "We have work to do. Let's get these in order of photos, and then matched pieces need to be next to each other."

I start lining the clothes on the rack, and Bree follows my lead.

"Jansen didn't look happy to see me coming here."

I glance over at her. "Jansen saw you leaving?"

"Yeah, I was trying to leave before I knew he would be home, but he must've left work early today. He looks so miserable without you. He hasn't left his house all week but only for work and back."

I continue adjusting clothing on the rack but in a more somber mood. Bree's words make me feel guilty again for giving this relationship with Jansen get a chance before coming here.

"We slept together, Bree," I softly say.

"What." She stops working.

"The night before I left town. I didn't get to tell you because I wanted to hear all about you and Kent getting back together. Then before I knew it, I needed to come back here before saying anything, and that wasn't a conversation I wanted to have on the phone with you."

"Well?" she crosses her arms again.

"It was...." I clench my teeth together and don't make eye contact with her. "Everything I thought it would be and more. I wasn't expecting us.... I don't know, to connect like that."

"No wonder he has been moping around all week. He's falling for you, and then you leave. How is this going to work out, Rell?" she uncrosses her arms and returns to work. I'm glad she isn't mad at me for waiting so long to tell her about this.

"Don't say he is falling, Bree. I don't want that kind of pressure. I feel bad already for being here without him. How is this going to work? I don't know. What's that saying? Distance makes the heart grow fonder. Something like that?" I wave my hand around.

"That saying is shit, Rell." she laughs. "You are screwed because if he is falling, he isn't going to want distance. He is going to want you. Every day, all day."

Bree could be right about Jansen. If he is already upset about me being gone for a few days, how will he want to be with me when seeing me every day isn't an option?

We don't talk about Jansen anymore for the night. After finishing all the preparations for tomorrow's photo shoot, we leave Thread's office and head to the hotel. No fun is to be had until this shoot ends. Then I am going to need all the trendy drinks I can take.

The photographer came to *Threads* and set up everything in a small studio at the office. Bree and I just rolled the clothing cart up to the shoot, and models are off to the side getting hair and makeup done. It's crazy to think they are all here for my work. It seems so surreal, and I feel like I'm dreaming.

  Having Bree with me means a lot, and I hope they can see Bree's potential. I want her to be able to come with me if I take the job.

  We work together to prepare the outfits and steamed for the models once they are ready. I spot Stacey off to the side, conversing with the photographer. She's talking with her hands and pointing at the backdrop, so I think they may be talking about what Stacey wants for this shoot.

  Bree hands the first outfit to one of the models, finished with hair and makeup. I know I will cry once she comes out with the clothing on. I haven't seen my clothes on anyone yet, only mannequins. I start gathering the following outfit for the next model when Bree smacks my hand, "Go away, I can do this. You just stand over there," she points towards Stacey. "And watch. Got it?"

  I smile at her and give her a quick hug before walking away. I don't walk directly to Stacey yet. Instead, I take my time to get myself together. I want to take this entire experience in today. When that dream you've dreamed for so long becomes a reality you never thought it would be: you take in every second. Experience it as if it could be the only time you'll experience it because you never know what will happen next. Life works itself out even though you sometimes experience curveballs.

  I feel my phone vibrate in my back pocket, and when I pull it out, I see a text from Jansen.

J- Baby, I'm so proud of you. You are going to do great today.

Baby. A nickname he started using on Sunday. I smile before sliding my phone back into my pocket. Instead of responding now, I want to call Jansen to hear his voice, but it will have to wait until later.

I lift my hand to look at the ring on my finger before twirling it around. Since coming here, I have been looking at it more than usual. It reminds me of what is back home. There is still a commitment to Jansen to be his fiancé. I'm excited knowing there isn't any more faking to our relationship regarding this commitment. We can finally be *us*.

"Rell," I hear Bree call out behind me.

When I turn around, there stands a model wearing a plain pale pink tee tucked into a matching layered floral skirt, both designed by me. They added a hat and white sneakers to her look, which looks like I imagine it would look on someone.

I look back at Bree, wearing a giant proud smile on her face, which makes me tear up some. Trying not to forget what I'm supposed to be doing, I run over to the model and check her over. Then I send her to start photos, and before I can even take it all in, more and more models show up wearing all the rest of my collections. There is no control over the tears; they start falling, and this moment reminded me why I'm doing this.

Bree comes up behind me as all the models start getting set up for their photos taken and wraps her arm around my shoulder.

"You did it, Rell."

"I did it," I whisper.

She lays her head over my shoulder. "All with the help of the greatest assistant ever," she laughs. Which then makes me laugh through the tears. "You're the best."

"I have this under control. If you want to go, maybe call someone about this special moment," Bree looks at me and winks.

"Really?"

"Go. If Stacey needs you for anything, I will get you," she takes her arms down from my shoulder.

Walking out of the room, I stand by the door and leave it cracked so I can still see what is going on. Pulling my phone from my pocket, I hit call on Jansen's contact.

"Hey, everything okay?" he asks after the second ring.

"Yes. They're doing the shoot now."

"How does everything look? Exactly like you imagined?" he asks.

I smile, "Yes. Better."

"Baby, I hate to do this, but I've got to go. I have a flight to board."

"A flight?" I say, surprised because I know we haven't talked much this week, but he never told me he was going somewhere.

"I'm coming to you."

"Jansen, you are?" I want to cry because this is such a surprise.

"Yes, I'll see you in a couple of hours."

"I've missed you. I'll see you soon." I say before hanging up.

He's coming to me. We will only have hours to spend with each other before he returns to San Francisco. *Hours, and I can't wait.*

Chapter Twenty-three

Jansen

When my flight landed, I went straight to *Threads*. Rell came running out the front door when I got out of my uber and into my arms. I wrapped her up tight before giving her a long-awaited kiss and spinning her around. Then she gave me a tour of all the offices. We then went into her office, where a rack of all her designs was hanging, and I couldn't be more proud after looking over them.

Bree is staying for the week here with Rell so they can prepare for the runway show and launch party this week, along with what they have planned for their *The Gram* account. Thankfully Bree is such a great friend, letting Rell hang with me for the rest of tonight and tomorrow while she hangs out in Los Angeles with Felicia and Shae.

Everyone is gone besides Rell and me. She's checking everything she cleaned up from the photo shoot while I sit in her office chair waiting for her.

"Can I ask you a question?" I ask Rell.

"Of course." she nods while continuing to organize the clothing on the rack.

"Did they ask you to stay?"

She turns to me with a straight face. Did I mean to get right to the point while I'm here? *No.* But sitting in this office with her made it feel like the right time to ask.

"It's okay if they did," I tell her to reassure her it's truly okay.

"Stacey offered, but I told her I wanted to think about it."

I hold out my arms for her to join me. "Come here."

Rell walks over to me, taking a seat on my lap, and I brush her hair from her face. "You have to take it, Rell. It's your dream job, and you've worked hard for this moment."

She leans down, kissing me on the lips, and I slide my hand through her hair, bringing her closer to me.

Pulling out of our kiss, she says, "What about us?"

"That's a great question, and we will figure it out." I kissed her once more. "But let's just enjoy what we have going."

Rell spends a few more minutes finishing up at the office before we leave to go to the hotel room. She does a quick clothing change before we explore Los Angeles together. After our short conversation back at *Threads*, I feel anxious about being here in LA. We will explore the city together, but soon this could be Rell's home.

Rell's in the bathroom changing while I lay across the hotel bed. I'll be sharing this room with her tonight when we get back and while sleeping together was great the other night, I want to spend time with Rell since our time together is short. What we have going isn't just about the sex for me. It was the sex that solidified I wanted to be with her. We got close that night, and that was all we needed.

Rell walks out of the bathroom wearing one of her pieces, a floral skirt and plain white shirt tucked in the front, with some white sneakers. She looks incredible.

"Ready?" she asks, standing at the foot of the bed.

"You're killing me, Rell. Since the night I picked you up for our first date, you've done things to me with what you wear out."

"So, that first night, you weren't just mad about my following. You didn't like what I wore to the dinner?" she laughs.

"Correct, and every night since then. No doubt, no one believes we are a couple. You, dear, are way above someone like me." I hop off the bed, wrapping my arms around her before kissing her forehead.

She may be out of my league, but I can't say I'm not enjoying every minute of it. She has had this grip on me since I met her in the rain.

Hand in hand, we walk out of the hotel together and down the street. We pass lots of bars and restaurants but keep walking just to sightsee.

Keeping up with this city alone would be hard for someone like me, considering I don't get out much or mingle with people. On the other hand, Rell will do fantastic here, and part of that scares me. She could come here and never want to visit San Francisco. There's a chance Bree's coming too, so that would leave only me as a reason to come back. Would I be enough for her to come back?

We come upon a bar that isn't as packed as the others, and Rell stops. "Want to try this one?"

I look at the modern black door and bright white letters above it saying *Moonlit.* Looks decent. "Sure."

We walk inside through a crowd of people to the bar to order drinks. When the bartender comes over, I look to Rell for her order, "What do you want?"

"I don't know. Felicia and Shae order my drinks."

I turn back to the bartender, "We'll have two beers on tap. What do you have?"

"I don't want a beer," Rell says.

I turned back to her, "Then what do you want?"

She yells over me to the bartender, "Espresso Martini."

I turned back to her again. Shaking my head. "Seriously?"

"Don't ask questions," she smirks.

After I order a beer, the bartender brings us our drinks, and we find seats on the patio. Rell takes a sip of her drink before staring at me with beautiful eyes and resting her head on her hand.

"Explain," I say, pointing to her drink.

"Trendy Los Angeles Rell drinks this. Felicia and Shae ordered them the first night we went out."

I nod and pinch my brow, "What did you order the other times you went out?"

"If it wasn't one of these, it was a spicy margarita. I didn't think that drink would've set well with you if I ordered it, so I got this," she points to her drink.

"So, there's Trendy Los Angeles Rell? What happened to Trendy San Fransisco Rell?" I lean in closer to her across the small table.

"There was never a trendy San Francisco Rell, remember? She was dull and uninteresting."

I reach across the table, taking her hand in mine, "That has to be the most untrue thing I've ever heard. You've done nothing but interest me since the day I met you. That night you told me that. It was like you opened up a deep dark secret to me, and I wanted to be there for you. So, as much as you irritated me, I kept wanting to know more about you. The distraction I didn't want while I was here, but I wouldn't take anything back."

"So, I guess I'm a great fiancé?" she laughs.

"Yes," I laugh, shaking my head. "You make a great fiancé."

"Are there any more events we need to attend together when I get back?" she takes another drink.

"There is, but we don't need to go."

"When is it?"

"Next Sunday, it's just a thing at the park for families. As I said, we don't have to go since you will get back into town. I'll be honest; taking you to something like that excites me because we are the real deal now."

"Was it ever really fake before, though?" she asks

"Ha," I shake my head, "Rell dear, you are asking so many questions. But I'll be honest again. No, maybe the first night we went out, but that was because I barely knew you. When you grabbed my hand under the table during dinner, I felt a sense of comfort from you, and I haven't looked back."

"I think we should go together next Sunday because I want to be that kind of girlfriend now. Also, it excites me not to fake anything in front of anyone anymore."

"Girlfriend?" I smirk before asking, "So you're saying you've been faking it with me?" I point to my chest.

She laughs, "Oh, Jansen, I hate to admit it, but I can't remember the last time I faked anything with you if I ever faked anything at all. You walked into my house the first day I met you, and I knew then I was in trouble. I knew every time you held my hand; it was for comfort. We have set rules with each other, and I didn't mind that you broke them the first night."

Neither one of us had barely touched our drinks while talking about all these things I knew we would talk about one day. I didn't think it would be today, and I definitely didn't think it would be here in Los Angeles. How I ended up in a place like this is just crazy.

I came to San Francisco to escape life. A life that I thought I had all figured out, and I was all wrong. Coming to San Francisco has shown me much more about my life. A job that seems to be going well now, and Rell. Someone I didn't know I needed, and now I can't picture my life without her.

We finish our drinks before heading back to the hotel hand and hand. I would've sat outside that bar to talk with Rell till morning, but I know she's exhausted from being here and overworking herself all week. So, now all I want to do is cuddle up with her in bed.

Once we are back at the hotel and in our room, we brush our teeth in the bathroom before crawling into bed. Rell cuddles up to my chest, wearing her matching pink silk sleep set, something I'm not used to since we both slept naked the last time we were in bed together.

"Thanks for coming," Rell says into my chest.

"I didn't want to go another day without seeing you," I say, kissing her forehead and hugging her tightly.

We both stay silent, and then before I know it, Rell is fast asleep against my chest. I roll over slightly, turning off the lamp behind me on the nightstand. Then roll back over and fall asleep myself, never letting Rell go.

I woke up to a tickling sensation on my chest and kisses on my neck. When I open my eyes, I see Rell straddling my hips, smiling at me. I poke her back, and before I know it, I have her pinned down to the bed. Kissing her, I whisper into her neck, "Good morning to you too."

"How rude of me. Good morning, handsome." She whispers back.

Slowly sliding down her neck, I start unbuttoning her sleep shirt. Once undone, I open it up, exposing her breasts. "Am I dreaming this?"

She laughs before saying, "Let's shower."

"Rell Campbell, do you enjoy having sex in the shower? Because if so, then we are going to have zero problems." I laugh.

"Maybe," she smirks.

Getting off the bed, I turn around and point to my back, "Get on."

Rell hops on my back, wrapping her legs around me, and I give her a piggyback ride to the hotel bathroom. I drop her down in front of the bathroom mirror. While she looks in the mirror at herself, I start a hot shower for us. When I turn back to her, she throws her long brown hair into a bun on the top of her head—walking behind her, looping my finger under her shirt. Then I slowly slip her shirt down off her shoulder, leaving kisses from her neck down to her shoulder. Once her shirt is completely off, I toss it on the floor before sliding her shorts down her legs. She steps out of each leg individually, and I throw her shorts to the side. When I return to eye level with her, she wraps her arms around my neck before our mouths collide.

I lift her, wrap her legs around my waist, and walk to the shower. Our mouths never leave each other. We make it into the shower without either of us missing a beat. Then just like last time, I give her all of me, but this time with much more emotion. I don't want to let her go and leave her.

After showering, we spend more time in the hotel room before grabbing lunch. Then it was time for me to get back to San Francisco. It was the first time I had to leave Rell. She has always been the one to leave me. I hate every bit of it but knowing we are just days away from seeing other again makes me feel only slightly better.

My time here in Los Angeles was short, but I feel like Rell and I took another step in our relationship, showing that distance will be okay and opening up to each other about those feelings we didn't want to admit some time ago.

I held Rell for a long time outside the airport before finally telling her goodbye and almost slipping words from my mouth that I wanted to say, but it was too soon.

Chapter Twenty-four

Rell

Bree and I unload all the clothing from the *Threads* van, hanging it on the clothing rack to roll into the studio for the runway show. Other designers from other companies are here showing their clothing along with mine. People are seated in chairs on each side of the runway, and the models are ready. We need to get inside, set up, and prepare the models, and we should be good. Right? Except we are running late, and I'm panicking that maybe my designs aren't good enough.

We make it through the doors, rushing to our area. Bree starts taking models along with Shae and Felicia. They throw clothes on them and check their looks before lining them up. Me, though. I'm just standing here watching and telling myself not to throw up. Running late was my fault because I looked over the office a million times, ensuring we didn't forget one thing before leaving.

"Rell, Hello," Bree yells out.

I snap out of my dazed state to look at her.

"Are you going to help? They only have a few minutes before they have to go out."

Running over, I start checking the model in front of Bree. "Sorry."

"It's okay if you need a minute, but can you wait until this is over? We're running behind."

"I'm a mess today." I straighten out the model's top.

Bree laughs, "At least you have a perfect reason to be a mess."

After finishing the rest of the models, they align with the rest. We check them all up and down one more time. I stand in front of the line, waiting for our turn. I take deep breaths in and out while trying to remain calm.

Since Jansen left on Sunday, my week has been messy. I was left feeling sad after he got on his flight. So, I stayed in the parking lot until I watched his plane take off. Usually, I would go to *Threads* to get some work done before Monday morning, but I wasn't feeling it, so I spent the rest of the night in my hotel room.

Then this week consisted of lots of preparation for this runway show and planning the launch party that will take place tomorrow night. Thankfully work has kept me busy, so I wasn't able to think about Jansen as much as I would've liked.

He will be here first thing tomorrow morning, and we will be together at the launch party tomorrow night at the *Threads* office. Once the party is over, we plan to return to San Francisco to attend his work event the day after.

"Threads." A lady with a headset yells out, waving her hand to me.

After giving her a nod and thumbs up, I turn to all the models, including Bree, Shae, and Felicia. "Alright, ladies. Let's go take care of business." I stepped to the side and let them walk by me.

Bree runs to me impatiently, "Ah, I'm so excited."

"Calm down. We can get all excited once we finish." I say with a sly grin on my lips.

She lowers her hands and rolls her eyes, and we follow behind the models to the stage.

They all go out individually as we watch from the side. Every model's look is the same as I drew up and the same as they styled at the photo shoot. Just a few tears fall from my eyes as I watch them. No, I'm not supposed to cry. I can't cry off any makeup because I have to walk out there with Stacey, who's just across the stage from me, beaming. I did this not only for me, but I did it for them, for *Threads*. This company has been good to me, and I want to work for them. I want to do this.

The last model walks off the stage, and Stacey looks over at me, smiling. We walk up the steps together, and once they call out, "*Threads by Rell*." Stacey and I take our places on stage. She takes my hand in hers as we walk down the runway. Lights shining brightly, people clapping. Stacey raises my hand in the air, and everyone cheers. It's then the tears flow. The hard work I put into this, the traveling, the hours, and the designs all went into this. It was worth it for this moment right now. I bow, and when I stand, Stacey hugs me.

I did it. I dreamed something, worked hard, and I got to live it.

After the show, Felicia and Shae insist we all must celebrate with drinks. We're all at the bar we had been to before, but Bree is with us this time. Felicia is again in charge of drinks, and part of me is excited to see what kind of trendy drink she orders us this time.

We're all seated on the leather sofas, Bree and I on one and them on the other. The waitress comes with a tray of drinks, all in copper tin mugs. After placing them all in front of us on the small table, the waitress walks away.

"Moscow Mules. Drink up." Felicia yells out.

I shake my head at her before taking a sip. "Not bad, I guess."

"Sorry, I have no real idea what I ordered us. I just told the waitress to bring us something popular that wasn't something we'd already had."

"So, you guys come here sometimes?" Bree asks.

"Sometimes here, sometimes other bars. This particular bar has better people and is known to have famous people come here occasionally," Shae says.

"Have you seen anyone famous before?" Bree asks.

"Not yet, but maybe one day," Felicia says.

I almost spit out my drink, laughing.

"So what do you guys do for fun besides bars?" Bree, with another question.

"They like to hang out at their condo, swim in their pool, and have one-night stands with guys who have girlfriends," I answer.

Shae gives me the evil eye, and I start laughing. Bree doesn't get it, but once she notices Shae's expression, she starts laughing. "Shae, not you?"

"It wasn't my finest moment in life."

"So, is this the life you will be living here, Rell?"

"I don't see myself making the mistake Shae made," I point to Shae, "No offense. I'm older than the two of you, so I don't see this as something I'd always do living here. Sorry, but I'll probably spend more time in my condo, reading a book, working on work things."

Bree smiles because she knows me and knows that this party life isn't a life I would live. It's been fun while I've been here for a short time but living here, I wouldn't want it to be different from my life now.

"How are things with Jansen?" Felicia asks.

Jansen hasn't been someone I've talked about this week. Now that we have been more official and it's not just been our fake dating relationship, I feel the need to keep our relationship more private.

"Good, he'll be here tomorrow."

"Are there any more chapters you want to read us?" Shae asks.

"There are no new chapters," I take a sip of my drink, so I don't have to say anything more.

Shae gives me another evil eye. She's on to me.

When he came to the city, what we shared was so personal and intimate, and I wanted to keep it all to myself. A part of me doesn't want to hear what they will say about our relationship if I move here. I don't want to hear anyone tell me it won't work.

"Can we talk about something else?" I ask.

"Yes, like how my best friend just killed her first runway show," Bree exclaims.

"Ahhhh.... wasn't it incredible?" Felicia says.

"Probably the best moment of my life so far."

We all finish our drinks while talking about the runway show and fall designs I might have in mind if I stay. Once we leave the bar, Bree and I walk back to the hotel together and go to our separate rooms for the night.

Jansen

My packed bag is on the bed, ready to go. My flight leaves in over an hour for Los Angeles so that I can be with Rell for her launch party. I'm taking a quick shower when I hear my phone repeatedly vibrating on the bathroom counter. I get out to dry off and see several missed calls from work.

"Fuck me," I whisper to myself. Now is not the time for this. It's a Saturday morning, so there has to be something going wrong.

After I throw on some clothes, I call back one of the men at the Jobsite of the condos. "Hey. What's going on?" I ask when he answers.

"There's stuff missing out here again. The camera is gone, and there's damage to the condos. We need to figure out this situation."

"You've gotta be kidding me. Who is doing this shit to us?" I look over at my bag on the bed. I've got to leave now, and there's no way I can't go with my job like this.

"We need you out here," he says.

I close my eyes, running my hand down my face. "I'll be there as fast as I can."

Grabbing my bag off the bed, I walk out of the bedroom and into my truck. I toss the bag into the passenger seat and back out of the driveway. Opening my phone, I look to change my flight to something later. I need to be there for her. If I miss this launch party, I'm only letting her down.

When I reached the condo site, I could see windows smashed and graffiti on the sides of the building. It all looks worse than I imagined in my head, and it's going to take time to clean this place up.

I get out of the truck, meeting some of the construction workers inside the condos, where we find more damage. Someone took a hammer to anything inside a few condos. I'll need to get to the office and order more supplies. There will have to be a phone call to Jay, and I'll need to explain everything. The worst part of all this is being unable to go to Los Angeles to be with Rell. That phone call will hurt the worst.

Walking the rest of the condo site, I write down a list of everything that I need to order. Luckily, somebody can fix the cosmetic things by ordering a replacement, but it will come out of my budget, and I'll be in the negative. I'm beginning to think someone has something out for me with the way this job is going. There must be someone who doesn't like me.

On the way to the office, I dial Rell.

"Hey, did you just land?" she answers.

"Baby, I can't make it."

"Did something happen?" she sounds worried.

"Someone trashed the condos, and I'm heading into the office to sort this all out. I still need to call Jay. I had my bag packed and ready. They called while I was in the shower. I'm sorry."

"Jansen, don't be sorry. It's alright. This isn't your fault."

"I wanted to be there."

"I'll catch a flight tonight after the party. Stay up, and come get me."

"No, Rell, stay. I'll come to get you in the morning at the airport." I say, pleading. She doesn't need to come home after a big night just for me. We will be together tomorrow. It's just one night.

"I've got to go. I'll talk to you later, okay?"

"Okay," I say before I hear the phone hang up.

I sit and open my laptop when I get to my office. Before getting here, I called Jay, and he told me not to sweat it. He told me to order all the same supplies we already had on the site and whatever else to fix the damage. We both agreed this has to be happening by someone within the office. Now I'm going to be looking for any clue on who it would be.

Shortly after I began working, I got a text message.

Rell- My flight lands at eleven tonight. I better see you there waiting for me.

The grip that Rell has on me. The cranky me wants to send an arguing text response, but I can't complain that she wants to spend more time with me. It never crossed my mind that maybe she wanted to come home. I'm ready for her to be home.

Chapter Twenty-five

Jansen

Watching Rell sleep next to me, I think about last night. After finishing up at the office, I had time to come home and clean my place before getting Rell at the airport. She talked about her launch party the whole drive home. It was a simple party just for her. They had everyone from the office celebrate the launch with champagne and finger foods. Tomorrow her clothing line will officially launch to the public, and I'm happy and nervous at the same time. So proud of her, but knowing if this goes well, she will be gone.

Once we got to my place, we showered together and fell asleep. Today we have a family gathering at the park for my work. The one I didn't care to go to, but Rell insisted we attend. Part of me is excited about being a real deal now and not having to pretend anything while we are there.

I quietly slide out of bed to the kitchen to make a pot of coffee, throwing on a pair of sweatpants before going to the kitchen. The coffee hasn't even started dripping before Rell comes up behind me, wrapping her arms around my chest.

"Morning," she mumbles with her head against my back.

I spin around, placing a kiss on her cheek. "Good morning."

"I'll take some." she points to the mug in my hand.

"Coffee?"

"Sure, I may not drink it all, but I want to have coffee with you," she gets on her toes to kiss me.

I turn around and grab another mug from the cabinet when I hear the tv come on in the living room. I pour two cups before walking to the fridge to grab creamer, pouring some into both mugs. Rell's bundled with a blanket on the loveseat when I get to the living room. I take the seat next to her and hand her a mug.

"So, what's the plan for today?" she says before taking a sip.

"The thing at the park isn't until later this afternoon, so we can stay here and relax. Maybe watch movies, or sports, or sleep. Whatever sounds good to you."

"All that sounds good to me. Maybe even read a book."

"I'm sure you'll want to go home sometime today." I rest my hand on her leg.

"Maybe later. Bree will be with Kent there all day," she takes another sip.

"Well, we can do anything."

She takes another sip before running her hand through my hair. "I want to be with you today, tomorrow, and the next day to make up for those days I couldn't."

Leaning in to kiss her."How did I get so lucky with you?"

"You made me jump over the fence." she laughs.

I shake my head, smiling. I don't love the way we started this relationship. It wasn't traditional, and I hated how I was to her when we started this. Since there won't be a redo, I will have to deal with it and instead make up for it.

Rell rests her head against my shoulder while we finish drinking coffee together. I could get used to this but knowing this isn't going to be like this for long makes me enjoy this moment more.

"Let's do something tomorrow night after I get off work to celebrate your launch."

"I don't want a party," she says, looking up at me.

"No party. How about dinner?" I kiss her forehead.

"As long as it's just us," she says, and I don't ask why only us. I know she's been around many people lately and going out. The Rell I know is a homebody, and I don't blame her for wanting a nice quiet night.

"I won't argue with that."

"I'm going back to bed now," she gets up from the couch and holds her hand out. "You coming?" I don't hesitate to grab her hand. Back to bed, we go.

———————

We got to the park. I get out and walk over to help Rell out. She wore a simple white sundress and looked beautiful. The weather couldn't have been better today, the sun shining and warm temperatures. We walk through the park holding hands, and I spot bouncy houses and picnic tables set up. It has to be it.

"Oh, shit," I grumble under my breath.

"What?" Rell says, looking around like she missed something.

"There are kids here."

"And?"

"I didn't think people would bring their kids to this."

Rell starts laughing, "It's a family thing, right?"

I don't answer because she's right I should've known. Kids just sometimes give me unwanted anxiety. I'm not around kids much, and I don't exactly know to act around them.

Rell gives our hands a shake to wake me up a little bit, and thankfully, there's comfort in holding her hand because I'll probably lose my shit sometime today being around all these kids.

"Jansen, you'll be fine. It's just other people's children."

When we come to the picnic tables, we see Jay and Laura sitting at one, and Rell walks us in their direction. "Hey," Rell says to Laura, and she stands from her seat to hug Rell.

"I wasn't sure if you'd be here with how busy you are these days," Laura says.

"I wouldn't miss this. It's been a month since I've last seen you, hasn't it?"

Jay stands, and I give him a shake but don't take my eyes off the fifty kids jumping in the bouncy house behind him. I scratch the back of my neck, then nod.

"You good, Jansen?" Jay asks.

"Yep, never been better." I lie.

"How did everything go at the office yesterday? Were you able to fix everything?" Jay asks, my eyes still looking at the kids. Rell gives our hand a shake, "Jansen?"

I look away and at Jay. "Sorry. Yeah. Everything's great now. We should be back to our normal schedule after this week."

"That's good to hear."

"Come with me, Rell. There are some people here I would like for you to meet," Laura says to Rell, and before I can react, Rell lets go of my hand to walk away with Laura. My worst nightmare is officially happening, the only comfortable thing here for me just walked away, and I'm alone.

Once Rell and Laura join a crowd of women, some holding babies, I can't help but keep my eyes on them. Then Jay puts his hand on my shoulder to get my attention, "We need to figure out whos trying to destroy you."

"Yea, I haven't thought about it much since yesterday, but I think it's someone within the office. Maybe someone who I haven't met yet."

Jay walks towards the bounce house, and even though my heart starts racing and sweat starts breaking out, thinking of getting closer to it, I follow. Jay continues talking about the office and my job, but I can barely hear him over the kids screaming while jumping up and down. I rub my forehead and look around. Where are these kids' parents? It's only me and Jay standing over here watching, and neither of us owns any of these kids.

"You think it could be Tim? He is a project manager like you, but he seems to like you. Maybe he could be scamming us?" Jay says, tapping my shoulder again.

"Oh yeah, Tim," I say, arms crossed over my chest. I watch a kid wipe the snot hanging from his nose with his shirt sleeve while he jumps. I closed my eyes, shaking my head. Someone get this kid a Kleenex. This bounce house has to be full of massive amounts of germs.

I turn my head back to look for Rell, but she's no longer in the area she was in not long ago, so I turn my attention to the bounce house while Jay continues talking.

"Have you met Conrad? He's about your age, a project manager on the same floor. I could see it being him. He always keeps to himself and works hard as you do."

"I think I've seen him in the breakroom once."

Conrad's the one who pointed out my hot girlfriend once and asked how I scored her. It could be him, but I don't understand why it would be him. I'm starting not to care who it is, as long as it's not Jay. He knows that the problem with my job is no longer my problem, so I could care less as long as they don't mess with my job again. I'll leave the detective work up to Jay and return to minding my business.

I watch as a kid pushes another down in the bounce house. The kid starts screaming and crying for its parents, and that's when I check out on this bouncy house watching. "I'm going to go look for Rell," I tell Jay before walking away.

There are people scattered around everywhere, and it could take me hours to get through this many people to find her. I see Laura standing with a group of women by one of the picnic tables, and that's when I see Rell holding a baby. Someone's kid. It's almost like she can sense me looking at her because she turns her head and starts walking toward me, smiling.

I meet her halfway, "Where were you?"

"I was meeting some of the wives," she says, bouncing the baby in her arms.

The baby she's holding is a girl who looks just under a year old. Just watching the baby in Rell's arms has my anxiety going crazy. I'm starting to sweat all over profusely.

"Don't you think the parents want their kid back?" I point to the baby.

"The mom had an emergency at the bounce house, so I offered to hold her. Isn't she so cute?" Rell says, fixing the baby's bow on its head before looking at me with a smile.

"I think you should take it back." I clench my teeth. I can't do babies.

"Jansen, calm down."

"Rell. This kid is making me nervous. What if it throws up or something? My ass will turn into *Vince Vaughn* from *Four Christmases* in two seconds flat. I'm not even kidding. I'll be out of here. You can catch another ride home."

Rell starts dying laughing as she bounces the baby. "You're the one being a baby. I think this is great practice for us."

"Oh yeah, great practice. You hold it, and I'll pretend everything is great. Just great. You can forget sex tonight. How do I know that you aren't thinking about making your own now that you're holding that baby." I say seriously.

"Fine. You tit bag. I'll go back to the women who don't have a problem with me holding a baby." She says, and the baby reaches for the hand she was using while talking.

Rell holding that baby isn't making me mad; it's making me think about something I've never thought about before, *having kids*.

She turns to walk away, and I stop her by putting my arm around her shoulder. "I'll come with you, but I won't hold that baby since you're doing such a great job."

"By the way," she says, walking back towards the bounce house. "It's adorable seeing you freak out a little over a baby."

"Did you do this on purpose, Rell? I feel you did this on purpose to see how I'd react, knowing I don't do kids." I say, looking at the baby in her arms, who's smiling at me.

As much as I don't want to admit it, it wouldn't be so bad. Rell can take care of it when it's a baby, and I'll help when it's a little older. Why am I even thinking about this?

"You like kids. You just don't know it yet."

She pauses her steps, turning in my direction. "Here, hold her for a second." Then proceeds to hand me the child. My body stiffens, but I somehow open my arms, and Rell sets the baby in them. "Better. Now relax a little bit." She straightens my arms, so I look like I know what I'm doing holding this baby. "There, now we look like we could be parents one day."

"Rell, who's kid is this?" I look at the baby in the face, and it stares at me with fear. I whisper. "Please don't cry, please." Then I bounce her just like Rell, giving her a fake smile.

"Oh, I don't know. The mom is friends with Laura." She looks around and then points to the lady holding a kid—the kid who got pushed down in the bounce house earlier.

"Some mom said, *here, I don't know you, have my kid?*" I say.

"Yeah. Pretty much," Rell looks over at the baby in my arms while we walk back and smiles at her.

I'm patting the baby's back, bouncing it, and trying anything so it won't cry before we get it to its mother. I don't even know why I'm holding the kid, but it isn't as bad as I thought it would be. "Why do I have the baby?" I ask Rell.

"I think you'd make a hot dad, so I handed you the baby to see if I was right."

"Is this a joke?" I ask, continuing to fear this baby in my arms.

She laughs, "Guess you'll find out in four weeks."

I stop my steps. "That's not funny, Rell."

"If you were wondering, you'd be freaking hot, baby daddy," She says, trying to sound serious but ends up busting up laughing

We continue walking in the direction of the group of moms. Laura is standing within the circle, chatting.

"I'll take that as a compliment."

The baby in my arms must find Rell and me fascinating because she hasn't been able to take her eyes off us while we talk. Maybe this isn't so bad, and everything Rell says should scare me, but it doesn't.

When we reach the group of ladies, Laura turns to me and can maybe sense the awkwardness I look and feel right now. She reaches her arms out, "Awe. I'll take her from you." I hand her over the baby easier than I did taking it from Rell, and it immediately starts crying in Laura's arms. I slowly back away and will let her take care of that.

"Well, this has been fun, but I think Rell and I are going to head out," I say quickly.

Rell flips her head at me, "We're leaving?"

"Yes, we have plans." I lie.

Rell screws her face up, confused. So I take her hand and pull her in my direction. She follows my lead.

"It was nice meeting all of you," she says, waving. "I'll see you later, Laura."

We turn to walk out of the park, then Rell asks. "Why are we leaving?"

"After all that, there was no other choice but to take you back to the house so I could have you all to myself."

She smiles, "Jansen Davis, you are something else."

Slowly but surely, I'm falling. Tonight was another level, seeing Rell around kids. There was never a time when I thought my mind would think about some of the things I felt tonight.

Chapter Twenty-six

Rell

I wake up to the feeling of Jansen's lips on my cheek.

"Baby, I'm going to work."

I moan, pulling the covers over my face.

"You're launching in an hour. Are you going to be up before then?"

My launch. I sit up quickly in bed. "Today."

Jansen looks at me, laughing. "Yes. Today."

"Have a good day at work," I tell him.

He leans over me on the bed, "Let me know how your day goes."

"I will." I place a soft kiss on his lips.

He walks to the door, wearing khaki-colored dress pants and a polo for work, and pauses before walking out. He turns back to me to say something and stops himself.

"I'll see you tonight," I say to break the awkward silence.

He points to me, "Yes, tonight," before leaving the room.

I can hear him walking through the house. Once I hear the front door close, I lie back in his bed. We were up too late last night, and I'm not ready for today. It is a make-or-break situation for me. If this goes well, I could have a great job opportunity. If nothing sells, then there isn't anything for me to worry about; I'll continue what I'm doing now. I'll stay here in San Francisco, and my life will be no different than it was before.

Not wanting to, I climb out of Jansen's bed, throwing on some clothing to go home to prepare for my launch. Bree and I had plans to share it on *The Gram* before it goes live for everyone. I use the backdoor to leave but still walk around the front of the house. Thankfully Margret wasn't out front early this morning to catch me going.

Walking up the stairs to my front door, I use my key to get in and find Bree on the couch once the door is open.

"The walk of shame?" she asks.

"Funny. Where's Kent?" I say, shutting the door behind me.

"He had an early workout class."

I walk past the living room into the hallway and hear Bree follow me. Once I get to my bedroom, she walks in behind me. "Ready for today?"

"I'm so unsure what I am right now," I say as I fall back onto the bed.

"Is this because of Jansen?" She sits next to me.

"I think I love him."

Bree squints her eyes at me.

"Am I crazy? Because this is not the right time to fall in love with my fake fiancé. My life is changing, and I'll have to make a choice I don't want to make."

"You're not crazy. Just don't make a choice, and choose both."

Oh, how I wish what she was saying was easy. How are Jansen and I supposed to work if he is always here and I'll always be in Los Angeles? Traveling hasn't been easy on me, and I know it won't be easy on him, either.

Bree and I don't talk anymore about Jansen while getting ready. I'm unsure if telling her I was falling in love helped me more than I already felt. Before Jansen left for work today, I was almost positive he wanted to tell me he loved me, and he stopped himself.

We are ten minutes from the launch time. Bree and I made some stories for *The Gram* reminding all our followers that today was the day. Now we are sitting on the couch playing the waiting game to see how everything goes. Stacey will be calling to keep us updated on sales, and I'll be so nervous when that phone call comes.

I still haven't told Bree I don't mind if this doesn't work out today. So selfish of me, considering this is something for both of us, but my mind is in a hundred places right now, and I'm just waiting for some direction. I've always wanted something bigger and better for us, but how do I know this will work out?

I glance at Bree, who's passing the time by scrolling through our account on her phone. She doesn't look the least bit nervous. I'm pinching my lip with my fingers and nervously tapping my foot. This day means everything.

"Okay. Here we go," Bree shouts.

I bite my bottom lip before saying, "We should do something."

"Now?" she says, surprised.

"Yea. If we sit around here, we'll just be waiting. Let's go to yoga or something. When's the last time we went to that?"

She shrugs, "Sure. Let's go."

We quickly dress for yoga and are out the door ten minutes later. We wave to Margret just out front before turning the corner to walk down a few places to the yoga studio. A new class starts in just a few minutes, and I couldn't have picked a better time to want to go. This class is all I need to help me relax.

When we walk into the studio, I turn my phone on vibrate before throwing it into my bag, and then we take our spots. I know there will be missed calls and messages, but I want time to put them away and not think about it.

The instructor comes in, and we're set in our positions to get started. I close my eyes, and I'm already feeling much better than I was at the house when I woke up and went to bed. This whole month has been nothing but stressful. I wasn't supposed to fall in love with Jansen. I was supposed to be a fake fiancé that doesn't catch feelings.

"Downward dog, ladies."

Well, this isn't a position Jansen's had me in yet. Maybe we should try this later. Brain, *shut it.* This is not the place to think about all the incredible lovemaking Jansen and I have been having.

"Standing forward bend."

I get in the best position possible and look over to see Bree killing her moves in the studio today. Maybe she's been coming without me?

I let out a small grunt trying to get my face closer to my legs, and I'm failing.

"Warrior pose."

This is one I can do easily. I stand in a sideways lunge, arm out in front and behind me. I close my eyes. That is when I hear a repeated vibrating noise, knowing it has to be my phone going off. I ignore it and peek over at Bree to see her silently giggling, which makes me smile.

Today reminds me how much I missed my time with Bree. There hasn't been much of that lately, either. We haven't had a conversation that didn't involve work or guys in such a long time. Most of our time together in Los Angeles the last couple of weeks has been at *Threads*.

While finishing class, I continue hearing the vibrating noise in my bag. Once we wrap up our hour in a half long class, I roll up my mat before grabbing my bag to leave.

"Going to check those messages?" Bree asks.

"There's so many. I think I can wait till we get home."

We stop for our usual smoothies before walking home. When we get inside, we set our yoga mats by the door, and then both fall back onto the couch. I slip my bag off my shoulder, taking my phone out, before setting the load on the floor. Opening my phone, I see that I have one missed call from Stacey, some notifications from *The Gram*, and *ten* missed calls from Jansen.

Yikes. I wasn't expecting Jansen to worry about me. I'll call him first before calling Stacey.

He answers on the first ring. "Where are you?"

"I'm home. Bree and I went to yoga," I say as Bree looks over at me sternly. She's probably wondering who's on the phone.

"Babe, I want to know these things. I was worried about you," he says, and my heart flutters. He cares about me.

"Sorry. I was overwhelmed with the launch and needed to get my mind on something else, so I asked Bree to go to yoga."

"It's fine. Maybe I shouldn't be so worried."

"Jansen, I should've told you."

"You're sold out, by the way," He says excitedly.

I sit up from the couch so fast. "Really?"

Bree scoots closer and mouths, "What?" so I shoo her away with my hand.

"Yeah. When you didn't answer, I thought you were busy with everything. I checked the website, and after refreshing the page several times, it's all gone. I'm so proud of you, Rell. You did it." Jansen's voice filled with pride, and I could hear it radiating through the phone.

"Are you sure? It's only been an hour and a half. There's no way." My eyes start welling up with tears.

Bree stands once she understands and throws her hands over her mouth.

"I'm positive, babe. Call Stacey to make sure, and I'll see you after work."

"Okay," I say before hanging up.

I stand from the couch, pacing between the tv and the coffee table.

"You sold out?" Bree asks.

I pause. "*We* sold out," smiling; I don't know if I should be excited or scared.

"Let's call Stacey."

I point to her, "Right."

I took a deep breath before hitting the call on Stacey's number.

We both stand there looking at each other while letting it ring on speakerphone. We wait for Stacey to answer, and after three rings, she picks up. "Rell."

"Yes?" I bit down on my lip.

"You did it, my dear. We sold out within an hour, and we have plans to have another launch in two weeks."

"Ahhhhhh…. Stacey, I can't believe it." I say.

"We knew you could do it. This line was just fantastic. It also helped with your following of people on The Gram."

"Thank you so much for giving me this opportunity."

"Our offer still stands, Rell. We would love to have you here. If you say yes, we would love to have Bree come with you as your assistant. What do you say?"

Bree throws her hands over her mouth in shock before shaking her head yes. Doing this with my best friend would be a dream come true. Jansen comes to mind, and I know he would be disappointed in me if I told her no.

"Yes. We would love to."

"Congratulations, Rell and Bree, you are officially team members of Threads. Can the two of you come here this weekend? We can talk next Monday about everything."

Looking forward to Bree, "We'll be there."

"Great, see you then."

Once I hang up the phone, Bree and I start jumping up and down together.

I point to her, "Is Kent okay with this?"

She shrugs before saying, "Is Jansen okay with this?"

"Yeah…. He told me to take it when he was in Los Angeles."

"Kent knew there was a chance, but we haven't talked about it because I wasn't sure what you would do. I thought you'd do it, but then I knew things were going well between you and Jansen."

Walking over to the couch to sit, I think about what Bree and I just agreed. I look around the house we will have to sell and the things that need to be packed away and moved to a new city that we don't know very well. Then it hits me that I'll leave behind someone I love for something I've always dreamt of doing. Why did the two best things in my life have to happen together when they can't go hand in hand?

Jansen

I haven't heard from Rell since we talked this morning, but I know we're having dinner together and celebrating this day for her. Before coming home, I stopped by the store to get something for dinner. I'm not a good cook, but I want to make something for her. I grabbed pasta because it's even I can't fuck that up and a bottle of wine. Not my favorite thing, but I know Rell likes it.

I've debated whether tonight should be when I let Rell know I'm falling in love with her. By the end of the workday, I decided to wait until that moment was special. She deserves to know, but when the time is right.

When I got home, all the lights except the back porch lights at Rell's house were off. I know that's where Rell has to be. Bree is more than likely away with Kent for the night.

I get out of the truck, walk inside, and lay the bag of groceries on the counter. I shoot Rell a quick text to let her know I'm home before unloading everything. I hear a knock at the back door when I have everything emptied from the bag, which surprises me since Rell always uses the front door.

I open the door to find a smiling Rell, "Hey."

"Hey." I smile back at her. She looks breathtaking, more beautiful than I've ever seen, a glow to her.

After she walks in, I close the door behind her. She walks to the counter by the fridge and hops on the counter to take a seat. Before I can even kiss her, she says, "I'm moving to Los Angeles."

I freeze up right there. Even though I knew this would happen, Rell's words are still shocking.

"No?" she frowns, "I shouldn't take the job?"

"No. No, that's not it. I *want* you to take the job. I'm just surprised. That's it." I walk over to her and place myself between her legs. I look into her deep brown eyes, "I'm so proud of you." I say before kissing her.

She wraps her arms around my neck, "You told me to take it, so when Stacey offered Bree and me the job again today, we took it."

I put a hand on both sides of her cheeks, "You're going to do great things in LA."

"Thanks."

Our mouths collide together, and I never want to stop kissing her.

She pulls out of our kiss, "What are you making me?"

"Pasta and wine, It's the best I can do."

"Well, you're lucky because I love pasta and wine," she kisses me once more before jumping off the counter as I walk away to start dinner.

I point to the cabinet to her left, "There should be glasses in there for the wine."

She turns around, opens the cabinet door, and pulls out two whiskey glasses since I don't own any for wine. After setting them on the counter, she reaches for the bottle of wine, unscrewing the top and pouring some into the glasses. I should be starting dinner, but I am enjoying the view of Rell making herself home in my kitchen.

Coming up behind her, I slide her hair to the side and place a kiss just below her ear before taking a glass of wine she poured from her hand. She spins around and wraps her hand around my neck. Looking me right into my eyes, "Jansen, will we be fine? If I move, we will make it work between us?"

Sitting the glass on the counter behind her, I grab her hips, "This will work. If it means I have to travel every weekend because I missed you every damn day of the week because I know I will, I will do whatever it takes, Rell. I'm falling…." I stop myself.

"I'm falling for you, Jansen, and it scares me."

She didn't hear me stop myself because the nervous look on her face told me that she was scared to tell me herself that she was falling. This is the perfect time to tell her I love her, but I can't. She's already worried about us.

I brush my hand across her cheek before placing some hair behind her ear, "Don't be scared. Falling is okay," I say before I kiss her.

Suddenly this dinner isn't my main priority tonight. Enjoying every second I can get with Rell is becoming greater to me than anything else.

She sits again on the counter, holding her wine, while I start dinner. Tonight she wore my favorite leggings and sweatshirt, and I like her best when she doesn't care how she looks. She's beautiful just as she is. Rell watches my every move in the kitchen, and while I look like I know what I'm doing, I don't. I've never cooked for a woman before.

I can feel her eyes on me, and it makes me smile without looking at her. I keep my eyes on what I'm doing, throwing pasta in boiling water, and a sauce in a saucepan.

"What?" I finally say, taking my eyes away for a second to look at her.

"You're just so cute, cooking for me."

"Not cute. There has to be a better word than cute."

She puts her finger to her chin, pretending she's thinking of a better word when I know damn well she knows a better word already. "Sexy?"

I laugh, "That's much better."

"You're sexy when you get jealous, sexy when you kiss me, sexy when you hold a baby, and you're sexy when you take me to the bedroom," she smiles, biting down on her lip.

"Are you trying to tell me something, Rell Campbell, or do you want dinner?" I walk up to her between her legs, slipping my hands up her sweatshirt.

She wraps her arms around my neck, "I'm trying to tell you something."

Sliding my hands from under her shirt to her butt cheeks, I lift her from the counter, and she wraps her legs tightly around me while laughing. We make it down the hallway before she says, "Wait, wait. We don't want to burn the place down."

I roll my eyes before walking back down the hallways to the kitchen, still holding Rell. She leans over, turning off the burners before we make our way to the bedroom, where I plan to savor every second with Rell.

Chapter Twenty-seven

Rell

Hello Los Angeles. This trip is different from the last, knowing that this will be my last time coming here before I move here. Jansen dropped Bree and me off at the airport yesterday morning. While the previous few days with Jansen hadn't been any different than they usually are, he wasn't ready to let me go on this trip. My heart is telling me that maybe I made a mistake taking this job.

Last night after arriving in Los Angeles, Bree and I had a girls' night in the hotel room, just watching movies and getting room service. We were both nervous about what Stacey would say today, so we didn't talk much.

We got ready together, wearing our usual trendy outfits for today. We've been waiting in my office for Stacey to arrive. I'm playing with the ring on my finger that I never take off, and Bree is scrolling through her phone.

We both hear a slight knock and look at each other before Bree stashes her phone away under her leg. The door opens, and it's Stacey. "Want to come down to my office?"

"Yeah, sure."

I get up from my desk chair and walk out of the office as Bree follows. She catches up to me as we walk together behind

Stacey. She grabs my hand and squeezes it. I'm so lucky to be able to have her here with me.

We walk into Stacey's office. Bree and I sit in the armchairs while Stacey sits behind her desk. "First off, I want to say Congratulations."

"Thank you," I say.

"This first round of the launch wasn't enough, honestly. We knew that. There will be a second round of all the same pieces for those who missed the first round."

"Okay," I say, and Bree nods.

"Now, we want to talk about the positions. You still accept, right?"

Bree and I look at each other and smile before turning our attention back to Stacey. "Yes. We want to do this."

"Great. We would love for the two of you to move here next week. We have condos available for you, and if you prefer to share one, we can do that too. We will provide a moving company to pack your stuff for you. Then move it here, so you won't need to worry about that. Sound good so far?"

Next week? It all sounds so soon. I feel gutted.

We look at each other again, and Bree nods.

"Yes, that's good. Two condos are fine," I say. Bree and I talked last night, and Kent will be following her here shortly after she moves and gets situated. I think they would like to have their own place. I don't want to live alone, but I don't have a choice.

"Great, I'll have everything set up. I would like to have you both here starting a week from today. We will work together to get this second launch up and going. Then we will go straight into a few summer pieces, then a huge fall line. You two will do wonderfully here, and everyone can't wait for you to start. How about your fiancé Rell? Is everything good there?"

I forgot she knew I had a fiancé, "Yes. He's staying in San Francisco. We will be doing long distance."

"Just don't let that get in the way of work."

"I won't," I say. I don't know what Stacey means by getting in the way of work, but I would like to think that being away from each other always doesn't interfere with work.

"Later today, I'll take the two of you over to the condos. It's the same place as Shae and Felicia. They will be able to help the two of you with the area and meet people here. Do you have any questions?"

Thinking for a second before answering, "I think we're good."

"Great. If you think of anything later, you can always ask me then. I want to thank you for accepting this. Both of you have a great future here at Threads," Stacey smiles.

Bree and I get up to leave but tell Stacey, "Thank you," on the way out the door. Together we walked down to my office. I walk in behind Bree and shut the door.

"Next week!" I say, trying not to freak out at this moment.

Bree takes a seat, "That will be okay, right?"

Walking around the desk, I sit on my desk chair and throw my hands over my face. This is the moment I want to cry, and I question if I'm doing the right thing. What am I even going to say to Jansen? We needed more time before I left, and the week in San Francisco I have left is not enough.

Gathering my thoughts, I think about Bree for a second. She wants this and is more than ready to move here for us. Take my hands away from my face, and wipe them on the skirt I wore to the office today. "Yeah. We will be fine. Thankfully they are helping us with getting everything here."

Bree gives me a quick smile, which helps me feel slightly better, but I need Jansen. The reassurance that he will show me, letting me know we will be fine and make it through this.

―――――――――

I'm standing in the middle of my new living room. The condos are lovely and have a very much Los Angeles feel. One wall in my living room is just windows looking over the city, and while the space is fancier than I imagined it to be, it's small. It isn't bad since I'll be the only one living here, but the reality of being alone hasn't set in. This apartment almost saddens me, but I know this is where I need to be. And Bree.

Bree and Stacey are down the hall checking out Bree's condo, and I'm thankful for a moment alone. Walking over to the windows and looking at the view I get of the city, I wipe away the tear running down one cheek. I haven't spoken to Jansen on the phone since coming here, and it's because I'm scared. I'm afraid to tell him I'm leaving him in a week, nervous about what he's going to say, and devastated thinking about what might happen between us. I'm also upset about leaving the place Bree and I called home for the last five years. The memories we made and the times we had in the house.

When I spin around, Stacey and Bree walk together in the condo. I quickly wipe away any tears left and try to hide my upset by putting a smile on my face when they look up at me.

"What do you think?" Stacey asks.

"It's nice," I answered with a slight smile.

Bree's face lights up like she's excited about this; I know she is.

I grab my bag from the kitchen island by the front door and slide it over my shoulder. Then we all walk out and down the hallway together. When we go out the back doors of the building, I see the pool and remember the conversation I had with Felicia and Shae. I wonder when summer comes if I'll even be down here hanging out with them or in my room waiting for Jansen's visits. I don't want to miss out on things. I wish I were experiencing this with him, too, not at a distance.

We get into Stacey's car, me sitting in the back, and drive off toward the airport. I informed Jansen earlier that we would be coming tonight so that he could pick us up from the airport. I know my heart won't be able to handle the smile he always has when he sees me coming from across the airport.

Jansen

After hardly speaking with Rell while she was gone, I can't wait to see her and hear all about what's new with her job at *Threads*. I'm standing at the airport waiting for her and Bree. Their flight landed not long ago. Once I get them back home, I'm hoping Rell will stay with me for the night. I don't know how much time we have left before time isn't an option for us anymore. I want to be with her every minute I can.

I see Rell coming down the escalator, and a giant smile draws across my face. My heart rate accelerates when she doesn't give me the same usual smile. I frown, knowing something is wrong with her.

Like always, I meet her at the bottom and take her bags from her.

"Hey," I say.

"Hi," Rell says, and Bree flashes me a smile standing behind her.

We quietly walk over to the baggage claim to take what has to be a small bag, considering they only stayed one night. Rell's still wearing the worried look on her face, and while I want to know what's on her mind, here's not the place. Bree looks as if she'll say something; it might upset Rell, so she's choosing not to talk. It'll be the most exciting ride home.

"How was the weather in LA?" I break the silence.

Bree spits out a laugh, which makes Rell smile just a little.

"It was nice," Rell says, giving a short answer.

The bags started coming out quickly, and I couldn't be more thankful since I killed the silence with the dumbest question I could ask. Rell and I have hardly been around Bree alone, so this is already awkward.

They grab their small bags, and I take them from them to roll out to the truck. I throw them in the back, and we all get in. Once I get the car started, the country music starts playing. Rell has never had a problem with it, but Bree seems to think it's funny.

We get on the road to head home, "You two need food?"

"I'm okay," Rell answers.

I look back at Bree through the rearview mirror, and she shakes her head no. So it seems like we are going straight home.

Looking over at Rell and then back at the road. She looks like there could be a chance that she won't want to talk about whatever is on her mind. I tap the gas a little harder to get us home quicker. I need Rell, and I want her alone.

Not a single word is said the rest of the short drive home that felt like the longest drive of my life. When we all get out of the car, Bree takes off for their house as Rell stands beside the truck waiting for me on her side.

I move around the truck, walk up to her, and kiss her lips. Her hands find their way up the back of my neck, and she brings me in closer. Once she pulls out of our kiss to catch her breath, I say, "Stay with me tonight?"

"Let me grab some things from home."

I kiss her lips again, "I'll be waiting."

She smiles at me before rolling her bag around me and heading home. I walk up the front steps to my door and walk in once I see she made it inside. Starting in the living room, I tidy my place up some and then make my way to the bedroom.

My heart is all over the place at the moment. Not knowing what's bothering Rell and the fact that whatever it is, I don't think it's good. I take a look at myself in the mirror in my bathroom. Tonight may be the night I tell her I love her. I can't take it anymore that I haven't told her yet. I want to be able to tell her anytime I want, so I can reassure her that she's mine.

I hear a knock on the backdoor, so I quickly walk down the hallway into the kitchen to answer. Rell's standing there in cozy clothes that she had to change into swiftly and a small overnight bag in her hand. She walks right in and drops the load on the kitchen table.

"Did you just jump the fence?" I ask.

"Yeah."

I walk over to her and wrap my arms around her waist, and she places hers around my neck. "I love you."

She drops her forehead to my chest. It wasn't the reaction I expected, and I was almost sure she felt the same way. "Jansen, I leave Sunday for LA, forever."

I close my eyes and hold her tighter, "Tell me you love me, Rell. That's all I want to hear."

She lifts her head to me, "I do, Jansen, but how are we going to go through this?"

"If we love each other, then nothing else matters. We will make this work."

Rell smiles as if the weight has been lifted off her shoulders, "I love you," and then her lips meet mine.

I lift her feet off the ground and make our way to the bedroom. I've wanted something like this, to love someone and never want to let that person go, and now I have it, but part of me has to let her go, which will be challenging, but I know she's my person. We will get through this.

Once we make it to the bedroom and I put Rell's feet back on the ground, she pulls off her clothes. I watch as she slides her sweatshirt over her head and our lips meet again. Trying to unbutton my jeans, Rell's hands find their way over mine, and she gets them undone herself, her lips never leaving mine. My jeans find their way to the ground, and I slip my feet out before pulling my shirt off over my head.

While I'm standing here naked, Rell's eyes wander over my body, and she shakes her head smiling. She slides her hands up my chest before pushing me to sit on the bed. She takes her place on my lap with each of her knees on either side of me. She wraps her arms around my neck and kisses me before putting her forehead to mine.

"I love you, and I mean it. Okay," Rell whispers.

I close my eyes as my hands reach the back of her head. Holding her close and tight, I want to bottle up this moment with her. "I love you more than I ever thought my heart could love someone." My lips connect with hers as she pushes me back onto the bed.

If this were the last moment I ever had with her, it wouldn't be enough. I don't want Rell for only right now. I want her forever. My heart has never desired or needed someone as much as it does her. Even forever is not enough.

Chapter Twenty-eight

Rell

As I lay here, Jansen's arm over me as we lie in his bed, my mind anxiously wonders about the future we have awaiting us. The outcome doesn't look good to me, breaking my heart. He's confident we will make it through the distance and the time away from each other. My heart wants to believe him, but it's hard. I slept maybe a whole hour last night. I watched him sleep peacefully throughout the night, and it was as if he was finally whole. This Jansen isn't the same one I met months ago. He's happy now. He's right where he wants to be, and I want to be with him, right here, waking to him every day. I want to share a place with him and a future, but how is that possible when we will forever be in two different areas?

Jansens alarm begins to go off on the nightstand, and I roll myself over to look at him when he wakes. He moans before reaching his hand over to turn off his alarm, his eyes still closed. Once it's off, he pulls me closer to him and places a kiss on my forehead. "Good Morning."

I wrap my arms around him, snuggle into his chest, and he holds me tighter. Something he's been doing a lot lately, and I know it's because he doesn't want to let me go. I don't want to let go, either.

"Tell me to stay, Jansen," the words fall right out of my mouth.

He's silent.

I release myself from him and sit in bed, pulling the sheets up. "Tell me to stay. You always tell me to stay, Jansen. Tell me not to go. Tell me I'm making a mistake."

He's shaking his head no, "I can't."

Tears start to fall from my eyes, "I want you to tell me you love me, and you can't let me go."

He sits up and takes my hand in his. "I love you. I'll never want you to go. I'll always be waiting for you here, but I can't tell you to stay. I'm not going to be that man that tells you to give up on your dreams to be with me. Those dreams were far before I came into your life. You have to go, Rell. You have to live your dreams and be happy."

"We won't make it, Jansen."

He wraps his arms around me, "Don't say that."

"You'll always be here, and I'll always be there. I want to believe you when you say we will make it work, but Jansen, I can't be happy if we live miles apart."

"Don't, Rell. Don't say that. You're going to be so happy and successful in Los Angeles," he kisses my forehead.

We sit there in silence for a few minutes before he gets up from the bed to get ready for work. I watch him as he walks into the bathroom, and then I get up to throw some clothes on. He comes out of the bathroom and takes one look at me. "Are you leaving?"

"Jansen, maybe this isn't a good idea. My heart's with you, and it wants to stay with you. I'll break into a thousand pieces missing you, and I won't be able to piece myself back together. If I can't be with you every day, I don't want to be with you. It'll kill me." I slide the ring off my finger and place it on the nightstand.

"Rell, stop it," he runs to me, wrapping his arms around me.

"I mean it," tears fall down my cheeks. "I can't do this."

Jansen wipes away my tears before kissing me.

"My last flight leaves at nine am on Sunday. That's your last chance to tell me to stay, Jansen. I don't have to go. I can stay here and be with you forever," I kiss him one last time before pulling out of his arms.

"Rell," he reaches for me as I walk over to the bed to grab my overnight bag from the floor.

"I'm sorry. I am, but I'm trying to save us from a lot of hurts that's going to take place." I say, walking into the doorframe. Jansen stands there, watching in disbelief.

"I love you, Rell."

"I love you too, Jansen," I say before walking down the hall.

Tears don't stop coming. I expected him to follow me and tell me to stay, but he never followed me. Instead, I walk out the front door alone.

―――――――――

Rolling tape across the last box in the workroom, I clip off the end before looking at the room filled with brown boxes. The moving truck will be here tomorrow to get everything while Bree and I hop on a plane. We've been packing for what seems like weeks, but in reality, it's been two days.

"Done in here!" I yell out to Bree.

She comes walking in, "Wow," she crosses her arms. "This seems weird."

"I know. This room holds lots of memories. We filmed our life here. We got ready for dates and had conversations that we hold near and dear to our hearts here," I frown.

"We also grew in this room. We started not knowing what we were doing with ourselves, and look at us now," Bree wrapped an arm over my shoulder, and I put mine around her. Our heads come together, and we take a moment of silence, taking in the room.

We've come so far as partners and friends. I would've never dreamed of being where we were today when we started all this five years ago. Part of me is sad that what's next will be different for us.

We have decided to continue *The Gram* together. We'll need something to help promote the clothing lines, and we want to make the extra money still if this line doesn't work out. We'll cut back on some sponsors, and our page will look slightly different when we move and settle.

Bree's phone starts ringing in her back pocket, and she lets go to answer.

"Hey," she says before walking out the door.

I pick up one of the boxes off the floor and stack it on another before leaving the room to walk into my almost empty bedroom. I plop down on my bed next to the suitcase I already have packed for tomorrow. It's all starting to become very real.

It took me two days to pack a box. I waited. I don't know what I was waiting for, Jansen to show up to tell me to stay or for me to take chances with the distance. It came down to me choosing the hurt now instead of being apart for months or maybe years. He hasn't showed or called. Perhaps he knows I'm right. We would never make it in the end. I'll never forget the short time I had with him. The time we had just wasn't enough. I'll love him always. He'll forever have my heart.

"Kent's on his way, and I'm ordering pizza. Sound good with you?" Bree asks, popping her head through the doorway.

I lift my head from the bed, "Yeah. Sounds good."

She walks back out, and I sit up. Bree was there for me the last couple of days, putting me together as I did for her when she and Kent had their short split. I apologized to her for thinking that staying would even be an option. I was in love and making selfish decisions while not thinking about what Bree wanted when I told Jansen I wanted to stay. Even though she said she understood, it wasn't right. We are doing this for us, and staying would mean we would continue dreaming for more.

When I leave the room and meet Bree in the kitchen, she's pouring the last bottle of wine from the fridge into two plastic cups. Taking a seat a the counter, she slides one of the cups over to me and lifts hers. "To new beginnings," I lift my cup, and we toast.

New beginnings. A new job in a new place, and living by myself. Something I haven't done in so many years. I'm scared and excited if that's two emotions you can have together, along with just downright depressed. I'm pretty much feeling every emotion.

Kent walks through the front door with a pizza box in hand. He comes over to set it down on the counter and reaches over to kiss Bree's cheek. Usually, their touches don't bother me, but this one makes me feel sick. I miss Jansen, everything about him and us. I know this is my fault, but I feel like I spared us both from hurting worse. I love Jansen too much to be in constant pain from being unable to see him. I don't want 'whenever' with Jansen. I wanted him *forever*. We deserved more than what was going to happen to us. The thought of never seeing him again pains me. I hope he'll be there tomorrow to tell me goodbye or our normal 'see you later.' I need to see him one more time.

I reach over to open the pizza box and grab a massive slice of pizza. Folding it half, I take a significant bite before getting up from the barstool. I lift my pizza in the air and the wine in my other hand, "Goodnight, you two," then make my way back to my room. Tomorrow's a big day.

Before getting into Kent's car to take us to the airport, I take one last look at Jansen's house. I think of all the times I spent with him there and how I'll miss this view. I wonder if he is looking at me right now or if he's sleeping. A tear falls, but I stop myself quickly because I'll be a mess traveling with tears.

The movers haven't arrived yet, but Kent will take care of everything when he returns from dropping us off. I get in the backseat and look back at our house one last time. Tomorrow there will be a for sale sign placed out front.

On the way to the airport, there's silence in the car, and I'm thankful for it. I sightsee through the window one last time, not knowing when I'll be back here. I love this city.

I walk inside to wait for Bree when we get to the airport. She and Kent say their goodbyes outside. Kent is coming to LA in a few days, but they always have to kiss before leaving each other. I can't help but look around while I wait, just hoping to see a familiar face.

Bree comes in, and we go through all the stops we need to before we get to our gate early. The airport was slow this morning, so that we could get through everything before schedule. Once we reached our gate, we sat in the chairs to wait until time for our flight.

"Are you good?" Bree asks me.

Looking around the airport, "I'm okay."

Bree places her hand on my knee, "Rell, I don't want you to get your hopes up."

"I'm not. Well, I'm trying not to."

She pulls her phone from her bag to look at while we wait, and I'm not interested in looking at anything on mine. So I cross my arms over my chest while we continue to wait.

I watch families with small children walk by and smile, thinking about Jansen holding the baby at the park. A time when we were so happy, and the one time we didn't have to pretend anymore.

Our section starts to fill up quickly, reminding me that we will be boarding soon. Bree continues passing the time on her phone while I still watch people walking by. Time is running out if he shows. If he comes, there will be no time to tell him what I want and need to say. Once again, tears begin to form, and I don't want to cry. I've cried so many tears since I left his place days ago. I whisper to myself, "Come on, Jansen. Show up."

The attendant's voice comes over the speaker. It's time for us to board. Bree stands and grabs her bag, so I do the same. I look around one last time, and no one looks like him. We walk towards the line of people boarding. I don't look back while we get in line. I knew he wouldn't show. I wanted him to and felt he would fight for us, telling me he loved me, but he didn't come. I can't blame him; I didn't fight for us either. I gave up, and I wouldn't say I liked that. I should've fought harder.

We scan our tickets and walk down the jet bridge before getting on the plane. I place my bag on the overhead and take my seat by the window. Bree follows, sitting next to me. I watch as people walk by and load onto the plane. He's not coming, and time has run out.

Chapter Twenty-nine

Jansen

It's been one month without Rell. I'm still living the devastating life that started when she walked out the door. I couldn't run to her and be the man she wanted me to be. It wasn't in me to hold her back from something she loved, which made her happy. I was something so small compared to the life she was going to live in LA. I love her, and if she didn't think we would make it, then she was right. We didn't have a fighting chance at making distance work for us when we'd only been together for a short time.

The day she left San Francisco, I made it to my truck. I started the car and was ready to beg her to stay, but I never made it out of the driveway. That wasn't who I was; it was who I wanted to be for her. She has a far better future there, and I can't stop her. Knowing she would wait for me to show up broke me. I never showed up for her. Instead, I sat there in my truck for an hour and cried as a piece of me left.

I've barely dragged myself around since she left. I get to work early, and I leave hours late. I don't enjoy driving into the driveway and seeing a for sale sign stand in the yard. I don't like walking out back, and the swing I once used to find her in reading is gone. I can't look at the house that was once hers. I can barely look at my home, knowing all the rooms I share memories with her.

The only people I've talked to in the last month are people from work. I've ignored Jay too often and know the time will come when I need to tell him this whole story. There was never a fiancé, although I feel that's what Rell was the entire time. She stood in for something I needed and gave me everything.

The hardest part of this last month was one week after Rell left. She made that breakup post she said she'd make if anything ever happened to us. I wasn't expecting it, and there it was. Loud and clear, she posted that we were no longer together. It said we were in two different places and posted a photo of us we took the night we were on the boat. I blame myself for it. I didn't fight hard enough for us.

Did we have a chance of making the distance work like I thought we would? I don't know. I want to believe we would have. I know Rell wasn't lying when she said she would break into a thousand pieces missing me because I would've too. I would've missed her every damn day, and I *do*. I love her more now that I miss her, and I can only hope she feels the same. If I never get the chance to see her again, I'll die a broken man. I don't think I could ever love anyone the way I loved her.

Walking into work today, the first one in the office since that's my new routine, I walk by Jay's office and see him sitting at his desk. I wave, walking by his door when he sees me. He nods to me and then continues typing away on his computer. When I reach my lonely, boring office, I take a seat and open up my laptop.

The condos have been doing well, and their progress is incredible. I've been able to divide all my attention to them so they will be ready in the fall. What's next for me here? I don't know, but I feel my time here is ending, and it'll be time for me to return to Kansas City. There doesn't seem to be any new developments here in San Francisco for me to stay here, and why stay when I don't have much of a life here? I didn't in Kansas City either.

My phone buzzes and the caller ID tells me who it is. "Hello."

"Can we talk for a second?" Jay asks.

"Yeah. Sure. I'll be right down."

He hangs up, and I close my laptop. I'd just walked by there, and it didn't look then like he needed to talk to me about anything, so there's no telling what he wanted.

When I reach his office, he points for me to close the door, so I do. Then I take a seat in one of his chairs.

"How are you?" he asks.

I wipe my sweaty hand on my pants. "I'm good."

"You seem as though something has been bothering you?"

Do I tell him that my life has gone to shit? No.

"I'm sorry. I've just been focusing on work."

"I won't complain about that," he leans forward, putting his elbows on his desk. "I wanted to tell you that we caught the person who damaged the condos."

I lean forward, "Really?"

I'd almost forgotten all the stuff that had gone down with my job.

"It was Conrad. We found the camera on his office desk and ran the card. We brought him in to talk, and he confessed, saying you just intimated him and how you work. We fired him yesterday afternoon."

"Wow," I ran my hands through my hair, "I would've never guessed him."

"There's more to the story. Care to explain?" Jay kicks back and crosses his arms.

Shit. Conrad knew who Rell was.

"You mean about Rell?

He nods.

"First off, I want to apologize. I'm sorry. Rell was my neighbor, and we made a deal with each other. I asked her to be my fiancé, and in return, I helped her with *The Gram*. It sounds crazy, I know, and that's because it is. I was never engaged. My girlfriend back home cheated, and when you invited me to dinner, I wanted to impress you, so I made a deal with Rell." I say, frowning.

"Your two no longer have this deal?" he asks.

I shake my head, "No. We honestly haven't had the deal for some time. Now she's off doing life in LA, and I'm here without her."

"First, I want to thank you for being honest with me. Second, I want to let you know that Laura and I knew you and Rell weren't together. Laura had followed Rell for some time on The Gram. She was taken by her the first night you brought her over. Laura got this idea that you two would be perfect together, so she kept inviting the two of you to things. She knew you weren't together any more weeks ago when Rell made her post." Jay says.

I'm shocked by his words and don't know what to say.

"The office also knew that you and Rell weren't together. Until rumors were about some kiss in your office that looked very real."

I shake my head, "I'm so sorry, Jay. I didn't know who she was when we made the deal. I felt like we were going to get caught, but I wasn't sure. I didn't know she had so many followers when we made this deal together."

"Did you fall in love with Rell?"

"I did," I confess. "I've never loved anyone the way I love her," I say as I drop my head.

"Jansen, I hate that I'm about to say this, but I think the time has come for you to go."

I stand from my chair immediately and throw my arms out at him. "Please don't, Jay. I'm sorry for everything. I'm sorry for embarrassing myself here at the office and with you. I didn't mean for that to happen. I'll work harder to make it up to you. I don't want to go back to Kansas City. I'll be that many more miles from Rell." I say as tears form in my eyes.

"Jansen, when you leave here, pack your office."

"Please, give me a second chance, Jay. Please," I'm standing begging.

"Jansen…."

"Yes?" I pause, pacing.

"We're opening a new office in Los Angeles. If you want it, we want to make you the new boss. We haven't started any projects, but some developments are upcoming there. The new office opens next week, and we have some staff hired. We need you there, that is if you want the job?"

I put my hands over my face, "Really?" I ask, shocked with a hint of embarrassment.

He laughs, "Really."

"Yes, yes. I want it. I promise you I won't let you down, Jay." I run my hands through my hair. This is happening. I pinch myself to make sure this is happening.

"Can you promise me one thing?" I look at him, "Promise me that you'll get her back."

I smile, "Oh, I'm getting her back, and I'm never letting go."

"You can go, and I'll email you all the details later."

"Thank you, Jay."

I get to the door, and Jay says. "One more thing."

I turn to him.

"Talk to people, Jansen. It'll help with your job," he smiles.

I nod and then walk out the door.

Walking to my office wearing the biggest grin, I head over to the window to look at the view for hopefully the last time. I'm going to get Rell back. We're getting the chance to start over, and I want to do it the right way this time.

When I get home from work early, I see a sold sign on the sign outside Rell's house. I get out of my truck and walk to the front of the house. While looking at it before it becomes someone else's, I think about the time I met Rell right here in the rain. I smile before turning around. Then I bump right into Margret. "Shit, sorry."

"She was here," she says in return.

"She?" I ask her.

"That pretty girl who used to live here. She was sitting on your steps today. I forgot her name. I used to see her at your house all the time."

"Rell? She was here?" I point to the ground.

"Oh yes, Rell," she points to my front door. "She was here for an hour today, pacing the front of your house, crying, and then she left."

Rell was here, and she was just outside my door. Does she still want me? She has to.

"Margret, tell me everything you saw today." I put my hand on her shoulder.

"Well, she was here with the new people who bought the house. Then when they left, she looked over to your house before taking a seat on the steps. Then she cried and started pacing the front like she wanted to go inside but knew you weren't home. Then after wiping away her tears. She left." she says, pointing to my house.

"Thank you, Margret."

She walked away and waved her hand in the air while leaving. I've never been into nosey Margret, but today, she gave me the necessary answers. I need to get to Rell. There's still that chance that I knew was there.

Rolling my overloaded suitcase out of the airport, I meet my Uber outside the door. I'm in Los Angeles to check out the new office and meet all my colleagues. I feel like I'm still dreaming or that I'm getting punked. Jay gave me this job, and it's more than anything I've ever wanted, yet I still feel like something's missing from my life. I haven't talked to Rell; she doesn't know I'm here or I'll be here for my new position.

I've wanted to call her. I've pulled my phone out many times and looked at her photo on my phone. I've typed messages and deleted them. We've been apart for over a month, and in reality, I don't know what she's doing or if she even wants me back. I couldn't get myself to call her to beg for her back. She deserves better than that, and I'm hoping my plan of slowly working my way back into her life works. We need a fresh start to what we started so many months ago.

The Uber drops me off at my destination, and I can't believe my eyes when I get out to see the new building. Jay's giving me the most fantastic office building to run. The office is smaller than we have back in San Francisco. It's a modern black one-story building on the city's outskirts. Other buildings surrounding it are of the same design. How did Jay never tell me about this? I don't know, but he couldn't have given me this opportunity at a better time. Well, maybe before Rell left me, but I see this chance at getting her back worth it.

Unlocking the front door, I walk inside the building, and it's already filled with furniture. I roll my bag as I walk down the hallway to my office. This building has glass walls like the other office, but I get privacy with walls for my office. It's almost like Jay knew I was the man for this job all along.

When I walk into my office, the back wall is nothing but windows, and the ample space is empty, but this time, I'll be making this office feel welcoming. It's already starting to feel like home, and I just got here.

After leaving the office, I walk to the hotel a few doors down to drop my bag. Today would be the perfect time to walk around and get familiar with where I'll be. So after changing clothes, I start a walk. I pass by the new office building and walk to the site where there's potential for some condos we could build within the city. Now that I'm taking on a new position, I need to look for places we could put our mark on.

I round the corner. Then I'm at the site after a few more blocks. Looking around the area to see if this is the right place to put some condos, I notice the *Threads* office just a few doors down. My heart instantly starts racing. Rell could be in there right now. I look back from where I just walked and then back at *Threads*. We are only going to be a mile apart. I shake my head in disbelief. This can't be real.

Chapter Thirty

Rell

Life has been challenging and different, but I'm adjusting. Bree seems to be taking the challenge better than me, but she has something to look forward to coming home every night. I have books and a makeshift office on my kitchen island that keeps me occupied after work.

Summer has arrived here in Los Angeles, and while Bree and Kent like hanging down by the pool with Felicia and Shae on the weekends, I usually keep to myself. I started retaking yoga classes here and found a great smoothie place. Both cost me an arm and a leg, but they keep me going. My summer pieces came out last week and sold out within hours again. We're working on getting some of my work into stores instead only on the *Threads* website, and I can't explain my excitement.

Last week, I had to return to San Francisco for one last time. We sold the house, and I needed to sign some papers. Giving the place away that held memories wasn't nearly as hard for me as looking at Jansen's house one last time. I sat on his steps, not waiting for him because I knew he was at work, but taking in every memory on those steps. I had put every kiss with him in the back of my mind, but they all came flooding back that day. I wanted to stay there, I didn't want to leave, but I couldn't let him see me. If I had seen him, then I would have been a goner. I would've left this life I'm living here in Los Angeles for him.

Tonight after work, Felicia and Shae want us to go out for drinks. There's a new bar opening just down from the office, and after some pleading, I told them I'd go. I can't blame them for begging me to go; I need to get out for once. I've been locking myself in my condo every night. Bree and Kent have already made plans not to join us.

Bree and I are sitting in the new conjoined office given to us when we started. While she's my assistant, she is more like my best friend who gets to hang out at work with me all day. We talk about everything in our office all day while I work on the fall clothing line.

"How are you and Kent doing?" I ask.

"I think we are doing better here than in San Francisco. It could be because we live together now, or that we put the wedding off for the move. We're happy here, and our jobs are the best. Kent loves the new CrossFit gym."

"I'm so happy for you guys," I say, continuing some sketching.

I'm glad for them. They've come a long way since living in San Francisco. I think they needed to live together. They're ready for marriage more now than they were then, and I couldn't be happier for my best friend.

"You'll get there, Rell. Someone will sweep you off your feet, making you so happy."

I lift my head, giving her a quick smile. "I know."

She's right, and I wouldn't say I like it. This life here in Los Angeles should make me happy, but I need more time to overcome what I left. Hopefully, my heart will find a way to piece itself together for fall and the next clothing release. I know going out more with the girls is just what I need to help me get going in the right direction.

"Are you coming?" Felicia says, popping her head through the door.

I look at the time on my laptop, and it's past closing time. "Yeah."

"You guys go have some fun. Kent and I are going on a date," Bree says.

I grab my bag under my desk and slide it on my shoulder. "Well, you have fun on your date."

Walking out of the office, leaving Bree to close it down, I meet Shae and Felicia standing by the front door. "We better have some fun because I need it."

Felicia laughs, "Oh, we're gonna have some fun."

Together we all walk out the front door. I pull my phone out of my bag to check it and know there's nothing new to see, but I always look anyway. Frowning, I slip it back into my bag as we walk down the sidewalk. Felicia and Shae walk side by side, with me behind them. They've been to the new bar already and said it's going to be a great place to meet new people tonight, but I'll believe it when I see it. I've been to many bars with them and have yet to meet anyone promising. We ran into Cameron once while out, but the breakup from Jansen was still so fresh that I ignored him most of the night. Maybe we'll see him tonight.

They continue talking about work while we walk; my mind is elsewhere, so I look around. We walk by a new development site, and there's a huge sign right by the sidewalk. I stop walking and read the sign. *New condominiums. Coming soon*!

My mind instantly thinks of Jansen. There's no company name on the sign, I don't even remember the company Jansen worked for, but it doesn't matter because there's no way these have to do with him. He's in San Francisco.

"Rell," Shae yells, "Are you coming?"

I look at them, yards ahead of me, then back at the sign. "Coming."

I walk quickly to catch up to them, and when I do, I pull my phone from my bag. I open it up and search for Jansen on *The Gram*. My heart will hurt since I haven't looked at his account in weeks, but I want to see if there are any new updates in his life. After searching for his name, I clicked on his photo, and there haven't been any recent posts. There's a new story, so I click, knowing he'll see that I saw it. It's a photo of glasses filled with something, sitting on a bartop, and a mirror backdrop. There are five glasses in the image, telling me maybe he's not on a date but out with friends. Then I smile, thinking that he's out, making friends. There's no location tag or anything else detailing where he is, but the photo still makes me smile. I close out and put my phone away.

We reach the bar, and all walk in. Felicia heads to the bartender to order us all a round of drinks. There's no telling what kind of drinks, but it doesn't matter to me. Shae and I walk over to a lounge area, and before taking a seat, I look around.

"It's so busy in here tonight?" I sit.

"It was like this the other night. Maybe it'll die down some before we leave and make it easier to meet people," she speaks up a little bit so I can hear her.

We get cozy on the couch, and Felicia walks over to us with two espresso martinis and someone following her with the other. She hands us ours before turning back to grab the one from that person's hand. When she takes it, they walk off, and she sits across from us in a leather chair. "Find any hot guys here?"

I smile before taking a drink. I haven't seen any good-looking guys here, but I haven't been looking. I'm more worried about the number of people in this bar. It makes me a tiny bit uncomfortable.

"We just got here. Give it time, and guys will show," Shae says.

I continue drinking the espresso martini. These seem to be the drink Felicia orders for us when we go out, which has been rare since moving here, but I appreciate that she knows my taste now.

Still looking around the room, not knowing what I'm looking for, I spot a group of men at the bartop. Their backs are to us. It seems like they are paying out for the night to leave. They are all wearing baseball caps and laughing around. When some of them move away from the bar, I spot the guy paying for their tab, wearing a flannel shirt and no baseball cap. From a distance, it looks like he has familiar dark hair. I sit my drink down on the table in front of me and keep my eyes on him hoping to see him turn around. My head is messing me with because, to me, he looks like Jansen. The men are around him, and it's almost hard to see him through them. He turns around before walking out the door, and that's when we lock eyes.

"Jansen," I say, standing. My heart starts racing.

I walk off to follow them. "Rell, where are you going?" I hear Shae say behind me, but I don't turn around. I keep walking through the group of people, trying to catch the men leaving the bar. I make it to the door, pushing people out of my way. I look both ways when I get outside, and he's gone.

"Ugh," I grumble.

Was it him? Is my head messing with me since I looked at his account before coming here? I think back, trying to remember how many men were around him. *Four or five.* I can't remember. I was so focused on thinking it was him that it all happened so fast.

Walking back into the bar, I meet with Felicia and Shae and retake my seat.

"Where did you go?" Felicia asks.

"I thought I saw someone. It was nothing," I say because they know my story with Jansen, and I don't want them to think I'm crazy. If he were here, he would've told me, right? He would try to find his way back to me. But why would he be here, in Los Angeles? My one night out in a while, and I feel like I've already ruined it. I won't be able to take that moment off my mind for the rest of tonight because I think it was him.

"You thought it was Jansen?" Shae says.

Playing it cool, "No," I pick up my drink and take a sip. "The guy just looked like him, that's all."

"So, you ran after a random stranger out the door because you thought it was Jansen. Someone who's clearly in San Francisco because he would've told you if he were here?"

"I know, I know," I take another sip.

If Jansen were here in LA, there could be a reason why he didn't tell me he was here. Maybe, he doesn't think I'm available anymore, or he's looking for the right time. What am I even thinking about all this right now? It's insane.

I ruined last night's out with the girls. We still had some fun and a few drinks, but it wasn't enough to get my mind off that I saw Jansen. I was pretty convinced by the time we left that it was him. I couldn't get him off my mind. While I didn't bring him up anymore the rest of the night, the girls still knew I was thinking about him. I hadn't thought about him that much since coming here. Of course, I've missed him more than anything. I've been trying my hardest to put him in the past. I can't. It's impossible when you love someone so much it hurts.

He was in my dreams last night, and I wanted it to be real when I woke up. Instead, I woke up alone in my small condo, reminding myself that my dream was just a *dream*.

I got ready, dragging myself into the office. I knew working and staying busy would be enough to take my mind off, Jansen. I've also been trying to keep clear of the girls so that they wouldn't bring up last night in front of Bree. I wanted to be able to tell her myself sometime today.

I'm sitting at my desk quietly sketching while Bree's sitting at her desk working on the computer. I think I've said five words since coming into the office. Bree hadn't even asked how last night went, making me think she knew we didn't have as much fun as we expected. I keep looking over at her, but she seems to be minding her own business.

"You want to get lunch together today?" I ask.

"I'll be busy, but you can grab something for us and bring it back. We can have lunch here while I finish this stuff on the computer today."

"That'll work. I can leave sometime soon. Does a salad from a few doors down sound good?"

She looks over to me, "Yeah. How was last night?"

"It was okay," I say.

"I'm glad you went out."

"Me too," I smile sheepishly.

I finish up my sketch and then gather my things to leave. I slide my purse onto my arm and then get up from my desk chair. "I'll be back," I tell Bree before walking out the door. She nods and then goes back to typing away on the computer. I walk down the hallway to the front door. Felicia and Shae aren't at the front desk, which tells me they went to lunch too. I walk out the front doors and turn down the sidewalk. I don't get far when I hear someone yell, "Rell."

When I turn around, there's Jansen—wearing dress pants, a button-up shirt, and nice shoes. I've never seen him dressed so handsomely. A smile comes across my face, and tears form in my eyes. I knew it was him.

I walk to him just as he walks to me, and when we meet, I don't know what to do, so I stand there. He reaches out to brush back a piece of hair that flew across my face. "I saw you last night."

"I know."

We stand there staring at each other. Neither of us knows what to say, so I look down. Just seeing Jansen makes me feel all the emotions all over again. I have many questions to ask him, but I don't know where to start.

"First," he holds his hand out. "Jansen Davis, I feel like we never officially meet."

I hold my hand and smile. I know what Jansen's doing. "Rell Campbell," I point to the *Threads* building. "I work here, and you?"

"I just moved here from San Francisco. I'm head of the new construction company that just opened. My office is just around the corner."

"Nice, Mr. Davis. I'm impressed. I lived in San Fransisco not long ago. It was okay."

"Just okay?" he raises an eyebrow. "I met this girl there. She was pretty amazing, but then she moved."

"Well, that's no way to get a girl," I smile slightly.

"I want to take you out. There's this bar here called *Moonlit*. We could get drinks, talk?" he tucks his hands in his pockets, nervous.

"I would like that," I blush.

"Tonight?"

"Yea, tonight's good."

He smiles at me, taking his hands from his pockets. I want to touch and kiss him, but we can't just return to what we were before. We need to take this slowly, just like he wants.

Rubbing his hand down my arm, he says. "I've missed you," his touch makes me close my eyes and hold back the tears I want to cry. I've missed him too and hearing him say those words. I felt sadness.

"I missed you too."

"I'll see you tonight," he says, and I'm not ready to see him walk away.

"Yes. Just message me the details."

He smiles, and I know it because I told him to message me, and I'll look forward to it when he does.

He starts walking backward, and I smile, watching him walk away.

"Later, Rell."

"I'll see you around, Jansen." I laugh.

"Don't say that."

I wave, and he turns around to walk off back to work.

When I turned back around, I almost forgot what I was going to do but then reminded myself that I was grabbing lunch for Bree and me. The conversation we will have during lunch just got a lot more interesting.

Chapter Thirty-one

Jansen

I'd been waiting for the right time to meet Rell again. I needed to run into her again, and I was starting to get impatient with the days. I was visiting places around her work for lunch and meeting colleagues for dinner, just hoping I'd bump into her. Then that night at the bar, I saw her just as I walked out the door, and that was it for me. Knowing she had seen me too, I needed to see her again, and I wasn't going to wait another day. Today I went straight to *Threads*. I was going to march right in the front door and beg her to meet me for dinner. My plan was horrible, but I saw her there walking before I even had to beg, and my original reintroduction plan worked. It couldn't have been better. She knew what I was getting at when I introduced myself.

I didn't mean to slip out that I had missed her, but I couldn't hold back the words any longer. I could've told her more, but I'll wait. I'm hoping I have all the time in the world to say how much she means to me, and I could never go another day without her. We need to take this one day at a time.

Offering to meet her at the bar, but she returned the message saying I could pick her up at her place. I wasn't expecting her to be so open to me right now. I thought this would take time for us to return to where we were, and I know some things will.

I park my rental outside her condo building and lock it after getting out. This place is fancier than I imagined it to be. I walk by a large pool area before walking through the doors. This is already so different from the life Rell and I lived back in San Francisco, and it makes me sad thinking about Rell not having the swing she loved so much.

I take the elevator to her floor and walk down to her door. Before knocking, I wipe my sweaty hands on my thighs. Then I wait.

The door opens, "Hey," she opens it more, "You can come in?"

I walk into her apartment. My eyes instantly go to the tiny white couch covered with pink pillows. All her furniture looks new from what she had at her old place.

"Cute," I say.

"It's different."

"It's small."

She laughs, "It is, but it's just me here."

"So, Bree and Kent share a place?" I ask.

"They do. They're down the hall," she joins me in the kitchen island and living room space. She closes the laptop open on the bar, picks up a mug by the computer, pours the liquid down the sink, and then sets the cup down.

"You like it here?"

"Like this condo or Los Angeles?"

"The condo."

She leans over on the kitchen counter with her elbows, "It's okay. Where are you staying?"

I take a seat on one of the barstools. "I'm staying in a hotel close to the office. I still have the house back in San Francisco."

"Oh," she frowns.

"No, not like that. I have it to hold my stuff until I find a place here. I haven't looked yet. The hotel hasn't been bad."

"When and how did you end up in LA?" she asks.

"A week ago. It's a funny story, actually," I laugh. "I thought I was getting fired. Jay had me come into his office. He told me Conrad was the one destroying the condos. Then I had to explain the story of our deal. Everyone knew we weren't together the whole time, including Laura. She follows you, by the way."

Rell laughs, "Really?"

"Yeah. Jay told me to pack up my office and that I was coming here. They had this new office in the works, and I knew nothing about it until right then. I flew out here a couple of days later, and here I am."

She smiles—the smile I missed seeing so much.

"The guys at the bar with me the other night now work for me. It's crazy to think I'm here and running a company."

"I knew you could do it. I'm proud of you." Rell stands from the counter. "Want me to get ready?"

"Oh yeah, just whenever," I say, almost forgetting we were going out.

Rell walks into her tiny room just off the living room, and she leaves the door open so I continue the conversation. "I'm guessing the island is your office?"

She yells from her bathroom attached to her room. "Yeah."

Looking around at the four-foot-long kitchen island, knowing this space wasn't comparable to the workroom she had. Granted, she has an office of her own at Threads. Rell's used to working from home, so I know she'd probably want something more significant than this.

She walks out of the room wearing a black fitted skirt paired with a white top and her long brown hair down. Looking at her so stunningly beautiful made my heart beat five times faster. It's still there, my love for her. It's still here.

I don't take my eyes off her as she slips on a pair of shoes before looking up at me, "Ready," she says.

"You look hot." I laugh, feeling first-date jitters. I know it's only been a little over a month since Rell and I saw each other, but she makes me nervous.

She rolls her eyes while shaking her head. Then she walks over to a hook behind the front door that holds her bag. So, I get up from the barstool and follow behind her. As much as I'd rather stay here with her, I promised her drinks, but more importantly, I wanted to talk.

We walked out of the condo together and down the hall. She doesn't talk, which makes me think she's just as jittery as I am. What were we nervous about? I have no idea. I follow her inside the elevator. I stand beside her, and just as the door closes, she looks up at me, smiling. I smile back just as the door closes. Then something comes over me. What are we doing? Not holding back any longer, I take her face into my hands and kiss her lips that I missed so much. Her hands find their way up the back of my neck, and she brings me closer to her. Our kiss is a mess, but I don't even care. I want her. She parts her lips to let me in and moans when I lift her off her feet by wrapping my arms around her. Rell drops her head back to catch her breath, and I place kisses down her jawline to her neck, then back up again.

"I love you," she whispers against my lips.

"Baby, you don't know how badly I've missed those words. I love you, Rell," I say before dropping her to her feet.

The doors to the elevator open, and we both look over at them, reminding me where we were again. I got lost in Rell, and now I don't mind where we end up for the night as long as we're together.

I pressed the button to close the elevator doors, "We're not going anywhere."

She smiles, wrapping her arms around my neck, "Good because I didn't want to anyway."

Once the doors are closed, our mouths collide again. My hands glide up Rell's back and tangle into the hair behind her neck. I've missed this all too much. We could kiss for the rest of the night, which wouldn't be enough to compensate for all the time we've lost in the last month.

Our lips leave each other once the elevator door opens. Rell takes my hand as we walk out of the elevator and back down the hall to her condo. After she unlocks the door, we walk in, and she tosses her bag onto the kitchen island before dragging me by the hand into her bedroom.

She falls back onto the bed, and I crawl over her. I kiss her soft lips quickly, and when I lift my head to look at her, I notice a tear rolling down her cheek.

I wipe it away with my thumb, "What's wrong?"

With a slight smile, she says, "I thought I'd never see you again."

I kiss her, "I'm here, baby."

She takes my face into her hands, rubbing her thumbs across my temples while smiling. "Stay with me, Jansen."

"I'm staying," I kiss her cheek and then her lips, "And I'm never leaving."

She grins before kissing me with everything that she has. It's almost like we were never apart. We picked up right where we left off, and I finally couldn't feel more at home with her in my arms.

I adjust my tie while looking into the bathroom mirror. Now that I'm the boss, I dress fancier for work besides my usual dress pants and button-ups while living in San Francisco. When I get it adjusted, I walk out of the bathroom to find Rell at the kitchen island waiting for me. She's wearing a white sundress, sandals, and her hair in a ponytail.

"Yum," she says before biting her lip once she sees me.

I kissed her, "We don't have time for that again this morning."

She frowns, getting down from the barstool.

"Don't forget I have plans for us after work."

"Got it," she says, grabbing her bag and meeting me at the door to leave.

I've been staying with her for two weeks. We get ready for work in the mornings before I drop her off at *Threads* on my way to the office. Things couldn't be better between us, so I have a surprise for her tonight. It's time we take the next step because I don't want to wait any longer.

We pull up outside *Threads*, and she leans over the console of the rental car to kiss me before getting out.

"I love you," I say.

"I love you too," she says before opening the car door.

She gets out, shutting the door, and I watch her walk through the front doors before driving off.

I'm the first person at the office when I arrive. After turning all the lights on, I walk to my office. I haven't been able to make it feel like home yet, but I have plans to once all my belongings arrive in town. Rell stopped by the other day for lunch, holding a photo of us in a frame, and she put it on my desk. It was a nice touch; I've looked at it every day since.

It still doesn't seem real to me that this is my office, and I get to run things. The first week here was tough without Rell. Since we've been together, it feels like my life is where it's supposed to be.

I take a seat at my desk and open my laptop. I have an email from Jay asking me to call him when I get a chance. I feel a sense of worry, thinking I already did something wrong.

After finding him on my phone, I hit send and waited.

After two rings, he answers, "Jansen. How are things?"

I lean back in my chair, "They're great. Everything couldn't be better."

"You got her back?" he asked.

Smiling, "I got her back."

"Great news," he pauses, "I was calling because there was something I wanted to tell you."

I lean forward and prop my elbows on my desk, "What's that?"

"I wanted to let you know that you've been doing a great job in the two weeks you've been there. When the guys in Kansas City told me you were the man for this Los Angeles job, I knew I needed to see it myself, so we decided to bring you to San Francisco for a trial run. You impressed me, which is why I was so hard on you when things went wrong," Jay says.

I pinch the bridge of my nose, "You mean I was supposed to be here all along?"

"Yes, I know I could've saved some heartache by sending you there sooner, but the office wasn't ready. You're doing great, Jansen. The guys there talk highly of you."

"Well, thank you," I say.

I don't know if I should be mad at him for never telling me this or happy that I was supposed to be here all along. The thought that Rell and I could've dealt with the distance until I got here makes me mad, but then again, maybe it was supposed to be this way all along. It's like we needed the chance to start over to make our relationship stronger. I don't know. Rell and I went hard quickly by starting backward. We were engaged when we barely knew each other. When she left, I felt like I lost her as my fiancé, and she was never that.

"Look, I'm sorry. I know you're probably mad at me, but I couldn't tell you until it was time."

I sit back in my chair, "It's okay, Jay, thanks for telling me."

"Have a good day," he says before hanging up.

Setting my phone on my desk, I look over at the photo of Rell and me. She chose the picture of us the first night we made our deal. The deal that's no longer there, and honestly, we've grown so much since then. I smile because, after all, that we went through to get here, Rell was supposed to be my future.

I've been anxious all day for work to end. My conversation with Jay didn't dampen my plans for Rell and me this evening. I look over at Rell, who has her hands over her eyes while I park the car. I get out, running around the car to open her door for her. I help her out of the car, and once she's placed perfectly on the sidewalk, I say, "Okay, open your eyes."

She takes her hands off her eyes and gasps, "A house?"

"Our house," I smile, looking over at her.

She looked confused, so I took her hand and had her follow me to the front door.

The house is a modern white home built by a notable architect in Los Angeles. It hit the market last week, and I knew I needed to get my hands on it. It's a two-story with tons of space for both of us.

I unlock the door, and we walk into an expansive entryway. The house has all-white walls and lots of modern wood built-ins throughout the house. It has a wealthy Los Angeles feel.

"Jansen. There's no way we could afford this place."

"Actually, yes, I can…. *we* can…. I sorta make a lot of money now," I say as I watch her walk around and take it all in.

She gives me evil eyes, and it's cute.

I take her hand, "Let me show you around."

We walk down the hallway to the main bedroom with a primary connecting bathroom. The glass shower is massive, and I know everything that will happen there. Rell's silent while looking around. I don't bother with questions. I'll wait until we finish the tour. We head upstairs, looking at three bedrooms and two more bathrooms.

Then once back downstairs, I take her out the back door. There's an oversized covered back porch, and I already have someone building a swing for Rell. We then walk out to a large grass-covered area surrounded by a tall black metal fence.

"Why's the fence so tall?"

I scratch the back of my neck, "Privacy, baby, and we'll need it."

We walked back into the house, "So, what do you think?"

She continues looking around, "I love it, don't get me wrong but don't you think it's a lot of space? We could get something smaller."

I walk over to her, wrapping my arms around her, "We could but then where are we going to put kids?"

She smiles, "But….Jansen Davis doesn't want kids."

I brush her hair back from her cheek, "I never said I didn't want *our* kids."

She gets on her toes, kissing me on the lips. "I like the house."

"Good, because I already bought it. It's ours in a couple of weeks."

She shakes her head at me, smiling.

Some of me thought she wouldn't like the house or I got it without her, but she seemed to love it. We are right where I want to be and on to the next step. I'm ready for this future with her and *forever*.

Chapter Thirty- two

Rell

Last week we made our last trip to San Francisco to pack up Jansen's house. It was a bittersweet goodbye to the house. The place holds memories of the beginning of us, and while it was hard to say goodbye, I'm ready for what's next with Jansen and me. We've made strides since he came to Los Angeles. Strides that I don't think we would've made staying in San Francisco or if we chose the distance. I know why Jansen didn't come that day. He didn't want me to stay. He never wanted me to resent him for staying and living the life I was already living. I'm thankful for that. While the first month here was hard for me to adjust to, it's felt like home since Jansen came back into my life.

Jansen told me how Jay said this job in Los Angeles would always be his. Despite the hardships, I can't help but think it all worked out the way it was supposed for us. We needed a fresh start. We fell in love during what was the most challenging time in our lives.

We moved into our home, and Jansen surprised me with a giant patio swing on the back porch. It's so much bigger than the one I had before. We've spent almost every night out there together since moving in. We christened it the first night since the large fence gave us all the privacy Jansen wanted.

My heart became a puddle hearing Jansen's words, *our kids*. He's been very sure that that was something he wasn't sure he wanted, and I fell in love with him one hundred times harder. While I know we'll get to it when we're ready, thinking about that part of our lives excites me. We have steps to take before then, but I know it won't be long before we get there.

Work has been going much better for me lately. My designs for the fall are ready, and next week we will start the photoshoot for them. Bree has been the best assistant helping me prepare everything. This time I couldn't be happier to have her there through the whole process. We still have *The Gram,* but we use it to share mostly our lives while preparing the clothing line. Most of our sponsors have dropped us since taking a step back from it, and I'm okay with that. My life with Jansen is more significant than working all the time.

It's the first weekend in our house, and Jansen let me sleep in, but the smell of coffee has awakened me. After sliding on my black silk robe, I walk down the hallway to find a shirtless Jansen pouring himself a coffee in a mug in the kitchen.

I sat on the counter behind him, "Good morning."

He turns, smiling before walking over to me, "Morning, beautiful," then kisses my cheek. "Want some?" he holds up his mug before taking a sip.

"Sure," I say.

He takes a mug from the cabinet, pouring coffee into it before handing it to me.

"What's the plan today?" I asked, taking the mug.

"We can finish unpacking the rest of our things," he leans against the counter across from me.

Frowning, "That doesn't sound like fun."

He laughs, "Luckily, it's only a few boxes."

When I moved here, I sold a bunch of stuff from Bree and I's house since we knew we wouldn't have the room for it in our condos. Jansen did the same, but he sold things knowing we could get new stuff together. It made the moving truckload more manageable, and we also have his truck here. I missed that truck.

"I'll shower soon so I can get started on that," I say.

"I'll take the deer to my office today," he grins over his mug.

Oh yes, the deer head made the trip to Los Angeles. I told Jansen I didn't mind if it was at the house, but he insisted it would stand out with the rest of our things. He felt the best place for it was his office. It should feel right at home there.

I set my mug down on the counter before jumping off. Walking up to Jansen, I kiss him before whispering, "You joining me?"

"Yes," he whispers back, "Why are you whispering?" he grins.

"I was trying to sound sexy."

He laughs, "Baby, you don't have to whisper to sound sexy."

I take the mug from the counter, "Come."

"Don't think there'll be a problem with that," he says.

I smirk, "Of course, you'd say that."

Jansen follows me as we walk to the main bathroom. I turn on the shower, and even though we have two shower heads, we only use one. I slide off my robe, and it falls to the floor, unveiling my naked body. Jansen came up behind me before I opened the shower door and placed a kiss on my shoulder.

"I haven't told you I love you today," he says, wrapping his arms around me.

I spin around in his arms, "I love you too."

He places a kiss on the tip of my nose before letting me go to take off his sweatpants. I'll never get tired of hearing those words from him. He doesn't let a day go by without telling me about his love for me.

While Jansen ran some things to his office, I put the finishing touches on the house before unloading the last boxes into the closet. We've been here a week, and we've already made the place feel like a home. I can genuinely say I'm happy for the first time in my life. I'm satisfied with where I am, with work, my friendship with Bree, and, more importantly, my relationship with Jansen. I've never loved anyone as much as I love him.

When I ran out of things to do, I took a book to the porch swing to pass the time until Jansen returned. The weather in Los Angeles is perfect for outside reading today. Not long after coming outside, Jansen pops his head through the back door.

"There's something I want to show you."

Turning my head in his direction, "Now?"

"We could wait, but I think this is something you'll want to see now," he grins.

Getting up from the swing, I set my book down so I could come back. Jansen takes my hand and leads the way when I'm inside the house. We get to the stairs, and he starts walking up them.

I don't know what he would want to show me up here. There's nothing up here yet. Since we moved in, I think I've been up here once.

He stops at one of the bedroom doors and turns around to me.

"Close your eyes, babe."

Smiling, I put my hands over my eyes.

I hear the door open and feel Jansen's hand on my back, guiding me into the room. Once he has me right where he wants me, he says, "Open your eyes."

I take my hands down from my face, but my eyes remain closed. I'm nervous about what Jansen has to show me. After a few more seconds, I open my eyes to see a wall of built-in bookshelves, a large white desk, and a velvet pink desk chair.

"Welcome to your new office."

"Jansen, I love it," I say, looking around at everything and taking it all in.

"The first night we went out, you called Laura's office a dream. I think since that night, it was something I've always wanted to give you."

Smiling at him, "Thank you."

When I turned around, I noticed a clothing rack with my clothing line hanging, and above it hung a neon pink sign that said, *boss babe*.

"Take a seat," he says, grinning.

Walking behind the desk, I take a seat in my chair. Pink supplies are on the top of the desk, along with a new computer. Then I notice a box sitting next to the keyboard. It looks familiar. Picking it up, I show it to Jansen without opening it.

"Is this what I think it is?"

He laughs, walking over to my side, "Open it."

I opened the box to a ring but not the one I thought. It's not the ring I once wore. It's a larger diamond ring. I gasp before tears begin to fall down my cheeks. Jansen gets down to eye level next to me.

"Marry me, Rell. Today, tomorrow, the next day, whenever you want, as long as I get to spend forever with you. You make me a better man. I love you, and what I feel for you only happens once in a lifetime. I never want to go another day without you."

I set the ring down on the desk before taking Jansen's face into my hands. "Yes. I've never wanted anything more than to spend forever with you."

Jansen wraps his arms around me before his lips fall to mine.

We're right where we need to be. Something we once were, but it wasn't real, and this time it's so very much real. I love Jansen more than I've ever loved anyone. He's my home.

As I lie here squished between Jansen's arm and the bed, the bed we haven't left almost the whole day, I think about how I got here. I'm not sleeping, not because I'm sad. It's quite the opposite. This entire time I've been looking for something more in life. I can't help but think that more was this person sleeping right in front of me. It wasn't a job. I got the job, but yet my heart wanted so much more. It wanted him.

Jansen and I fell in love when we weren't supposed to. We were in a relationship that had rules and wasn't real. There was more distance between us than time, yet we never stopped wanting each other. I should've known the minute I saw him in the rain, but it doesn't work that way. Jansen didn't want distractions, yet he never stopped himself from falling in love with me. It was always supposed to be him and me.

That small part of our relationship where we weren't together hurt, but I knew in my heart that we'd find our way back into each other's arms, and we did. Now the love I have for him, not even one life, is enough time to spend with him.

My hand cups Jansen's face as I watch him sleep peacefully, and I smile. He stirs a moment, wrapping his arm tighter around me while sleeping, so I drop my hand to snuggle into his chest and try to close my eyes. Being in his arms is one of my favorite things, and it started all those months ago during a night in San Francisco on a swing. Now we are in a place that was so foreign to us then, but now it all feels like home.

Snuggling closer, I finally decide to close my eyes feeling content.

Felling lips wander from my neck to my chest, and I groan. Usually, waking to this sensation excites me, but today's work day for the both of us after an incredible weekend, and I'm tired. His lips work their way up my neck again, the feeling bringing a slight smile to my face.

"There is she," he whispers.

I look at Jansen, opening my eyes, "Let's do it today."

Confused, he laughs, "Whatever it is, is that what kept you up last night?"

Sitting up, I lean my back against the headboard, bringing the covers up. Jansen kisses my cheek, still hovering over me.

"Can we skip work?" I ask.

"I think I know where you're going with this," He sits on the bed, taking my face into his hands. "I love you, Rell. Trust me, and I want to do everything right now with you. We don't need to rush this. I want to give you the wedding you deserve. Then we can make babies and fill the house. Okay?"

Smiling, I lean in to kiss him, "Okay."

"Plus, if we had done it today, then you wouldn't have got to design your wedding dress with the help of Threads. That would've been devastating to Stacey, considering how excited she was about it when I asked."

"No way," I say, shocked.

Jansen grins, "Yes. She wants to help you expand your brand."

Pouting my lip as tears began to form in my eyes. "Have I told you how much I love you?"

"Every day, Rell," he smiles, "You don't have to tell because I know. I see it, I feel it, and you make the luckiest man alive daily."

A tear falls down my cheek as he leans to kiss me. "I'll never stop loving you, Rell."

The End
Or not, the end?

Acknowledgments

First and foremost, I want to thank my amazing family. They let me take time away from them to write this book and never complained. They mean the world to me and have been so supportive. Secondly, I want to thank all of my fans and supporters. You are the people who keep me going and never let me second-guess myself. I have thought about you guys a lot while publishing this book. I'm so thankful for every single one of you, and you know who you are. Stefanie K. Steck, you girl are my absolute rock. Writing this book with you by my side has been the most fantastic ride. The countless text, calls, and everything else you have done for me have not gone unnoticed. You're stuck with me for a lifetime, friend. I couldn't have asked for a better person to walk along with on this author journey we are taking. Thank you for everything you have done for me, my biggest fan. I also thank Chelly @books_tea_and_fantasy for taking the time to beta-read for me at the last minute. I'll forever be thankful for your kind comments and laughs. Thank you, Aleshka, for being my first-ever beta reader and giving me honest and sometimes hard comments. It wasn't easy, but you were so helpful. Celia E. Ochoa @readwithceo, thank you for believing in me and answering all my crazy questions. I met you during a vulnerable time and your encouragement has meant the world to me. You haven't only helped me become a better writer, but you sent me the best music recommendations, and the playlist for this book was so many amazing songs sent by you. Jessica Costello, I want to thank you for your encouraging words, and laughs. I couldn't be more thankful to have crossed paths with you. All of those that have believed in me thank you. This book is for all of you. I couldn't have asked for better bookstagram friends, fans, and supporters. I have tears to wipe away writing this because I'm just so appreciative. All the love was felt during the process of this book, and I am forever grateful.

CPSIA information can be obtained
at www.ICGtesting.com
Printed in the USA
JSHW022015050223
37301JS00002B/93